Thunder crashed on the mountain

The cabin was storm-tight, and the rain pounding against the glass was soothing. To Cassandra, even the rumble of the thunder was comforting. She stared out the window, her fingers tracing the cool pane.

A triple-pronged fork of light blazed across the noisy sky, illuminating the edge of the woods. There a lone figure stared at the house.

The scream caught in Cassandra's throat. His hands hung down his sides, empty fists dangling. Buckets of rain fell on him, but he didn't move. He just watched the darkened house.

"Adam." Cassandra whispered the name. "Adam!" she cried, but it was only a harsh whisper. Her voice wouldn't work. She couldn't tear her gaze away from the man. It was almost as if they were bonded together.

Familiar jumped to the windowsill beside Cassandra. His back went into a tight arch, and a deep, guttural hiss escaped him.

ABOUT THE AUTHOR

Caroline Burnes is delighted to bring back Familiar, the black cat who solves crimes, for his second Harlequin Intrigue novel. He was first introduced in *Fear Familiar*, Intrigue #134.

The owner of three cats—as well as dogs and horses—Caroline is a firm believer that animals are highly intelligent and quite capable of solving or creating turmoil. A member of People for Ethical Treatment of Animals and the Humane Society, she urges all pet owners to have their pets spayed or neutered and to get involved in making the world a better place for animals and humans alike.

Too Familiar

Caroline Burnes

Harlequin Books

TORONTO • NEW YORK • LONDON
AMSTERDAM • PARIS • SYDNEY • HAMBURG
STOCKHOLM • ATHENS • TOKYO • MILAN
MADRID • WARSAW • BUDAPEST • AUCKLAND

This book is dedicated to Eugene Walter—cat lover, writer, chef, musician, poet, traveler and the most generous of friends.

Harlequin Intrigue edition published February 1993

ISBN 0-373-22215-7

TOO FAMILIAR

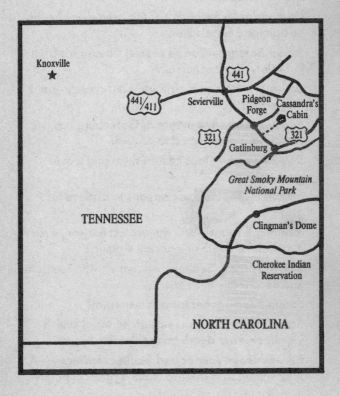

CAST OF CHARACTERS

Familiar—An act of violence puts the feline on the road in Tennessee.

Cassandra McBeth—Prophetic dreams set her up as bait for a serial killer.

Adam Raleigh—Can he protect Cassandra from the killer—or from herself?

Bounder—He and his friends want change—and they want it now.

Ken Simpson—The mayor of Gatlinburg has secrets he's determined to protect.

Ray Elsworth—Does he love them and leave them—dead?

Martin West—He'll use anyone to achieve his goals.

Running Stream—Will she protect her son, even if it means the death of innocent women?

Sheriff Harvey Beaker—A lawman who seems to make too many mistakes.

Joann Reed—Is her taste in men fatal?

Sarah Welford—Is she one of the serial killer's victims or is her death an accident?

Billy Buckeye Tanner and Stalker McKinney—Are they willing to murder to make a political point?

Chapter One

She looks dead, slumped over the steering wheel.

Hard to say from my vantage point on this bluff. My body feels like a punching bag, but I guess I'd better mosey on over to her car and take a peek. Snazzy little red convertible, a sign that she's got a bit of class. She hit the bank pretty hard, and for no apparent reason. Not another car in sight. She just swerved and slammed on the brakes. Almost as if she fainted or something.

Pretty little thing, for a blonde. Doesn't look a bit like my Eleanor. My Eleanor who might be injured. Or worse. And Dr. Doolittle, too. I'm even worried about him. Worry about those two has tormented me for the past three days— ever since I woke up in that moving van somewhere south of Washington with a hideful of glass and bruises. My hearing is still messed up from the blast.

It had to be a bomb. That's a hard thing to accept, that my family has been devastated by some explosion. But I've thought and thought about it, and that's the only possibility that makes any sense. The last thing I remember, I was walking to the refrigerator. Eleanor, the doc, and that funny-talking houseguest they were so excited to see had all gone to bed. There was the sound of a window breaking, the thunk of something on the living-room floor and a concussion that felt as if all the air were being sucked out of the house. The kitchen window shattered when I went through it, and that's it. I musta crawled into the Hendersons' mov-

*ing van and passed out. Since I woke up, Eleanor's been the
only thing on my mind. She couldn't have been killed! She
couldn't! Not her or Dr. Doolittle. Even as we speak, I'm on
my way back to Washington to find out what happened.*

*Right now, though, it looks as if I'm going to have to take
a little detour. No self-respecting guy can just walk away
from a damsel in distress. If the dame buckled tight in her
car seat is still alive, she might need some assistance. I can't
do the fireman's carry, but I might be able to wake her up.*

*Hey, she's moaning! Now she's crying. Good grief! She's
turning on the faucets over a little car wreck. I need to tell
this kiddo to buck up! Tears won't help. Best thing to do is
get up and get moving. Never set yourself up as a sitting
duck, babe. This calls for action.*

*Hey! I nudged her hand and she didn't do a thing. That's
not exactly the most response I've ever gotten from a good-
looking woman. This calls for more dramatic pressure. A
little sandpaper tongue on the old bend of the elbow. Yep!
That's the ticket! She's lifting her head and beginning to
look around.*

*Dig those blue eyes! It's Goldilocks, I do believe. Those
eyes look like a summer sky that stretches forever. Big and
deep and intense. And filled with pain! Great, now that
makes two of us. She's hurt; I'm hurt. This looks like the
beginning of a mutual need relationship. Uh-oh, she's going to speak. Let's hope and pray it's English.*

"CAT." Cassandra McBeth let the word fall from her
mouth. She was surprised that she still had the ability for
speech. Struggling to release the seat belt that had saved her
life, she popped the button and felt her body sag. This seizure had been the worst of all. It had caught her unexpectedly. Before she could pull her car onto the side of the road,
she'd been in the throes of. . .

"The murder." She finished her thought out loud. There
was no other way to describe what she'd witnessed. A
graphic, horrifying murder. Alfred Hitchcock couldn't have
done a better job of capturing the young woman's terror.

Cassandra felt the shakes take over her body as she reacted to what she'd envisioned. The girl had been looking out at a mountain view. The killer had come from behind. His fingers had circled her neck, caressing, before they began to press. It was as if Cassandra had been standing at the killer's shoulder.

"I'm losing my mind," she whispered. The tears threatened again and she fought them back.

The strange black cat sat beside her on the car seat and gave her a knowing look. It was only then that she noticed the blood matted in the cat's fur. It looked as if the injury had occurred several days before.

"You poor old tom," she said. Without any fear, she reached across the seat and stroked the cat's back. Her sensitive fingers found the matted gash along his left flank. When he didn't flinch, she explored further. The wound was deep, but it hadn't gone to the bone. The cat was remarkably calm. As she examined him, he held her with his steady, amber gaze, as if he knew she was trying to help him. Animals had a way of knowing things—just as she did.

"You're going home with me. I have a poultice that will clean this wound. Too late for stitches now, so we might have a scar, but it won't hinder your movements." The cat listened, as if he understood. She shook her head. Her nightmares were having a telling effect—she actually believed she was communicating with a cat.

Gripping the wheel firmly, she cautiously started the engine and put the car in reverse. When the seizure struck—and that was the only way to describe the thing that happened to her—the car had shunted off the road, crossed a small ditch and stopped against a soft embankment. She didn't care about the damage, she only wanted to get home, doctor the cat, and prepare a steaming mug of soothing herbal tea. The trip into Sevierville could wait.

But what if another girl dies?

That question came from her worst fears, and she quickly pushed it out of her mind. Even if she went to see Sheriff Harvey Beaker, he'd never believe a word she said. After all, she was Cassandra McBeth, daughter of the "famous" fortune-teller Sister Sylvia, reader of the stars, tarot, cards, Celtic runes, palms or auras. The prophet of Highway 441!

Cassandra felt the familiar anger begin to rise and she shut it off. At present, she had to concentrate on driving home. That in itself was chore enough after nearly wrecking her car. The little Mazda Miata, her one true extravagance, was pulling horribly to the right.

THERE'S SOMETHING definitely weird about Goldilocks, here. I'd feel a lot better if the first words out of her mouth hadn't involved an act of violence and death. But she has the kindest, most sensitive hands of anyone I've ever met. And those eyes—almost haunted. Yep, she's piqued my curiosity. You all know the old saying about that, but I'm still figuring that I've got at least five lives left.

I guess I've cast my lot in with Goldilocks, at least for the moment. She looks as if the hounds of hell have been chasing her all over this mountain. Before I head down that long highway home, I want to make sure things are okay with her. I also need a little medical attention and some rest. A Washington Post *or a television station with political news would also be appreciated. I don't mind helping Miss Locks, but I need to check on the home front. I've been completely out of touch since I jumped the moving van at that truck stop.*

I might as well make myself at home here on the front seat of this little sports car. It's nice to feel the wind in my ears after walking for three days. Limping, I should say.

Goldilocks has me worried. The skin between her brows is puckered tight enough to please a lemon. Something's on her mind, and it ain't visions of a Hawaiian vacation. At first glance, I thought she was a girl, but she's older. There's something about her that makes her seem young, and so vulnerable. It's not just her long, curly hair, or her size. It's something I can't put my finger on just yet. I'm a sucker for a helpless broad. I guess I'm just walking proof that chiv-

alry isn't dead. Whatever is bothering Miss Locks, I'll help her out with it before I get on the road home.

All this excitement has tuckered me out. I'll curl up and take a little nap until we hit the house. I sure hope Miss Locks is prepared for a feline visitor. Travel gives a cat such an appetite.

"THERE YOU GO." Cassandra smoothed the last piece of tape into place. The large black cat looked as if he were half mummy, but his multiple wounds were cleaned, medicated and dressed.

"I wish you could tell me what happened to you," she said as she poured a saucer of fresh milk and put it on the floor for him. "Looks like you went through a window somewhere. I'd guess car accident, but if there had been any wrecks near Gatlinburg, I'd have heard about it, especially this time of year. Bad news has a way of finding even the most remote places."

Like the murder of a twenty-five-year-old waitress.

With that thought, Cassandra felt the beginning of a dull headache. The body had been found two days ago, thrown down a ravine. The young woman had been in Gatlinburg for a week, one of the first of the summer help that flocked to the Smoky Mountain resort town. Janey Ables had been her name. Cassandra knew about the murder. She knew more than she'd ever wanted to know.

She looked out her large kitchen window. The small meadow was touched with the first green of spring, but the mountain only a few yards distant still wore its bleak winter attire. "We have another week of peace, and then the tourists will hit town in droves," she said. Her eyes welled up with tears. More young women would arrive, and more would die. She had to do something to try to stop it.

She could delay her trip to Sheriff Beaker's for another day, but then she had to go. The visions were getting more and more intense. Deny it as much as she wanted, she knew what they meant. Even if no one believed her, she had to try to tell the sheriff.

This wasn't the first time she'd experienced such an occurrence. Once was twenty years ago, and even now the memory made her heart constrict. Fear and guilt.

She'd been thirteen years old, a gangly, blond teenager who was more forest creature than child. She'd run wild in the woods while her mother pulled in customers off Highway 441 for a glimpse into the future and her daddy ran the enormous apple orchard that was now her overgrown upper meadow.

She'd been in the woods, tracking down the source of a small stream, when she'd been nearly blinded by a pain in her head. The leafy branches of an apple tree had suddenly surrounded her. She'd heard and felt the sickening crack of the limb. Clutching desperately, her fingers found only leaves that slipped through her grasp. She'd felt herself falling, before impact with the earth. Impact and darkness.

Her father had died that afternoon in a freak fall from one of the apple trees that grew near the edge of the mountain. Somehow she'd shared with him the final moments of his life. Across a distance of more than a mile, she'd connected with his thoughts and the horror of his death.

Cassandra had been stricken mute by the incident for three days. She'd thought she was going insane and had been afraid to speak to anyone. When she finally talked, her family's reaction had not been what she'd expected.

Her mother had called it a gift. Cassandra felt differently, though. The second sight was a curse, and one she never wanted to experience again. Never!

But it was happening now. Only this time it was worse than ever.

Four nights before, she'd found herself sharing death with a woman she'd never met. A girl whose long, dark hair had trembled in the wind as someone's fingers squeezed the life from her. A girl named Janey Ables.

Cassandra felt the familiar panic. The dream had come to her, as real as any moment in her life. The first news of the murder came on the television. Janey's strangled body had been found by a passing motorist. Cassandra couldn't be certain, but she was willing to bet the murder had taken place just as she'd witnessed it in her dream. She had to go to the sheriff, just in case there was something she'd seen that might help them find the killer.

What she couldn't see was the killer's face, or the victim's. Twice in the past week she'd suffered the same death vision. That was why she was going to Sheriff Beaker.

She was determined to tell him of the visions, even if he laughed at her and called her crazy—as most of the town had since she was a little girl. She was Crazy Sylvia's crazy daughter. Mountain girl, or, behind her back, goat girl. That was what they called her when they were being kind. Goat girl, because she lived far up the mountain among the rocks and trees.

Her childhood had been full of taunts and names. Now it was even worse. In local gossip, Cassandra knew that she was thought of as a witch. Young children were warned to steer clear of her. Teenagers were often dared into making a visit to her house late at night to obtain some herb or flower from her extensive gardens. The fact that she was a famous writer, gardener and herbal healer cut no slack with the locals. Her international reputation didn't make a dent in the way the local people viewed her. They'd known her for too long. And they were afraid of her. That was the one thing that no one in town could forgive—she made them afraid.

Cassandra sighed as she stroked the cat's back. At least he wasn't afraid of her. He was making himself right at home, digging into the milk and the can of tuna she'd opened for him. With an appetite like that, he'd be back on his four feet in a matter of days.

The cat had almost devoured the entire bowl of milk when Cassandra heard a soft noise at her door. A smile touched the corners of her mouth. She didn't move; she waited.

"Come in, Running Stream," she said softly. She noticed that the cat had also turned his attention toward the front door. He showed no surprise or anxiety when the screen opened and a tall, statuesque woman stepped into the room.

The woman's brown eyes saw the cat immediately, and there was an imperceptible nod of her head. "So, at long last you have heeded my advice and taken a pet," she said softly. Her voice was as gentle as falling rain. Dark braids hung down her back, and her lightly browned skin revealed no age. Only her eyes were ancient. It suited her that she had adopted a traditional Indian name, as some of her people did.

"I found him." Cassandra saw the look the cat gave her. "Or he found me." She smiled when he went back to eating. "He's rather extraordinary."

"He *is* a cat," Running Stream answered. "His species has much magic, much power."

"He has much appetite," Cassandra said, laughing at her friend. "He can hang around until he gets well. He looks as if he were flung through a glass wall."

Running Stream said nothing, but her expressive eyes narrowed. "And you? You look as if you've been in trouble."

Cassandra's protests were cut short with a wave of the other woman's hand.

"It's the visions again, isn't it? You saw that woman killed."

Cassandra went to the stove and turned on the big kettle. "I was going to the sheriff. I had another attack, and I'm nearly wrecked." She could hear the emotion in her voice growing beyond her control. "It's another young woman. I can almost see her. She has this beautiful neck, and short, dark, curly hair. She's wearing these very unusual earrings."

"Does she die?" Running Stream asked.

Cassandra nodded. "She struggles. She reaches behind her and claws him a little, but it doesn't do any good."

The tall Indian woman ignored her hysterics. "So the killer is a man. You're certain?"

Cassandra was shaken by the other woman's calm intensity. "Yes, I guess he is. He's strong. Too strong for a woman."

"For a rational woman," Running Stream emphasized, "the irrational have great strength."

"It's a man. I can feel the texture of the hair on his arm." Cassandra felt her body tremble. "It's almost as if I were him!" she blurted out. "I feel the struggle of the victim, and I feel the killer's power, his desire to kill. Victim and killer. It's terrifying!"

"You can control your own person," Running Stream said calmly. "That is what you must remember. You cannot control your visions, but you can control your actions. If you don't remember this, then you'll suffer more than is necessary."

"What I want to know is why? Why am I having these visions now? I don't know these women. I don't want to know them. I don't know anything about any of them. When my father died, he was part of my life. Why am I involved in these other people's lives, these strangers? And why, after all these years, am I dreaming like this again?"

Running Stream walked to the center of the room. She knelt down and held out her hand to the cat. Without any hesitation, the cat walked toward her and brushed against her fingers. "You shouldn't question the source of a gift."

"Gift!" Cassandra's fiery temper jumped. "You and my mother! Some gift! I get to experience my own father's death, and now I'm involved in the horrible deaths of women I don't know. You can't imagine what it's like to feel those fingers close on her throat! This isn't a gift, it's a curse." She sat down on the sofa. "I'm sorry," she apologized in her next breath. "Just don't call whatever this is a gift."

Running Stream smiled. She was busy stroking the cat. "He's very fine. He'll make an excellent housemate."

"Meow!" the cat said.

"Black isn't the color I would have selected for you," she added when Cassandra didn't comment.

"Why not?" Cassandra was surprised. She hadn't given the cat's coloring a single thought. In fact, she hadn't considered the possibility that he would stay with her. Her friend's observation intrigued her.

"The people in town already view you with some... trepidation. They think you are a witch. A black cat..."

"A familiar."

Before Cassandra could add more, the cat flipped onto his back and mewed loudly.

"Familiar," Running Stream said. The cat got up and went to her, rubbing against her hand. "I think we've named him, Cass."

"He seems to respond to it," Cassandra said a little doubtfully. "I was thinking of Lucky or Blackie."

Running Stream shook her head. "The Cherokee people believe that each animal knows his own name. Watch." She drew away from the cat. "Familiar, come here."

Tail straight in the air, the cat hobbled toward her. He rubbed his face on her hand. "I think he's telling us that he already has a name."

"Okay, his name's Familiar, and I'm stuck with prophetic visions. I hate to go into town and talk with Beaker, but I don't know what else to do."

"It's a shame the police in Gatlinburg can't intervene. It's out of their jurisdiction. I've had dealings with Beaker before. He won't believe you." The first hint of anger was in the Indian woman's voice. "The people in town aren't capable of understanding. They shut out all ideas that make them uneasy. Go to the sheriff and tell him, Cassandra, because there's nothing else you can do. Remember, though, he won't believe you and there's the possibility he will only bring trouble to you."

"And what about the women? I see a murder. I have to try and stop it." All of Cassandra's anger was gone. Only a thin edge of desperation made her words sound harsh.

"Can you stop it?"

"I can try."

Running Stream shrugged. "You have a strong will, Cassandra. It isn't my intention to step between you and your fate. As a friend, I warn you to deal with Beaker very carefully. The townspeople can never understand. They'll blame you."

"A case of shoot the messenger." Cassandra knew her friend was right. The officials of Gatlinburg didn't want trouble, and when they got it, they were always looking for a convenient scapegoat. Sheriff Beaker was a reasonable man, about fifty percent of the time. But he didn't hold with dreams and visions, and during his long tenure in office he'd driven out on Highway 441 plenty of times to warn her mother about complaints. He didn't personally care what Sylvia McBeth did, or whose money she "conned." He just didn't want trouble.

"Get some sleep, Cassandra."

"Yeah, great idea." She couldn't help the sarcasm. She'd love to sleep—if she could forego her little trip through dreamland.

"I'll send Bounder over tonight to sit with you."

"That won't be necessary." Cassandra sighed. "I don't need your son to take up baby-sitting."

"Bounder loves to visit you." Running Stream smiled, and the severity of her face was radically changed. "He views you as his oldest sister, a wise woman with much grace and beauty."

"You can't flatter me into letting your twenty-two-year-old son spend his free time taking care of me."

"Then do it for me, Cass. I'm worried. You asked why the dreams have come back to you now, at this time. The answer to that question concerns me."

A chill touched Cassandra's skin. "What are you saying?"

"Like it or not, you're involved in those murders. Until we find out why, I've got a right to be worried."

Chapter Two

The green of budding leaves gave the rolling foothills a crisp newness that belied the age of the stony, gray peaks that hovered above them. Adam Raleigh was taken by the sight of spring in the mountains as he drove his rental car along the narrow paved road that wound to Gatlinburg, Tennessee.

He enjoyed the countryside. The clapboard houses with lanky dogs sleeping in the front yard and the land tilled for the first planting were more interesting than the homogenized highway eateries and service stations. He liked the way the road snaked and curled, slow and easy, symbolic of the kind of life he intended to enjoy—when he got old enough and rich enough to retire.

He smiled at that thought. If Cassandra McBeth would cooperate, then he might be a lot closer to his goal than he'd ever been before. All he had to do was convince a woman, whose reputation for reclusiveness made Carmelite nuns seem downright outgoing, to go on a national promotional tour for a breakfast cereal. For a man such as himself, gifted with persuasive abilities, it was going to be a piece of cake.

Let his employees laugh. And they had when he'd told them he was going to Tennessee to bring Cassandra McBeth back as spokesperson for Good Stuff Cereals. They'd laughed and laughed. Well, he was nearly at Gatlinburg, and they wouldn't be laughing long.

He saw the sign pointing the way to the heart of the resort town, and he took Highway 441 north, away from town. He'd scoped out Ms. McBeth's habits, her habitat and her well-known desire for privacy. When Adam Raleigh wanted something, he went after it in a big way. He didn't do anything by half measures.

In the back seat of the car was a video camera, tapes, ten boxes of Good Stuff all-natural, high-in-fiber, no-salt, no-sugar cereal, and two suitcases of clothes. He was staying as long as it took. Ever since the day, two years ago, when he'd made a special trip to Nashville to attend one of Cassandra's book signings—the only signing that she'd ever given—he'd known she was perfect.

His attention was focused on the road as he looked for the narrow path that served as Cassandra's driveway. The local resident he'd talked with in the Black Bear Diner had given him very clear directions. The man had been a trifle odd after Cassandra's name was mentioned, but an Andrew Jackson had finally prized the information loose.

Adam could feel his determination harden as he drew closer and closer to Cassandra.

So far, she'd thwarted all his efforts. He'd sent letters, contracts, video packets—featuring his own sincere beliefs—more letters, checks, even his personal credentials and long, detailed news clippings praising his cereal as a genuinely healthy product. He'd reminded her of their brief meeting. All had been ignored. But he wasn't even close to giving up. Cassandra McBeth was going to get a rare treat, a personal presentation of Good Stuff.

Part of his determination to see her was personal. The writer, whose books on herbs and remedies were revered by more than a million readers, was a woman with long blond hair and blue eyes that captured his imagination. Sure, he had his business reasons, but he'd also been captivated by something in those blue, blue eyes.

He was almost past the driveway when he noticed the bright orange vine that grew on the mailbox. That's what the man at the diner had told him to look for. Some sort of orange flower. Adam slowed the car and turned right. He was immediately under a canopy of dense trees. He felt as if he'd gone from bright daylight into early dusk in a matter of a few seconds.

The road, which was little more than a narrow path cut through the forest, wound up and away. He eased the car forward and began to prepare his opening strategy. He'd park away from the house and arrive on foot. That way she'd be less inclined to run him off. If he could just talk with her for a few minutes, he knew he could win her over. It was the first ten minutes that would be crucial to his success.

Alert for any signs of a house, he drove on and up. He felt as if he were tunneling deeper and deeper into the forest. The thought crossed his mind that perhaps the man at the diner was having a laugh on him now. Adam felt as if he'd gone several miles, and yet there was no house. He was about to give up when he saw the split-rail fence almost overgrown by honeysuckle. He pulled into a narrow break in the woods and got out of the car. Cassandra's house had to be nearby. He started walking.

Forty minutes later, through the trees, he saw the slate roof of the log cabin. His shins were aching and his cotton shirt clung to him. All physical pain disappeared as Adam stopped and took in the scene. He could immediately visualize the first commercial—Cassandra walking out of the cabin, the camera at wide angle taking in all the verdant foliage, the wildflowers that surrounded the house, the wholesomeness of the entire scene! Then the camera would close in on her, and she'd take one of the old cowhide rockers on the front porch as she prepared to breakfast on a blue bowlful of Good Stuff.

It had all of the downright goodness of *Little House on the Prairie* combined with Cassandra's own unique sensuality. He could see her in a white cotton dress with all of that hair tumbling about her shoulders.

The pleasant image was shattered by a low, anguished cry. Adam stepped toward the house, then checked himself. He had no business invading Cassandra McBeth's solitude. He was a trespasser. He realized with an unpleasant shock that he'd assumed Cassandra was single. What if she was involved with someone, and what if the two of them were having a spat?

On the other hand, what if she were injured? Or someone was possibly hurting her?

Adam needed no further encouragement. He was running across the meadow with every ounce of energy in his lean frame.

The cry came again, broken by sobs, and Adam paused long enough at the front door to verify that it wasn't locked. Then he was inside and confronting the sight of a struggling, quilt-covered woman on a sofa.

At first it didn't register on Adam that Cassandra McBeth struggled alone. There was no one holding her or assaulting her. The only other creature in the room was a strange black cat that had jumped onto the back of the sofa and was mewing loudly.

Adam froze for a moment, but Cassandra's terrified struggles and moans made him step forward. He forgot that he was in a woman's house uninvited, that he could be arrested for criminal trespassing. His only thought was to capture the anguished Cassandra McBeth and hold her close until she woke up from whatever nightmare was frightening her.

He went to the sofa and eased down beside her. "Cassandra," he said softly as he gripped her shoulders.

Her head tossed back and forth, her blond hair frothing about her face. "Please! No!" she whispered. "Oh, God, please don't!"

The terror in her voice prodded him to act more forcefully. He shook her lightly. "Cassandra," he said loudly. "Wake up!"

She arched against him, thrusting with her arms in a blind, desperate fashion.

"Cassandra!" He felt his own panic begin to rise. He couldn't seem to wake her. Instead of calming her, his touch seemed to make her struggle more.

"Let me go!" she hissed. Her hands came up like claws and she drew one across his cheek.

Adam ignored the blood that trickled down his jaw. He concentrated on capturing both of her hands and holding them tight.

"Meow!" the cat interjected along with an angry hiss.

"Get out of here," Adam said quickly. "I'm not going to hurt her." Before he could do anything else, the cat leaped across the sofa, landing on his chest with full force. Perched on the edge of the sofa, Adam lost his balance and fell. Instead of losing Cassandra's hands, he pulled her with him. She was light as a feather and she landed in his arms with some force. Cat, man and woman tumbled to the floor in a heap.

"What?" Cassandra's voice registered shock. For a moment she lay atop Adam without making any effort to move. She was half in the dream, half out. Looking around her, she saw the features of her own home. She could hear someone breathing beneath her. Strong, controlled breaths. Tentacles of the dream reached out to tug at her.

"Ms. McBeth!"

She could hear someone calling her from far away.

"Cassandra, I'm Adam Raleigh."

She felt the man move, and she tried to connect with what was happening. She could see him, and his features were vaguely familiar. He was talking to her, but she couldn't understand what he was saying.

Adam knew the woman was in a stupor. Had she had an epileptic seizure, or possibly an insulin reaction? He looked around the room for medication.

"Are you sick?" he asked.

She could understand that question. She shook her head no, but it seemed too heavy to move. She tried to react, but she couldn't.

Adam scooped her into his arms and put her on the sofa. With quick efficiency he picked up the comforter and tucked it around her. "You're going to be fine, Ms. McBeth. Shall I call a doctor?"

"No." This time she managed to speak, but it was barely a croak. "I had a nightmare."

Adam sat on the edge of the sofa. "You're looking better now. The color is coming back." He placed his hand on her forehead. "No fever. You really gave me a scare."

As he talked, Cassandra tried to shake off the final fringes of the nightmare. "Adam Raleigh?"

"Yes, I've been trying to reach you."

"The book signing." She remembered. Occasionally, when she was daydreaming, he'd slip back into her thoughts. What was he doing in her home? Was he really there, or was he part of the dream? She was completely disoriented.

"Are you ill?" He repeated his question. She was pale, and appeared to be in shock. Her eyes went from rational comprehension to fear in split seconds.

Cassandra tried to focus on the man before her, but she felt her panic return with all the force of the dream. She remembered now. She remembered the girl, her earrings dangling in her hair. She remembered the way the world swung around her, dark green and filled with the sounds of life.

Adam watched those incredible blue eyes widen to proportions of complete fear. Very carefully he reached down and pinned her arms beneath the comforter. If she went into some kind of fit, he didn't want her to hurt herself.

Cassandra tumbled back into the dream. The attack had come from behind. The young woman had been standing…where? There was the sensation of great height. There had been a view, she was certain, but she couldn't pull it back into focus. The girl had been standing, looking at the view.

"Cassandra." Adam tried to coax her back.

The killer had come up behind the woman. He was watching the way her hair moved in the breeze. The woman's earrings had jangled. Then the woman had begun to struggle as hands closed around her neck. Strong hands. Big hands.

"No!" Cassandra bolted into a sitting position. "No!" She held out her hands as far as her arms would reach. "No," she whispered. "Not these hands!"

Adam knew he'd lost Cassandra completely. She was no longer in the same room with him. Her body was there, but her consciousness was somewhere else. Someplace terrifying, if her expression was any clue. She was looking at her hands as if they were the foulest, most contemptible things on the face of the earth. Such small, incredibly delicate hands.

"Cassandra," he said softly.

She gave a shuddering sigh and held her hands to her face. Sobs broke from her body as she moaned.

Very gently, he gathered her into his arms. He knew she wasn't fully aware of him, of the fact that a stranger was in her house. So he waited until the sobs began to subside. When he thought she could understand him, he told her he was president of Good Stuff Cereals and why he was in her home. He reminded her of all the letters he'd sent. He talked on and on until she drew several ragged breaths and he knew she was over the worst of it.

When he quit talking, she indicated her desire to get up. She didn't look at Adam and she didn't ask any questions. She walked to the kitchen window and looked out, but her eyes didn't register any of the familiar sights.

"I was with him," she said softly. "I was with him." The tears started without warning. They drifted down her cheeks unnoticed as she continued to stare into the unseen meadow.

Adam closed the distance between them and put his arms around her. Very gently he turned her away from the window and into his chest. "It's okay," he said softly. "Whatever happened, it's okay."

The emotions he felt were strange and overwhelming. That he was holding a woman whose mental balance was precarious, at best, didn't matter. He felt only a strong desire to give comfort to someone who seemed so much in need of a friend.

"My hands," Cassandra said softly. "My hands were on her throat."

He felt her fists curl against his chest and he pulled her tighter. "You're safe. Whatever happened, you're safe now." He led her back to the sofa and sat down with her.

"Why?" she asked again and again. "Why now? Why me? Why?"

Adam had no answers for her. He didn't even know what the questions meant. He only knew that somehow he was involved. Good Stuff Cereals was still very much on his mind, but it had taken a back seat to whatever problem faced Cassandra McBeth.

The black cat jumped up on the sofa as if he were used to such privileges. He went to Cassandra and rubbed his face against her hand.

At last she drew a shuddering breath and reached out to stroke the cat. "It was only a dream, Familiar," she said softly. "Just a bad dream."

"Cassandra, you have to try and sleep," Adam said. She looked as if she was on the verge of collapse.

"I'm afraid. The dreams."

"I'll stay here with you. If you begin to move around, like you're dreaming, I'll wake you." Adam took her hand and held it. "I know you have no reason to trust me, but you can."

She turned exhausted blue eyes to Adam. "I haven't slept in three days," she said. Her lids were so heavy, she couldn't help herself. She knew she shouldn't put herself in such a vulnerable position, but his voice was so soothing, his touch so reassuring. And she was incredibly tired.

"Sleep, Cassandra," Adam said softly. "Sleep."

Her lids closed, then opened as if she were fighting. When they closed the second time, she was asleep.

Adam held her for a long while. She slept soundly, and peacefully. As he held her, he studied the delicate features of her face. The high cheekbones accented the pointed chin.

She had an elfin, magical look with her big eyes. But there was a stubborn tenacity in her jaw that promised that despite her current disability, Cassandra McBeth was her own woman.

In contrast to what he'd told his employees, convincing Cassandra McBeth was not going to be a piece of cake. He looked at the face of the sleeping woman he held and knew instinctively that nothing about her was easy.

Well, he wouldn't have it any other way. He was a man who liked a challenge. Cassandra McBeth would be a big one.

WELL, GOOD GRIEF, I practically had to knock Lancelot off the sofa to get any assistance from him, and now he's back on the sofa again, sitting like a stuffed toad. Left to his own devices, he would have let Miss Locks go into a convulsion before our very eyes! And I thought Dr. Doolittle was not as bright as the average cat. This guy makes the doc look like a brain surgeon! Oh, well, we cats learn to work with what we're given in the way of human helpers. If Lancelot is going to assist us, and the look on his face tells me I couldn't drive him away with a black bear attack, then I'd better figure up a way to make him useful.

I don't know what's happening with Miss Locks, but she's deep into something bad. She needs my help, and I'm here to give it.

If Lancelot will just push over a bit, I can click on the television. It's time for the news, and there's a chance I can learn something about Eleanor.

Let's see, the remote was around here somewhere. Under the sofa pillow. Well, a flick of my paw, and it's on the floor. Now a little stand on the button and voilà! News!

ADAM JUMPED when the television sprang into life. Tired from the long drive and hike, and lulled by the feel of Cassandra sleeping in his arms, he'd drifted into a light doze. He was unprepared for any noise except the chirping of the birds outside the window and Cassandra's light and peaceful breathing.

He saw the cat standing on the remote control and almost reached for the device. Such a move would disturb Cassandra, though, so he resisted. In a state of uncharacteristic passivity, he sat still and watched the five o'clock national news.

Turmoil in Russia; destruction in Bangladesh; educational system in crisis; tax revolt. He watched that segment with more interest. Protesters in Washington were holding their 1040 tax forms and burning them. They were refusing to pay their taxes.

"Boston Tea Party," he said softly with a grin. The American people were an amazing lot. They had a strict standard of fairness, and once it was breached, then revolution was a distinct possibility. "Congress beware," he added under his breath.

He tuned out the news as Cassandra stirred groggily.

"... No new evidence in the bombing of several Washington, D.C., activists. Although the home of Dr. and Mrs. Peter Curry was destroyed, there has been no trace of their bodies, or of the man who was allegedly staying with them, Kirk Ranager, a well-known activist who has engineered numerous raids to release political prisoners in foreign countries."

Adam was vaguely listening to the news when his attention was drawn to the cat. The arrogant feline stood at attention, every hair on his body raised. A low growl came from the cat's throat as he stared intently at the television. It was one of the more amazing things Adam had ever seen.

The television newscast shifted from national to local focus, and Adam gave it a closer listen. He knew little about Gatlinburg, except that it was a summer town for tourists and that it was in the Smoky Mountains. Someone in his office had mentioned that there was a Cherokee Indian reservation nearby in North Carolina.

The scene on the tube showed men with dogs traversing a rocky segment of mountainside. Adam watched with mild interest. The camera swung up to a young female reporter who stood, hair whipping in the wind, at the top of the cliff.

"Authorities have increased the search for Carla Winchester, a twenty-two-year-old Clemson University graduate student who came to Gatlinburg last week to take a job as a waitress at Whitley Resort. Ms. Winchester has been missing for two days and her family has offered a reward for any information regarding her whereabouts."

The camera shifted from the reporter to pick up a shot of a blue compact car parked in a scenic overlook.

"Ms. Winchester's car was found today near this overlook. Authorities have begun a ground search of the immediate area."

The scene changed again to reveal a head shot of a young woman.

"She is a brunette with blue eyes, five foot five, a hundred and twenty pounds, and was last seen at the Kettle Inn. If you see this woman, contact the local authorities. That's all the details here, Ted, back to you."

Adam felt Cassandra stiffen and he loosened his hold.

"That's her. The woman from my dream. She's dead. Or she will be soon."

Cassandra's voice was so calm, so matter-of-fact, that Adam continued stroking her hair.

"The police found her car up near the lookout point on a road called High Ridge, I think." He forced his voice to be as calm as hers.

Shifting her legs to the floor, Cassandra sat up. As she felt the full blast of the headache, she put her hands to her temples.

"Are you okay?"

"No, but there's nothing either of us can do about it now," she said. "I know you're Adam Raleigh, and I know your cereal company. What are you doing in my home?"

"I came to speak with you and sort of stumbled in on the middle of..."

"My most recent seizure, dream, nightmare, take your pick of words. I should have gone to the sheriff earlier.

This—'' she waved one hand at the television but didn't look up ''—is all my fault.''

"The pending revolt in Russia, or the local missing person?'' Adam had a smile ready for her when she cast him a sour look.

"I suspect I know what you want. The answer is no, so think about getting out of my home.'' She started to stand, but the throb in her head sent her back to a sitting position.

"Your cat can turn the television on.''

"He isn't my cat.''

"Who does he belong to, then? You aren't exactly overwhelmed with neighbors.''

"He doesn't belong to anyone. See if you can get this straight. I'm a witch and he's a familiar. See, he's a free agent. He hangs out here when there's something on the tube he wants to watch. Now get out of here before I entertain him by turning you into a toad.''

"I thought that only worked on princes.''

As miserable as she felt, Cassandra had to fight to keep the smile from her face. Adam Raleigh was an audacious man. But he wasn't freaked out by her, and he'd seen her at one of her very worst moments. "I'm sure there's something else sinister I can do to you, but before I give it some thought, tell me what you saw here, today.'' It occurred to Cassandra that she might glean some valuable information from the stranger. Maybe she'd said or done something that would help her understand what was happening. "Start from the very beginning.''

"Okay, I was outside and heard you scream. When I ran in, I found you thrashing about on the sofa, having a nightmare.''

"What did I say?''

" 'No,' and you struggled, as if you were fighting someone.''

"That's it?'' She felt deflated. That much she could remember herself.

"Sorry. You were deep in the dream. So deep I almost couldn't wake you. If it hadn't been for that cat attacking me—'' He broke off and gave Familiar a curious look. The black cat was sitting at the end of the sofa cleaning his back leg.

"Yes, he is rather unusual," Cassandra said. "And so are you. Since you've come all this way, I'll listen to what you have to say. By the way, I received all of the materials you sent, and I did read it. But I'm not going to have anything to do with your product. Now tell me why you're here and then leave.''

"I'm president and owner of Good Stuff Cereals, I want you to be spokesperson.''

"No, and I don't want to. I don't believe in processed foods. Cereals are ruining the health of children. Sugar. Preservatives. Salt. Nasty, sticky candy that floats in tepid milk and rots children's teeth. Ick!''

"Good Stuff isn't like that. In fact, it's marketed for adults, not children. It's totally nutritious and completely healthy and all natural.''

"I'm impressed, Mr. Raleigh, but I'm not interested.''

"I came all the way here from Michigan to ask you to represent my company.''

Cassandra stood at last. The movement made her a little dizzy, but it soon passed. "Have you read any of my books?''

"Every single one—the natural way to eat and live.''

"Your product is the antithesis of what I believe in.''

"I knew you'd say that, but it isn't true. If you'll give me ten minutes of your time, I can prove that my cereal is as healthy as anything you could pick from the woods around us.''

"If I could help you, Mr. Raleigh, I would. I'm in your debt for helping me. But what you're asking is impossible. I'm sorry you came all this distance for no better result.''

"I'm not going to leave unless you agree to at least try my cereal.''

"No thanks.''

Adam settled back into the sofa. "I don't have anywhere else to go. My car broke down on the way up your drive."

"It's a long walk to the highway, but it won't kill you."

"What do you know about the woman who disappeared?"

Adam's last question was a showstopper. Cassandra turned away from him and went to the stove. She put the kettle on for a cup of hawthorn tea. She felt nervous, itchy, as if her skin were suddenly too tight.

When she had the kettle on, she turned back to face him across the open room. "It's getting late, Mr. Raleigh. I'll drive you down the mountain to town. I need to go and see the sheriff anyway."

Adam nodded. He hadn't meant to make her blanch so. He'd only wanted to throw her off stride for a moment. His words had upset her far more than he'd intended. Maybe it would be wiser for him to take a room in town and try a softer approach.

"I'm sorry," he said. "It was brutal of me to press you that way."

"Yes," she agreed. There was a sincere concern in the man's face, and she suddenly remembered his hands stroking her hair, the way he'd held her with such compassion and strength. "Let's have a cup of tea before we go," she said. "I'm sorry, too. I can't endorse your product, but there's no sense in being rude about it."

"I couldn't help but notice the blackberry leaves you've dried. I'd be delighted to have a cup of that tea. I've read about it in your books, but never tried it."

Cassandra's lips tilted in the slightest suggestion of a smile. "My pleasure," she said.

"I really have read all your books. I'm a fan of yours," Adam said as he stood up and joined her in the kitchen.

"Give it up, Mr. Raleigh," she said.

"Okay," he agreed easily, "if you'll tell me about your nightmare. I know enough to figure out that you were dreaming about the missing woman, Carla Winchester. Whatever you dreamed has deeply upset you.''

"Carla Winchester," Cassandra said the words and felt her hands begin to tremble. It was always this way after a dream. There would be a few moments of calm, then the shakes and a headache. The dreams were becoming more and more frequent.

"Hey," Adam caught the cup before it slipped from her limp hand. "Sit down and I'll make the tea." He guided her toward a kitchen chair.

Cassandra allowed him to seat her. As he set up two cups and prepared the tea, she watched him. He was a tall man, well muscled but not heavy. He moved with a grace and agility that she enjoyed. His chestnut hair was neatly cut, his brown eyes intelligent with a hint of concern for her. Well-controlled concern. He probably thought she was an escapee from a mental institution and he was trying hard not to provoke her. She smiled at the thought.

"Feeling better?"

She nodded. Talking would only ignite the headache she knew was waiting. She took the cup of tea he offered. "Honey's in the cabinet," she said.

He got honey, lemon and milk, and put them on the table. As they drank their tea, he talked of his impressions of the mountains and of his admiration for her work. He kept the conversation light, quick, and without any requirement for her participation. As he talked he watched the tremors pass through her body, and he saw the pain and fear in her eyes when she raised them to his. Not for the first time, the thought crossed his mind that Cassandra McBeth was not a stable woman. She might be a brilliant writer, but she also might not be completely sane.

Looking at her, he felt a strong compulsion to make sure that she was okay. No matter what happened with the cereal, he wanted to be sure that nothing hurt Cassandra. Not even herself.

"We'd better go," she said shakily.

"It could wait until tomorrow," he suggested, seeing the way her body shook again.

"No." There was iron determination in that one word. "That girl is probably already dead, but if she isn't, then I have to do something. I have to try and stop her murder."

Her blue eyes were crystal clear, and completely tormented, as she stared at him.

Chapter Three

The FBI Wanted posters fluttered against the bulletin board in the sporadic gusts of an oscillating fan. Cassandra watched the papers move up and down, avoiding the penetrating stare of Sheriff Beaker. He was looking at her as if she'd escaped from a mental institution.

"You say you saw Janey Ables's murder, and now you've seen Carla Winchester strangled, too."

Cassandra nodded. Against all of her adamant insistence, Adam had accompanied her to the sheriff's office. In fact, he'd driven her when he saw the condition of her car. The right fender had been damaged when she ran off the road.

Adam's car had miraculously cured itself. The motor turned over on the first try, and Adam did have the decency to blush—a little. Cassandra had graciously let his fib pass. She was simply glad he'd come with her. He'd heard her story for the first time, along with Sheriff Beaker. While Beaker thought she was mad, Adam was watching her with calm deliberation. He probably didn't believe her, but he was willing to listen.

"Ma'am, we appreciate your help and all, but so far, we have no evidence that Ms. Winchester is in any danger. Lots of young women come up here for a vacation and sow a few wild oats. We're thinking Ms. Winchester might have met some friends and gone off with them."

"She had a job," Cassandra said softly. "She was a college student who needed summer employment. A good student from what you say. Not the kind to go running off without some consideration for her responsibilities."

"Young folks make mistakes. It's their prerogative, Ms. McBeth." The sheriff's voice was tired. "Now thank you again for your help. It's late and my wife has been holding supper for me for two hours."

Cassandra stood. "And if I have another vision, should I contact you?" The sarcasm was sharp in her tone.

"Yes, ma'am." Beaker stood, too. He was tall and thin. His sharp eyes watched Cassandra with a new speculation. "If you have any revelations about where the body might be, I'd be interested in hearing that, too."

"Of course."

Adam opened the door to the sheriff's personal office, and he and Cassandra stepped into the main room. A dispatcher watched them with open curiosity.

As Adam opened the outer door for Cassandra, he heard the woman question the sheriff. "Wasn't that Sylvia McBeth's daughter, that hermit who writes?" Adam shut the door as fast as possible, but he could tell that Cassandra had heard the question.

"It's okay," she said, and shrugged. "It's part of the price of having a fortune-teller for a mother."

"How about something to eat?" Adam could see the tension in Cassandra.

"I'd better go home."

"Is there anyone who can stay with you?"

Adam's obvious concern was the final straw. She had no desire to appear like some pitiful half-wit scorned by her own community. Cassandra stiffened her spine. "I'm not a child, and I'm not a lunatic. I don't need a baby-sitter. I want to go home, alone."

"This way," Adam said as he steered her toward the car. Ms. McBeth was headstrong, and a bit surly, but he wasn't ready to give up. Not by a long shot.

Night had fallen, giving the mountain a solid blackness that made Adam think of the people who had carved a trail through the wilderness and settled the area. There was a savage beauty to the countryside around Sevierville. They'd had to drive to the county seat to talk with Beaker. As they drove back to Gatlinburg, silence filled the car.

At times the road twisted and the shoulder fell away to empty space. Two or three lights winked far down the side of the drop-off, someone's homestead in a meadow. It made him feel small, and very alone.

They were turning up Cassandra's drive before Adam spoke again. "Unless you can get someone else to stay with you, I am." He wasn't leaving her alone. The area was too isolated.

"You'll do no such thing."

"Of course I will."

"Not in my home."

"In my car. I'm not leaving you alone on the side of this mountain. You believe a killer's loose. You need some protection." Adam felt his jaw muscles clench. She was a damn stubborn woman. He felt as if he'd fallen into a briar patch.

"You believe me?"

He swung his head to look at her. Her voice had such a plaintive note, he couldn't help but stare. The truth of the matter was, he hadn't thought about what he believed or didn't believe. The story she'd told Sheriff Beaker sounded like something out of a supermarket tabloid. Precognitive dreams, visions, murders. If the tale had come from anyone except the small, worried woman sitting beside him, he would have said that person had a rich fantasy life. But Cassandra—and he'd seen her in the throes of her nightmare, or seizure as she called it—wasn't the kind to exaggerate or lie for effect.

"I believe you believe it," he said at last.

"But you don't believe it's real."

He hesitated. "I don't know. I haven't given a lot of thought to this kind of thing before. Off the cuff, I'd have to say I was a skeptic. That was before I saw you, though."

"Maybe I'm just a damn good actress." Her temper flared and she couldn't help it. Why was she concerned whether this man believed her or not? He was a businessman out to make a deal. Her sanity wasn't up for him to judge.

"Maybe," Adam agreed. He cast her a devilish look. "If that's the case, all the more reason you should do a commercial endorsing my cereal. If acting is your career goal, a commercial might help."

She felt like telling him to take a flying leap off the side of the mountain, but she held herself in check. It was only another mile to her door. Another few minutes and she'd send him packing. The only trouble was, she didn't really want to stay alone. Maybe Running Stream would send Bounder over after all. The Indian woman was smart, and sensitive. She often did the exact opposite of what Cassandra requested—she knew Cassandra's heart and ignored her mouth.

"Mr. Raleigh, you've been very kind." She thought about the way he'd held her. "Much more than kind. I appreciate everything you've done, and if there was any way I could help you without betraying my own beliefs, I would. But I can't. It would be best if you went back to Michigan."

"Best for you, or best for me?"

In the glow of the headlights, Cassandra could see the last turn in the road to her cabin. "For both of us." She was bone tired.

"If you'll call a friend, I'll be glad to go."

She heard the finality in his voice and knew that further argument was useless. It was, after all, a smart request. She wasn't certain if she could wake up again if she had another seizure. As much as she disliked the idea, she could call Running Stream.

"Okay," she agreed as Adam drove into her yard and cut the engine.

Inside, Cassandra didn't waste any time. She stopped only long enough to give the big black cat a friendly stroke before she picked up the telephone and dialed. A few seconds later, she was pressing the switch hook up and down. There was no dial tone.

"Service is unreliable," she admitted. "Lots of miles of line and lots of storms." Uneasiness tingled the small of her back. Local teenagers sometimes sneaked up on her property, hoping for a glimpse of the "mountain witch." Sometimes they committed small acts of vandalism. The idea of being alone, without a phone or a reliable car, was scary.

"The local kids like to play pranks on me sometimes," she said aloud.

"If you need me, I'll be parked outside," Adam said. "I know you don't want me to stay, but I'm going to, anyway. For my own peace of mind. Have a good sleep."

His hand was on the knob when he yelped and jumped back. "Wait a minute!" The cat's claws dug sharply into his calf. "That blasted cat!"

"Familiar!" Cassandra was shocked. "Stop that."

Familiar unhooked his claws one by one. He held his paw in midair, contemplated it a few seconds, and then began to clean it.

"That animal has it in for me," Adam said. "He attacked me on the sofa earlier."

Cassandra looked from the cat to Adam. "I think he's trying to tell you to stay. It would seem that Familiar has more sense than either of us." Her smile was self-deprecating. "I am a bit uncomfortable staying alone, Adam. It's silly for you to sleep in the car when I have a guest room. Please stay."

Adam hid his victory grin. The cat was a pain in the neck, but he had perfect timing. The strange idea that he and Familiar were working together to protect Cassandra flitted through his mind. "I'll get my things." He looked at the cat. Familiar held his gaze, then slowly closed one eye.

ADAM HEARD THE RATTLE of the car engine and the slamming door before he was fully awake. He opened his eyes to the blast of morning sun that came in the window of his room. It was a room that perfectly reflected his hostess—

quilts and handwoven rugs, polished antiques and the smell of fresh flowers. He closed his eyes and thought of Cassandra. She was a beautiful woman, in an odd sort of way. Her eyes. That's what drew him to her. They were unusual in the depth of their honesty. She looked and didn't flinch. Nor did she hide her own troubles. All of her emotions were there to see, reflected in the sky blueness.

The sound of breaking glass had him out of bed and scrambling down the steep stairs from the guest room in the loft. "Cassandra?"

There was no answer, and he hurried into the kitchen, heedless of his state of near undress. He was wearing only his pajama bottoms. The house seemed empty, and he almost ran to the front porch. He was out the screen door before he saw the sheriff's car.

Cassandra was holding on to the porch railing as she talked with the lawman. Pieces of a broken water glass were around her bare feet, and she ignored them. Both she and the sheriff turned as he came out the door.

"Mr. Raleigh," Sheriff Beaker nodded. He glanced knowingly at Adam's bare chest.

"Sheriff," he said, but his concern was for Cassandra. She was pale and obviously holding on to the railing for support.

"They found Carla Winchester's body. In a ravine. She was strangled," Cassandra said slowly. "The sheriff wants to know where I was night before last."

"And I'd like to know your whereabouts, too," Beaker said as he stared at Adam. "I didn't realize you and Ms. McBeth were such good friends." He said the last word with a twist. "I got the impression you'd only met yesterday."

Adam went to Cassandra and bent to pick up the broken glass before she stepped on it. "I was in Knoxville at the Marriott. I checked out about eleven a.m. and started driving this way."

"I'm sure the hotel can verify that."

"I'm sure they can." Adam had the big pieces of glass gathered in his hand. He stood up and went to the edge of the porch. "Ms. McBeth went to your office trying to help. Why do I get the impression that you're accusing her of something?"

Beaker didn't move. "Maybe not her. Maybe you."

Cassandra's hand on Adam's arm was light, almost fluttery. "It's okay," she said softly. "He's only doing what he has to do. I know too much about the murder. I described it perfectly, didn't I? Carla Winchester was strangled from behind. The fingers pressed into her throat, just to the side and below the larynx. She struggled, going down on one knee in the gravel as she tried to get away. One hand clawed his face. There was tissue beneath the nails of her right hand, wasn't there? That would mean the scratches are on the right side of his face."

Both men were staring at her in fascination.

"Where did you find the body?" Cassandra asked.

"A hiker found it on a trail in a shallow ravine. It had been covered with brush."

"She wasn't killed there," Cassandra said. "It was somewhere with a view. High up."

"Ms. McBeth, if you're withholding anything, you could be charged as an accessory to murder." Beaker's hand had moved to his gun belt, where it hung loosely beside the grip of his gun.

"In case you've forgotten, Ms. McBeth went to your office voluntarily," Adam interjected.

"Where did you get those claw marks on your face?" the sheriff countered.

Adam touched the traces of the scratches Cassandra had given him. Since he hadn't shaved yet, he'd forgotten about them.

"When I was dreaming yesterday I accidentally scratched Mr. Raleigh," Cassandra said. "Those marks were made from the front, with my left hand." She held out her hand to show the short, well-cared-for nails.

"And where were you night before last?" Beaker asked her.

"Here. Alone."

"No alibi?"

She shook her head. "None."

"I thought Mr. Raleigh might say you were in Knoxville with him." Beaker let the accusation hang in the air.

"We weren't acquainted until yesterday," Cassandra said with complete dignity.

"Don't leave the area," Beaker said as he turned back to his car. "Either of you."

Adam and Cassandra watched the sheriff walk away. He got into his car, pulled around and left in a cloud of dust.

"He thinks you're involved in this," Adam said with amazement. "He really believes you did something wrong."

"I am involved," Cassandra said slowly. "Unfortunately, you are, too."

CASSANDRA EXAMINED the spoonful of cereal. She knew Adam was watching her as she lifted it to her mouth. Adam and a very interested black cat. She took the bite. It was crisp, not sticky sweet. She could detect the subtle flavors of the grains. Bits of dried apple gave it a naturally sweet taste.

"Well?" Adam prodded.

"It's not as bad as I thought it would be." The cereal was good. And if Adam's claims about the ingredients were true, it was a healthy cereal. It was just the idea of dry cold cereal that made her cringe. All of those innocent children munching down on sugar puffs with marshmallows and goo. The idea of what cereal had become was what she rejected. How could she make Adam understand?

"It's a good product," he said. "If children would eat Good Stuff..."

"But they won't. Given a choice, they'll take the candy-coated junk, and by marketing a product like Good Stuff, you encourage parents to buy cereal."

"I'm giving them a choice, Cassandra. A healthy product over things that are bad for their children."

"Adam, I tried your cereal. Now I have work to do on a book. I appreciate everything you've done, all the trouble I've caused you. But it's time for you to go." She picked up

Familiar and held him in her lap as she checked his wound.
The gash had begun to heal, and with the application of her
herbal remedies, even the scar would be minimized. He'd
taken the bandage off as soon as she'd put it on, and luckily, it wasn't necessary anymore.

"What about tonight?"

"You don't have to worry about me anymore. I'm not
afraid. I'm home. The phone service will be repaired. I'll be
fine."

"I mean, would you have dinner with me?" Adam picked
up the box of cereal and put it on the counter, out of sight.
"No business, no pressure. Just dinner. I'll pick you up and
bring you home. That way I can check around your house
and make sure you're okay."

"Don't you have a life in Michigan? I mean, shouldn't
you get back to your company?" Cassandra got up and put
a bowl of milk on the floor for Familiar. The black cat settled down to a leisurely breakfast. Adam disconcerted her.
He'd moved from a professional to a personal plane in one
giant step. Did she want him to stay around? She honestly
didn't know, and that troubled her.

"I haven't had a vacation in five years. I think I can afford to stay around a day or two and learn about the Smok-
ies. I was hoping you might show me some of your plants."

Cassandra felt the pull of conflict. Adam was adept at
putting pressure on her, and she didn't like it. He made
everything he said sound so reasonable.

Yet she found his company very pleasurable. He'd been
a perfect gentleman in her home, but there was something
in the way he looked at her that made her heart jump. He
was a handsome man. When he'd walked out the front door
clad only in his pajama bottoms, she hadn't reacted, but her
mind had registered the image. Lean torso with a light covering of brown hair on his chest. She remembered the feel
of that chest as he'd held her. It was strong and gave her a
sense of security.

Even more important, he didn't flinch. He'd taken everything that had happened in the past twenty-four hours

and none of it had rattled him. He was remarkable. It crossed her mind that she liked him more than she should. He was passing through her life, a man who'd come on an errand and would leave as soon as he realized he wouldn't get what he'd come for.

"In your third book, you write about a meadow not far from your house. I was hoping we could go there."

"We can." She looked at him, pleased by the open enthusiasm he had for life. He did know a lot about her writing, and her ideas. What would it hurt to take a walk with him? "We can go now. In fact, let me pack a picnic and we'll have lunch there." The truth was, she didn't want him to leave. There was something about Adam that attracted her. If she were being honest with herself, and she tried to be at all times, she wanted him to stay.

They talked about herbs, spices and natural medicines as Cassandra packed a picnic lunch. Adam did, indeed, know about natural foods and medicines. As they talked, she picked up tidbits about his past that intrigued her more and more.

The son of a corporate banker, Adam had rejected a handpicked invitation to work at a large bank and started his own company. Good Stuff was small, compared to the larger food companies. The breakfast cereal was their first product, but Adam was ready to expand. In the past few years, Adam had fought off several attempts at leveraged buy-outs. He was determined to keep Good Stuff small and accountable.

When the basket was packed, Cassandra held the door open for Familiar. "Coming with us?" she asked.

"Cats don't go for walks," Adam told her. "Cats are notoriously arrogant and never do anything like go for a walk."

"Meow," Familiar said on a throaty purr as he walked out the open door and went to the steps to wait for them.

"Familiar isn't an ordinary cat," Cassandra reminded him with a smile. "Don't ever underestimate him. He has some uncanny powers."

"Like you?" Adam teased.

"I'm not certain." Cassandra's brow was slightly furrowed. "Maybe not exactly like me, but Familiar's smart, and he knows a lot more than anyone thinks possible. Maybe all cats do."

"Meow," Familiar said, looking up at her. "Meow." He led the way down the steps and toward the meadow.

"See," Cassandra laughed. "We'd better hurry and catch up."

As they left the cabin behind, Cassandra pointed out the many different types of trees and wildflowers.

"Spring hits here suddenly. One day the land is gray, the next, tiny green buds are showing, and then the next day, it's spring."

"I've spent too long at my desk." Adam looked around him and sighed. The beauty of the mountains made him want to forget his work. For a split second he entertained the thought of moving. A cabin tucked high on the side of a mountain, like Cassandra's. Rich meadows and orchards around him. What would he do? He'd always dreamed of using his knowledge of herbs to make natural medicines. Cassandra wrote about cures and remedies handed down for generations. He wanted to make the actual salves and medicines. His cereal company was one aspect of that desire—healthy foods. But there was so much more he wanted to do.

"This orchard has been in my family for generations," Cassandra said as they walked. Her voice, naturally husky, deepened even more. "Like any other piece of ground, it continues when those who love it die."

For a small person, Cassandra took long strides. Adam couldn't help but notice the way her jeans tightened and relaxed as she walked. She used her entire leg to move forward, and she set a pace that made Adam hustle. The terrain was uphill, and he felt perspiration break out on his forehead even though the morning was still cool.

"The McBeth family has been in these parts for as long as the mountains have been settled," she continued, unaware of his scrutiny. "My dad's folks came over from Ireland, and they laid claim to this part of the mountain. My dad was the last, though. Or I should say that I am. He was an only child. I understand it was a bit of a fray when he married my mother."

"She wasn't from these parts, then?"

"Not by a long shot." Cassandra laughed. "My mother is European. It depends on her mood which country she's from, but always European." She laughed again. "She is exotic."

"How did she learn to tell fortunes?"

"Family trade. Her mother and her grandmother had done it. She said it was a gift, and she believes it. She does have an... ability to know about people. It's extraordinary."

"Where is she now?" Adam had wondered at Cassandra living alone. He'd assumed she had no relatives.

"Traveling. The last I heard, she was in Poland. I guess we have relatives all over the place. After my father died, she stayed here as long as she could. I don't think she ever wanted to stay in one place long. She was like a tumbleweed marrying a fence post. As long as Dad was alive, he kept her anchored to this place. Then—" she waved one hand in the air, palm up "—she was gone."

"And you stayed." That fact was more than a little interesting to Adam. "Why?"

"I guess I'm like my father in the way that I love this place. Even after the folks in town treated him badly about Mom, he still loved this land. He couldn't have left it, and I'm like him that way."

An hour had passed and they had covered several miles. Cassandra showed no sign of tiring or fatigue. The path split in two directions, and Familiar stood patiently at the intersection. Adam's natural inclination was to go right, but Cassandra tugged at his sleeve.

"Not that way."

"Why not?"

Cassandra's blue gaze was direct. "Bad memories. There's an overlook there that goes all the way down the mountain.'' She could tell by the way Adam's eyes brightened that the idea interested him.

"My father died there when I was a child,'' she added.

Chapter Four

Ah, a simple country meal of chicken and cheese. None of that fancy sauce that I was eating in Washington—ruining my figure, too. No, this is the life. Fresh air, sunshine, exercise, a little snooze on the quilt Cassandra brought.

My leg is getting stronger and stronger, and along with watching out for Miss Locks, I've been putting a lot of thought into what happened with Eleanor.

She's alive. I know it. If she weren't, I'd be able to tell. Hanging around Miss Locks has given me a new appreciation for my feline instincts. Well, it isn't totally my instincts. The news report said no bodies were found in my bombed home. Eleanor is alive, but I think she's hurt. That bothers me. Where is she? What can I do to help her?

Chances are Dr. Doolittle would get her out of Washington, if at all possible. He has contacts in the medical profession. But where would he take her? How can I get there? I'd never admit it to anyone else, but there are times when being a cat has distinct disadvantages. I mean, I'm a better driver than most of these maniacs behind the wheel of a car, but do you think they'd give me a license? Besides, I can't really see over the steering wheel. And who designed the automobile, anyway? The pedals are too far down on the floor. The upshot is that I have to figure out a way to catch a ride back to Washington. Getting in a car might not be that difficult, but getting it to go where I want, and then getting out of it again, will be tricky.

First, though, I have to figure out what to do. I tried to dial the phone the other day, but the line was dead. I guess that's the next step. Get the phone repaired and make an effort to get Dr. Doolittle's office. I remember the number. If I can just get him to answer instead of that battle-ax Lucille. She'll hang up on me. Dr. D. might have enough savvy to figure out my voice.

Get the phone fixed. That's the first step. Eat, rest and keep a watch on Miss Locks. From what I can see, Lancelot is quite willing to keep an eye on her. I'll bet he'd like to put a hand on her, too. Hey, hey. At least I haven't lost my touch for puns.

ADAM LEANED BACK on the quilt. The pattern was the Rose of Sharon, one her grandmother on her father's side had made for her hope chest when Cassandra was still an infant. It was a thought that interested Adam. Why hadn't Cassandra married? She was one of the most beautiful women he'd ever seen—not just in body, but in spirit. Why had she chosen to lead such a solitary, isolated life?

"More bread and cheese?" Cassandra asked. She cut another piece of cheese for Familiar. The cat's appetite was ravenous.

"I can't eat another bite," Adam said, stretching even longer on the soft quilt.

"You'll be hungry again—when we walk down the mountain." Cassandra was on her side, resting on one elbow. Adam's eyes were closed, and she studied this unusual man who'd broken into her life. He'd come when she was in the throes of a dream, when all of her defenses were trashed and useless. Otherwise, he'd never have gotten his toe in the front door. But she had to admit, it was odd how he fit in so easily—almost like the cat. She smiled slightly. Running Stream would say that the gods had sent her a gift when she needed him. To the Cherokee woman, every action had a purpose.

"Meow," Familiar said, as if to insist that it were true. He went to Cassandra and flopped onto his back at her side. Motor running, he demanded a rub.

Still stroking the cat, Cassandra lightly cleared her throat. "Thanks for being with me. Beaker's a difficult man, and he didn't believe a word I told him."

"No thanks necessary." Adam kept his eyes closed by an act of will. He felt Cassandra was going to say something. If he looked at her, she might shy away.

"I've been alone since my father died. That's the emotional reality if not the physical truth. My mother..." Cassandra paused. "Well, we're just very different. It was odd having someone on my side. Thank you, Adam."

He wanted to take her in his arms and hold her, but he knew he couldn't. He'd done it once, only because she'd been trapped between consciousness and a terrifying dreamscape. If he tried it now, she'd run away from him. "I'm not in the habit of traipsing around the mountains helping out women in distress, but I have to say, it made me feel good, Cassandra. You gave me something, too, an opportunity to help another person. One, I think, who doesn't often accept help from anyone." He opened his eyes and smiled at her. "Thank you."

The rush of warmth that Cassandra felt toward Adam made her want to lean over and kiss him. "We'd better go back," she said, her voice slightly roughened from the many emotions she held so tightly in check. She stood up quickly and began repacking the basket. Adam Raleigh troubled her—because he'd pierced her barriers and made her feel.

Adam carried the basket down the mountain with Cassandra at his side and Familiar pouncing from one clump of brush to another. The sun warmed their backs, and the silence they shared was companionable. They both had lots to think about.

At the cabin, Cassandra took the basket while Adam retrieved his things. It would be better for all if he left immediately. "Thanks for everything, Adam. I'm sorry I couldn't represent your cereal." Why was this parting so hard? She wanted Adam to leave. He disrupted the serenity she valued so much, and yet she was so drawn to him. In a rare impulsive gesture, she took the two steps that separated them and kissed his cheek. The sensation made her lips tingle. His skin smelled of sun and orchard. "Good luck with your company." She retreated behind the screened door, waiting for him to leave.

Adam squelched his desire to take her in his arms and kiss her properly. "Please check the phone before I go and make sure it's repaired." Every instinct in his body told him to stay with Cassandra. Yet he was packed and ready to leave. He had no valid reason to stay, and she'd made it clear that she preferred him to go.

Cassandra motioned Adam inside as she stepped into the den. She put the receiver to her ear. "Still dead." She gave it a puzzled look. "That's odd. There haven't been any severe storms. Usually they get the service back on in a few hours."

"I'll check the line," Adam offered. He dropped his bag before she could protest. A loose wire wouldn't be a problem, but it might be an excuse to delay his departure. He walked to the back of the cabin, tracing the line from the pole to the house with his eyes. When he found the wall box, he stopped. The line was cut—clean and straight. Whoever had done it meant business. A chill of apprehension tickled his neck. This wasn't a premonition. The damaged line was a fact. He wasn't leaving, no matter what Cassandra said.

Determined to stay, Adam went back into the house. To his amusement, the cat was sitting on the sofa watching television with Cassandra stroking his back.

"The line is—"

"Listen." Cassandra held up a finger for silence. "It's Martin West. He's doing a show on the strangled women."

Adam's attention went to the screen. He recognized Sheriff Beaker, but he'd never seen the two women who were sitting on either side of the lawman.

"One is a psychologist specializing in violence against women, Dr. Libby Smith. The other is Janey Ables's mother," Cassandra explained.

On closer inspection, Adam could see that one woman had obviously been crying. She was talking about her daughter's dreams and ambitions, all gone now.

West moved skillfully between his interviewees, building a picture of two young women who happened to be in the wrong place at the wrong time. Then he shifted the focus to the lawman.

There was no reason behind the killings, as far as Beaker could determine. Under West's probing questions, the conclusion was chilling: a killer who killed for the pleasure of inflicting pain and death, a person acting out some fantasy over and over again.

"He's a smart man," Beaker said. "FBI profiles of this type of killer show that they're usually of very high intelligence. They don't think they'll ever get caught. Sometimes, it becomes a game with him, tricking the authorities or anyone else who tries to track him down."

"Him?" West questioned.

"Him," Beaker said. "It's a man."

"You're very positive on that point. In fact, that's the only thing you've been positive about, Sheriff." West grinned at the camera. "You mentioned before the show started that there is some . . . disfigurement to the bodies."

Anger touched Beaker's face. "You agreed not to mention—"

West abruptly jumped in. "What do you make of the fact that the killer removes hair from the victims?"

"We have specialists studying that fact." Beaker was upset.

"It isn't a scalping, exactly," West continued. "The hair is cut close to the scalp, in the front, correct?"

"Yes." Beaker's voice was rigid.

"Based on your other deductions, perhaps we can assume that the killer is a bald man who is so self-conscious he thinks women don't like him so he decides to strike back."

Cassandra's fists clenched in her lap. "He's making a joke of all of this. Women are dying, and he's using it as a stage to mug."

Adam eased down onto the sofa beside her, and the cat inched closer so that he purred against her leg. Martin West didn't interest Adam; he'd seen a hundred fame-hungry television personalities who'd perform any indignity in the hopes of getting noticed. It was Cassandra who worried him. She was at the breaking point.

"I could sense part of this," she said softly. "He doesn't mean to kill. At least not at first. He thinks he isn't going to do it this time. But then he does. He has to win, he has to be dominant over the woman. And the sheriff is correct. Now it's becoming a game of who's smarter. You know Beaker could become a target himself."

"Yeah, well, Beaker's going to start a panic for sure," Adam said. "I'm no director of tourism, but this is the beginning of the summer season here in Gatlinburg. I suspect the town is swarming with young women earning money for college. If they think a killer's on the loose preying on young women, it's going to turn this town into total chaos."

"Beaker must be very concerned to risk going on television. He must not have a single lead."

Cassandra watched as the camera closed in on the sheriff's face. Beaker was speaking calmly of the need for all young women in the area to practice sensible precautions. He was reminding the citizenry to lock all doors and windows, to avoid dark and dangerous locations and above all, not to talk with strangers.

"Because of the high influx of tourists into Gatlinburg at this time of year, we're looking for a stranger in town, a transient," Beaker said. "Gatlinburg is a small community for most of the year. We know our neighbors. This is a problem that stems from outsiders," he said grimly.

Adam shifted uneasily on the sofa. "Beaker's doing the best he can, but that Martin guy has really painted a frightening picture. There's nothing worse than a killer who has no motive, who kills for the pleasure of the kill. That's what West has projected. Some kind of monster."

Cassandra nodded. "Yes, a brilliant monster. Martin West has become very popular with this kind of tactic. I seldom watch his show. He seems to have a penchant for attracting controversial guests with emotional topics."

"I've seem similar shows. Women who are married to men who have had sex change operations to become women." Adam shook his head. "The public desire to confess, to anything, is amazing."

"Martin West is good at it. He gets the audience stirred to the point of panic. There have been fights on his show, members of the audience hitting each other. It's apparently a great rating gimmick. I hear he's even getting some nibbles of interest from the networks."

Adam clicked off the set. "West may benefit from this kind of story, but no one else does."

"You're right about that." Something about Beaker was nagging at Cassandra. "What about the phone?"

"The line is down." Adam twisted the truth, for the moment. Cassandra had enough to worry about. Since he was staying, she didn't have to know the line had been cut. "Until you have phone service, you have a guest."

Cassandra calmly met his gaze. She could see the hint of belligerence in his eyes, the set to his jaw. It would be useless to argue. "Okay. Until the phone is repaired." Adam could stay, but she refused to probe her reasons for allowing it.

He couldn't believe her easy acquiescence. "Are you okay?"

"My car has been towed to town. My phone line is down. It would be really stupid of me to send you away, wouldn't it? I like my privacy, but until I can get in touch with some of my friends, it's nice to have another adult around."

"Meow," Familiar agreed before either could speak.

Adam checked his watch. "I need to run back into town before it gets dark. Can I bring anything?"

"No." Cassandra picked up Familiar and rose from the sofa. "We need to do some work out in the garden. I have some buds that must be protected. There's a cool front coming in."

"I have to make some calls to my office." He also had to report her cut line. "I'll be back."

Cassandra nodded. It was strange. Her feelings were mixed as she watched him leave. There was a sense of relief, and just a small tingle of…regret. The thought that he would return made her smile. She'd spent so much of her adult life alone, it was a new experience to anticipate another's presence. It was something she wanted to think about as she transferred her plants to a warmer environment. Gloves in hand, she went to the back door with Familiar at her heels.

Three hours later, her knees and back tired, she started for the house. She wanted a bit of her mint for iced tea. She'd planted it near the spigot on the side of the house.

The leaves were tender as she pinched off a few. Rising, she glanced at the hookup for the telephone. She knew immediately that the line had been cut. Her fingers tightened on the delicate leaves, crushing until the minty odor seeped from her hand. The line had been cut. By whom?

More importantly, why had Adam lied?

The obvious answer was so frightening that she refused to acknowledge it for a moment. Turning stiffly, she walked toward the house. She didn't allow her mind to think until she'd closed the door and taken a seat at the kitchen table.

If Adam had cut the line, then he was deliberately trying to isolate her on the mountain. Why?

Because he was . . . Beaker's words of warning came back to her like a second, cruel blow…a stranger in town. When Carla Winchester was killed, Adam had claimed to be in the Knoxville Marriott. He'd *claimed* to be there. Even if he had been, it was close enough that he could have driven to Gatlinburg the night of her murder. And Janey Ables? He could easily have been in the area for a week or more.

Cold sweat spiked the small of her back. She felt fear tightening around her rib cage, squeezing off her lungs. Forcing a deep breath, she held it until she felt the stricture relax. Now was no time to lose her nerve.

But why was he coming after her? That didn't make any sense at all. She pushed her panic down a notch. No, it didn't make a bit of sense that Adam would seek her out and that she would suddenly be having precognitive dreams of the murders.

Unless the dreams had recurred because he was somehow linked with her!

For a second she thought her heart would stop. Her scalp began to burn, as if thousands of ants had suddenly started biting her. She dropped her head between her knees and drew in long breaths.

This was the thing that had most disturbed her about the dreams. Why her? Why now? She had nothing that she knew about in common with either of the victims or the murderer. So why was she having the dreams? Before, with her father, it had been a strong link, a bond of love. And the dream had occurred simultaneously with the event.

Could it be Adam? He stirred emotions in her, there was no point denying it. He made her think of things she'd long ago put aside, intimate things. Had he upset some delicate balance that opened her to the "talent" she had so long buried?

The dreams had come before his arrival. Perhaps his presence in the area was enough. If he was the killer...

The sound of his car in the drive held her frozen. She knew then the feel of a rabbit in the road blinded by the headlights of a car. She had to move, to act normally. She was alone with him now, for the night at least. Unless she could get his car keys. But if he suspected anything, he might kill her.

Footsteps echoed along the front porch. Wiping her hands on her jeans, Cassandra put a smile on her face.

Adam came through the front door with his arms loaded with grocery bags.

"Since I'm an uninvited guest, I thought I might at least bring some food. I also got some wine." He put the bags on the table. "What's wrong?"

"Uh, a little scare in the garden. Snake." Cassandra laughed, but it was a ragged sound. She forced her gaze away from his. She wanted to stare at him, to see if she could ascertain the truth by looking at him. "It's a little early in the season, and I wasn't expecting a reptilian visitor."

"Poisonous?"

"No, just a rat snake. He went his way and I went mine."

Adam unloaded the sacks. With a start, Cassandra moved to put the food away.

"The company is running smooth as silk. They said for me to stay away as long as it took."

"That's wonderful."

"I also stopped by the phone company and asked them to come up and make the repairs."

Her fingers clutched the bread in her hand. "Oh? What did they say?"

"First thing tomorrow." Adam took the bread from her hand. For a long moment he stared at her. "You found where the line was cut, didn't you?"

Cassandra had never felt so alone in her life. Dusk had settled around her cabin, the home that had always felt like a fortress against disappointment and loneliness. She had never been more in danger. With his dark eyes examining every nuance, she knew it was pointless to lie. He knew the truth. "Yes," she whispered.

"I didn't tell you because I didn't want to frighten you." She swallowed. "I see."

"You think I did it, don't you?"

He didn't move, but Cassandra took a step back. "How long have you been around here?"

"Cassandra, I didn't do it. I found the line cut and I did report it. That's why I went into town. I didn't tell you because I didn't want to frighten you. I knew I would be here, and you've had enough on your mind."

"Who did it?"

Adam folded the paper sack and placed it carefully on the table. "When was the last time you used the phone?"

"I don't know," Cassandra answered. "Days ago."

"You said teenagers come up here to steal things. Could it have been one of them?"

"Yes, but that isn't likely. They take plants and knick-knacks from the yard or porch. Cutting the phone wouldn't help them. By the time the sheriff got here, even if I called him, they could walk off with most of the house."

Adam nodded as he accepted the truth. "Well, whoever did it meant to cut your connection with the rest of the world. For whatever reason."

"Did you do it, Adam?" She held her gaze steady on him. She couldn't read the truth in a person. Not always. But she could try.

"I did not."

She didn't completely believe him. Not at all. But she did believe that if he intended to hurt her, it wasn't at this particular time. If he was insane, then his madness was momentarily at bay. That thought sent a chill down the length of her body. She forced herself to focus on the positive aspect—at least she had time. There was a chance she might escape.

"I'm going to stay in my car," Adam said. He could read the fear in her eyes. It was evident in the way she stood, her arms so motionless she was terrified to make even the slightest move.

"No!"

The vehemence of her denial startled him. "Why not?"

"Stay in here. I'd rather be able to see you."

"Okay," he agreed. "But you have to stop acting as if I'm going to do something dastardly if you even breathe. I know it's hard for you, and I don't blame you, Cassandra, but I'm not going to hurt you."

"Give me your wallet."

He drew the billfold from his hip pocket and put it on the table. "I am Adam Raleigh. In the morning, when the phone is repaired, you can call my company. Until then, I guess you're going to have to take my word. Now will you let me prepare some dinner, or do you think I'm going to poison you?''

Cassandra picked up his wallet and stepped out of his way. In a moment she had out his driver's license, insurance card, credit cards and several photographs of a teenage girl.

"My niece," he said without looking up. "My sister's child, Bethany. She's a pretty girl, isn't she?"

He'd picked up catfish fillets in the local market and was busy preparing them. He cut a sliver of the white meat and put it in the cat's dish on the floor. When Familiar walked over to sample the morsel, he stroked the cat's back. "I'm who I say I am, Cassandra. Be wary of me, if you must. But don't do anything to get yourself hurt."

The rumble of thunder seemed to underline his words.

"The cold front," she said softly. Oh, great. She needed a storm now! With her nerves pulled as tight as piano wire, she'd never survive the booming and crashing of a mountaintop storm.

"We'll eat, batten down the hatches and wait for morning," Adam said. "You're safe . . . I can promise you that, but I can't make you believe it."

She put his billfold back on the table. "If you're who you say you are. If you did send all of those contracts. If you're telling the truth, maybe I am."

"Trust me," Adam answered.

"Said the wolf to Little Red Riding Hood."

THE STORM HIT the cabin in the early hours of the morning. Cassandra sat huddled at one end of the sofa watching the lightning fork against the graying windows. Dawn was coming, and she was glad. She'd slept fitfully, on and off, amazed that her body would betray her so when she wanted to stay awake.

Sleep held its own torment. The dreams were always lurking, always possible. She hadn't slept soundly in at least a week, and the deprivation was beginning to take its toll on her.

In contrast, Adam had taken his former space in the loft bedroom and was snoozing soundly. Cassandra had checked on him to make sure. He'd effectively hamstrung her plan to escape by pointing out that if he weren't the one who cut her phone line, then the real culprit could be hiding out somewhere in the dense woods around her house. Rushing about in the dark, she might accidentally encounter the one person she didn't want to meet. He'd pressed that point home to her with emphasis. It was better to stay with the devil she could see than to brave the devil she didn't know at all. At least for the night.

Walking to the window, Cassandra watched the showy display of electricity. She loved thunderstorms on the mountain. Somehow, it put life in perspective. The cabin was storm tight, and the rain pounding against the glass was normally soothing. Even the rumble of the thunder was usually comforting. Tonight, it only confirmed Cassandra's imprisonment. She stared out the window, her fingers tracing the cool pane.

A triple-pronged fork of light blazed across the noisy sky. At the edge of the woods, a lone figure stared at the house.

The scream caught in Cassandra's throat. She put her hand to her mouth, holding back silence. The figure, and it was a man, stood watching the house. His hands hung down at his sides, empty fists dangling. Buckets of rain fell on him, but he didn't move. He watched the darkened house.

''Adam.'' Cassandra whispered the name. ''Adam!'' she cried, but it was only a harsh whisper. She wasn't afraid the man outside would hear. The storm was far too loud. But her voice wouldn't work. She couldn't tear her gaze away from the man. It was almost as if they were bonded together.

Outside, the storm raged, but the only sound in the room was the movement of Familiar. The cat jumped to the windowsill beside Cassandra. His back went into a tight arch, and a deep, guttural hiss escaped from him.

"Familiar," Cassandra said, and it broke her vocal paralysis. "Adam!" she called out loud. "Hurry!"

Her cry was greeted by the sound of footsteps on the stairs. She turned to motion Adam toward her. "Quick. There's someone in the yard."

"What is it?" Hair tousled, Adam hurried to the window. "Where?" He searched the grayness. "There's no one there. What are you talking about?"

Turning back to search the grounds outside the house, Cassandra, too, found emptiness. Only Familiar seemed to see, or sense, the stranger. He remained arched on the sill, his lips curled back on low growls.

"There was a man there," Cassandra said quickly. "It was the killer. I know it was him. He was watching the house." She took a shaky breath. "It was almost as if he knew me and was watching me."

"Did you get a good look at him?" All traces of sleep were gone from Adam's face. "I'm going out to take a look for some clues."

"The rain," Cassandra said bleakly. "It'll wash everything away."

Adam took four long steps across the room to the door. "Flashlight?"

"On the shelf beside the door. Be careful."

The din of the storm entered the house for a split second as Adam opened the door and rushed barefoot into the rain.

Taking up her watch at the window, Cassandra saw him searching the edge of the woods. She watched with her heart in her throat. What if someone came out of the trees and attacked Adam?

When he turned back, running toward the house with long-legged strides, she felt relief. She hurried to the bathroom, grabbed a towel, and met him at the door.

"Nothing," he said as he dried the cold rain from his face and head. "The ground is an inch deep in water."

"I saw him," Cassandra answered. "I swear it."

"Can you describe him?"

Cassandra thought for a moment. "Not really. He was bigger than average height. Muscular."

"Hair?"

"I couldn't see."

"Clothes?"

"A long-sleeved blue jacket. Dark pants, long. Jeans, maybe." She paused. "Nothing, really, now that I try and tell you about it. I didn't see enough to be of help at all. And I stared at him."

"From a long distance through a rainstorm," Adam soothed her. He brushed back a curl of her hair. The triangle of skin between her eyebrows was furrowed with worry. "At least you saw someone, and now you know it isn't me."

"I saw someone," Cassandra said, turning away. "And I'm more confused than ever. I don't know who to believe. I don't even know if I believe my own eyes."

Chapter Five

"You're very pretty, you know. Since you're new in the area, I'd like to show you some of the better views."

The voice seemed to come from under water. Dark and undulating, it penetrated her ears and nose and mouth. Cassandra felt herself drowning and struggled to get to the surface, but she could not move.

"I have to be at work in a couple of hours. Besides, I'm not really new here anymore. I've been here three weeks."

This voice, light and feminine, held the echo of death. Cassandra had to warn her, to speak, but she was weighed down by water.

"Just a ride around. Take in a few of the scenic views. There's one really special one...in the park."

"I shouldn't."

"But you want to."

The young woman's laughter was light and easy. "Sorry, mister, maybe another time. I'm new here, and I have to have this job. Besides, my mother told me never to take up with strangers. Especially not when murders are happening."

"Your mama was right. But I'm no stranger."

"Yeah, you're familiar. Too familiar. You act like we've known each other for years." The laughter came again, rich and carefree. "Ask me again, another time."

The voices faded. Penned under the murky depths of the water, Cassandra felt the lull of the waves. The danger was over. The voices were still. She slept.

ADAM PUT HIS HAND on Cassandra's forehead. She was cool and apparently sound asleep. For a moment, he'd thought she was going to have another nightmare. She'd begun to struggle fiercely, mumbling words under her breath he couldn't understand. Now, though, she settled back into an easy sleep.

He debated whether to wake her and decided against it. It was late morning. After breakfast, Cassandra had finally stretched out on the sofa and taken a nap. She'd had only a few hours' sleep, and he could think of no reason to awaken her.

The storm had detained any phone repair crews. The rain had slacked off, and he'd searched outside the house for clues to the man Cassandra had seen. There was no sign of any intruder. If there had been any, the rain had washed it all away.

He was about to doze into a light sleep himself when he heard a noise at the front door. His body tensed, his ears straining for any sound.

Yes, there was a distinct noise coming from the door. He eased off the sofa, careful not to disturb Cassandra, and tiptoed to the front of the house. When he inched the door open, he was met by the dark, intense gaze of a powerfully built young man.

"Who are you?" the young man asked with hostility in his voice. Dark eyes narrowed. "Where's Cassandra?"

"Ms. McBeth is safe. Who are you?" Adam kept his voice level. The young man was glowering at him. He noticed the man's hair was long and dark, tied at the base of his skull with a leather thong. His features were distinctly American Indian.

"My name is Bounder. Who are you?" He jammed his foot into the crack in the door. "Where is Cassandra?"

"She's asleep," Adam answered. The young man looked dangerous, but he also acted as if he had a right to be on Cassandra's property. "I'm Adam Raleigh, a business acquaintance of Ms. McBeth's."

"I need to speak with her." Bounder flexed his leg enough to let Adam know that he wouldn't back down from a physical confrontation.

Adam studied the young man, taking in the features that marked him as Indian and proud of it. What the young man lacked in manners and social graces, he made up for in physical strength and fierceness. All in all, maybe he wasn't a bad friend for Cassandra to have. If he were a friend.

"She's asleep," Adam repeated. "She had a rough night. I don't want to wake her."

A half smile touched Bounder's features. "I'll wait. I have something important to tell her."

Before Adam could respond, the young man withdrew from the door and took a seat in a rocking chair on the front porch.

"She may sleep for a while," Adam said. He was taken aback by the young man's sudden show of docility.

"It doesn't matter," Bounder said slowly as he rocked back in the chair. "I must speak with her, so I'll wait." He turned to face Adam directly. "The Cherokee people are used to waiting, Mr. Raleigh. We wait, but we do not forget." He closed his eyes as if he, too, intended to nap.

"Great," Adam mumbled to himself as he closed the door. There was a serial killer on the loose, an intruder in Cassandra's isolated mountain yard, and now an Indian rebellion on her front porch. What else could happen?

"Meow!" The cry and the hook of sharp claws into the calf of his leg came simultaneously. Adam looked down at the intense yellow eyes of the black cat.

"Breakfast?" Adam inquired. "Would you care for eggs Benedict, perhaps a little caviar and champagne?" He sighed. "Okay, let's check the refrigerator and see what Cassandra has for you to eat. If you won't tattle on me, I might even see if I can find some coffee. Tea's great, but coffee really gets the blood kicking in the morning.''

Together, Adam and Familiar settled in the kitchen as Cassandra slept and Bounder waited.

CASSANDRA STRETCHED her aching muscles. She was surprised by the texture of the sofa beneath her. Falling asleep on the sofa wasn't one of her bad habits. She awoke completely when she heard voices in the kitchen. Adam, yes, but who was he talking to?

She got up and padded on bare feet, noticing that someone had removed her shoes and put them neatly beside the sofa, to the kitchen door. Her full lips curled into a genuine smile at the sight of Adam talking to Familiar. The cat watched him, as if he were listening to every word. There was an empty bowl on the floor, indicating that Familiar had finished his breakfast, and Adam was sipping a cup of coffee.

Cassandra walked into the room, took a cup and poured herself a full measure of coffee. She was further amused by Adam's startled expression. ''It only makes sense that I drink it if I have it in my home,'' she said, lifting the cup in a toast. ''To caffeine, in a very pleasurable form.''

''I was surprised to find the pot and the coffee,'' Adam admitted. ''I hope you don't mind that I took the liberty...''

''Not at all. Did I miss anything?''

''There's a young man on your porch. He said his name is Bounder.''

''Why didn't you ask him in?'' Cassandra asked quickly. ''Why is he on the porch?''

''I didn't know exactly what to do. He's rather fierce.''

Cassandra's laughter was surprisingly light. ''He can be. Honestly, though, he's the most gentle person I've ever known. His looks are a great defense.'' She put her cup on the table and went to the front door. In a moment she returned with the young man in tow.

She made the introductions. "Adam thinks you're fierce," she told Bounder as she gave him a hug. "I told you not to scowl at people. You do look as if you could swipe their heads off with one angry blow."

"I intended to look fierce, just in case he meant you harm," Bounder said. He looked at Adam and spoke to Cassandra. "I was surprised to find a man in your home."

The comment put a slight stain on Cassandra's face. "Life has a way of handing you lots of surprises, Bounder." She gave him a cup of coffee. "Now, where is Running Stream?"

"At the reservation working in the trading post. She sent me. She was worried about you. When she tried to call, the phone was dead. The drive to your house was roadblocked when I came up."

"What?" Cassandra looked quickly at Adam. "What do you mean?"

"One of those orange and white sawhorses, like road crews use. It was across your driveway with a sign saying the road was out."

"That's absurd!" Cassandra said.

"I know that now." Bounder smiled. "I walked up here and there's nothing wrong with your road. So who put the barricade up?"

"Good question," Adam noted. "And why?"

He caught Cassandra's eye. They were thinking the same thing. The stranger from last night. The man had no doubt driven in, put up the barricade, and then come up to the house. Why? There wasn't a single answer to that question that Adam liked.

Cassandra told Bounder about the intruder. The young man insisted on checking the area, even though Adam had gone over it thoroughly.

"No offense," Bounder said with the first real smile on his face, "but historically, I'm better at this."

Adam laughed. "I'll go, too. There's always the chance I can learn something new."

Cassandra returned to the window as Adam and Bounder went out into the warming sunshine to look for clues.

Alone with her thoughts, she felt a growing dread. Something was happening around her, something that she had no real part in, but she had been pulled into it nonetheless. Fragments of her earlier dream returned to her. The images were watery, flickering in and out. The girl. She'd been young, vivacious. For some reason Cassandra had an image of shoulder-length brown hair. Straight and shiny. A happy face with eyes that crinkled. Who was she? More importantly, was she the next victim?

An idea formed in Cassandra's mind. The girl in her dream said she had a job. The other two women who had been murdered had been in the area to work, too. If she could drive around, maybe visit a few shops and restaurants, she might find the girl and warn her. It was a straw to clutch at, but so far the only one she had.

She rushed into her bedroom and began pulling out clothes. She found a casual dress and flats, something suitable for an afternoon in the shops. By the time she heard the front door open and close, she was ready to go.

"We have to go into town," she said before Adam or Bounder could say anything. "I have to find the young woman."

"Cassandra," Adam said slowly, "have you lost an earring?"

She automatically reached up to her ear. The tiny stud was still in place. She checked the other one. "No. But listen, we have to go to town."

"It isn't hers," Bounder said, his eyes hard and speculating. From his pocket he withdrew a shiny, dangling bit of metal. "Cassandra doesn't wear this type of jewelry. No hoops or dangling things. I knew when I found it it wasn't hers."

Cassandra took two steps toward the earring. The sun, which was fully out now, caught the bits of metal and glinted from them. The tiny pieces clinked together as Bounder held it aloft.

"It's Carla's earring," Cassandra said. She recognized it immediately. "I saw it in the dream. It almost touched her shoulder. Her hair was short..."

Adam was at her side, his strong arm around her waist. She wasn't going to faint, but she liked his support anyway. "You found that in my yard?"

Adam answered first. "I missed it completely when I looked. It was buried under some dirt and leaves from the rain. Bounder found it."

The Indian walked forward and gave the earring to Cassandra.

"Is there any way we can find out from Sheriff Beaker if Carla Winchester was wearing earrings?" Cassandra said. "I'm certain this is hers, but I want to know for positive. From a source other than my dreams."

"You saw the earring clearly?" Adam asked.

"Yes. It was unusual. I remembered it." She hesitated. "I liked it, the way it hung from beneath her short hair. This is it, I'm certain. Dead certain."

"I doubt Beaker'll tell us much of anything," Adam said.

"We could take him this earring. If she had only one when they found her, and if it matched this one, he'd have to believe us." Cassandra examined the earring in her hand. It was inexpensive, but pretty, a mixture of shiny metal and light-catching crystals. She could picture it dangling from Carla's short, curly hair, just above her shoulder. Tears threatened suddenly and she blinked them back.

Adam's grip tightened around her. He gave a gentle squeeze of support. "We could do that, but it might only convince Beaker that you're involved in the murders. He did imply that, you know."

"Damn!" Cassandra exploded. "You're right. I can't take this to him and try to help, because he suspects me. What am I supposed to do?" Her frustration was evident.

Bounder and Adam exchanged looks. They had no simple answers.

"Why did you want to go to town?" Adam asked.

Cassandra told them her idea about looking for the girl in her dream.

"It's a long shot," Adam acknowledged, "but so far, it beats sitting here and waiting. We'll take the earring. Maybe we'll think of some way to approach Beaker with this."

"You could take it to the shops and ask the clerks if they remember someone buying it. It is an interesting piece of work. Those crystals are not expensive, but many of the local craftsmen are using them for jewelry," Bounder said. "Many Flowers makes jewelry from them. I've been helping her. If someone bought the earring as a gift for the dead woman, then you have a lead."

"That's a great idea," Cassandra said. "If we could find the shop, maybe they'd remember the earring, then..." She paused. "Then I could reasonably assume that the man who was watching my house is the killer."

"Or that Carla was here, on your premises for some reason shortly before she died," Adam added. "That's what I'm afraid Sheriff Beaker will assume."

"Let's go before I lose my nerve," Cassandra said. "Bounder, tell Running Stream that I'm fine. I'll stop by to see her on my way home, if Adam will take me. My car's in the shop."

"I will," Adam agreed. "And we'll give Bounder a ride to his car. I want to take a look at that barricade with him. He does have an eye for details."

The two men exchanged a smile, and for the first time in hours, Cassandra felt a moment of satisfaction. It was her strong opinion that Bounder needed to know more men away from the reservation. He was heavily involved in political movements within the Indian community and some of the men who influenced him were spoiling for trouble. Bounder had a right to make his own choices, but Cassandra wanted to be certain they were informed choices, not emotional ones. He needed to learn that not every white man was evil.

"Watch the house," she instructed Familiar as she started out the door behind the men.

"Aren't you going to lock it?" Adam asked.

Cassandra shook her head. "There's no point. If someone wants in, they'll get in. I've never locked my door."

"It might be time to start," Adam said. He took Cassandra's keys from her hand. "No, let's rephrase that. This is absolutely the time to start taking precautions."

"I CAN'T EAT ANOTHER thing." Cassandra pushed the cup of frozen yogurt over to Adam. They were in their fourth restaurant of the afternoon. They'd had coffee, tea, and a sampling of different menu items, all in an effort to watch and talk with waitresses. They'd also made a quick tour of most of the shops along the main drag of Gatlinburg.

They'd seen several young women who looked like the brunette in Cassandra's dream. On closer inspection, though, none of them had seemed to be the right girl.

"There are resorts all over the area. Ski lodges, candy shops, craft shops, antique stores and firecracker stands..." Cassandra wanted to march to Sheriff Beaker's office and demand help in her search, but she knew she couldn't, and the frustration was tying her in knots. "We'll never be able to search everywhere. That girl could die. And I might be able to stop it."

"You're doing everything you can," Adam said softly. He took her hand from the table and held it. It was so small and dainty, yet the texture of the skin showed the work she did outdoors. She was a charmingly petite woman, but her spirit was gritty and filled with energy. She was no piece of fluff. Adam's fingers closed over hers. "And I'll do everything I can to help you."

"My mother told me once that whenever I needed someone in my life, they would be there for me. She said I would never be alone in a time of need. And she said that those who came to me at those times would be special and unique people, people I should value." Cassandra looked down at the table for a moment as she struggled for composure. "I thought at the time that it was just something she said to me because she was leaving me alone. You know, some sort of pat voodoo solution so she could take off and lead her own life.''

Adam saw the conflicting emotions cross her face. He was more drawn to her than ever.

"The first time I thought about those words my mother said was when I met Running Stream and Bounder. The second time is now, with you. Perhaps my mother had more wisdom than I ever gave her credit for.''

"People respond to your own generosity of spirit, Cassandra. You could ignore these dreams you're having. Sure, they frighten you, but it really isn't your concern, is it?''

"I don't know that I could do anything else except what we're doing. But I want to thank you for being here with me, Adam. Thank you for believing me.''

"I do believe you. I do. I'm going to be completely honest and tell you that I'm not certain what I feel about your dreams. The earring—" he patted his shirt pocket where it was "—I just don't know. I'd like to ask Beaker about it myself. What I do know is that you need all of your... friends around you now. I intend to be here.''

"Let's go,'' Cassandra said, putting her napkin on the table. None of the waiters or waitresses in the Kettle Inn had known a girl who looked like the one Cassandra described. None of them had known Carla Winchester, either.

"Ready to go to the reservation?''

"No.'' Cassandra stood up, stretching to her full height of five foot three. "To Beaker's office. So, let him suspect me.'' She didn't wait for Adam's objections; she led the way to the car.

They were almost at Sevierville when Cassandra spoke again. She'd been watching Adam's profile, wondering how she'd been lucky enough to meet him at this time in her life. "If the earring plays a role in this, then you'll believe me,'' she said softly.

"It doesn't matter what I believe. Beaker won't put any weight in your dreams, and he's the one who matters.''

"Yes, but not completely. If you're going to spend your time helping me, I want you to believe.''

"Cassandra." Adam touched her shoulder. "Isn't it obvious that I care enough to help, whether I believe or not?"

Cassandra searched his face. The emotion she saw there made her skin tingle. "That may be the most valuable gift anyone has ever given me," she said, her voice a husky whisper. "Why?"

"That question keeps popping up in all our conversations." Adam signaled left to turn into the courthouse parking lot. "I don't have an answer to that question...yet." The clear blue of Cassandra's eyes had captured him. Was that why he was so determined to help her? He'd come to get her to endorse a product, a business arrangement. He hadn't thought of Good Stuff Cereals in days. What was happening to him?

"I hope Beaker's at work today." Cassandra was uncomfortable with the emotions Adam unleashed with such simple honesty.

"Let's go to the reservation and find Running Stream," Adam suggested as they stood in the parking lot.

Cassandra's smile was slow and tired. "After coming all this way? We'll visit the sheriff's office, and then try to find Running Stream."

The skinny dispatcher was still at the desk when they entered. "Sheriff Beaker, you got someone here to see you," she called to the back office.

Beaker's pleasant expression changed immediately when he saw Cassandra. "I don't have time for dreams and visions, Miss McBeth."

"Was Carla Winchester wearing a single earring?" Cassandra took the aggressive stance. She walked to the counter and stopped directly in front of Beaker.

"We're not revealing any details of the murder."

"A single earring, bits of metal and crystal?"

"Why?"

Adam brought the earring out of his pocket and put it on the counter.

"I have to know. Was she wearing the mate to this earring? If she was, then it proves I saw the murder before it happened in my dream."

"Where'd you get the earring?" Beaker asked. There was little interest in his voice.

"I found it," Cassandra said. She looked at Adam for support.

"Well, I'm going to tell you this, Miss McBeth, you and your friend, so maybe you'll go home and leave me alone to do my job. Miss Winchester's ears were pierced, but she wasn't wearing any earrings at all." He smiled. "Are you happy now?"

"Is this the truth?" Cassandra asked. She felt as if the air had been knocked from her. She'd been so certain it would match, so positive.

"It's the truth," Beaker answered, suddenly angry. "Now if you don't mind, I have work to do."

"Sheriff Beaker, is it possible that in the fall down the ravine, where the body was found, the earring might have come loose?" Adam asked. He wanted to put his arm around Cassandra but he checked the impulse. Now wasn't the time. Such a gesture would only make Beaker think she was weak, when she certainly wasn't.

Beaker gave Adam a long look. "Sure, that's possible. And she could have given the earring to the murderer as a keepsake."

His sarcasm drew a laugh from the radio dispatcher, and he grinned.

"My men combed that ravine. We took dogs. We had metal detectors. We spent three days working that site. We found nothing like an earring."

"The next victim will be a young woman with shoulder-length brunette hair. She has a soft drawl, maybe Georgia. She's about two inches taller than me. Her eyes crinkle when she laughs, and she likes to laugh."

Beaker looked at her as if she were mad.

"If I have my way, there won't be another murder," Beaker said slowly.

"I hope you have your way," Cassandra answered, not backing down an inch, "but I don't think so. Unless you find the killer, soon, that woman I just described will die."

Chapter Six

"The sheriff has no understanding of the power of a dream." Running Stream put three cups on the table and began to pour the hot tea. It had a pungent odor. "I knew he'd react this way."

"What can I do?" Cassandra asked. She and Adam had gone to the Cherokee reservation trading post, but Running Stream had already gone home. They'd tracked her down to her small cottage just over the Tennessee/North Carolina border.

Sitting silently at the table, Adam could hear the desperation in Cassandra's voice. He hoped the Indian woman might have answers, because he had none. He had only a bad feeling that Cassandra had made an enemy of Sheriff Beaker. The touchy lawman did not care to be questioned about his investigative tactics, especially not by a "crazy psychic."

"Listen to your dreams," Running Stream said as she took a seat with them at the old wooden table.

"I hate them," Cassandra said fiercely. "I hate all of this. I don't want it. I don't want to feel responsible for something I can't understand or stop!"

"You must not fight it," Running Stream said softly. "I know you don't want to hear this, but it is a gift. Your mother was correct. Among my people, the dreamer is honored."

"I want to work in my garden and write my books," Cassandra said. "A simple life. Not this."

"You have been given a great chance. A human life has been handed to you, Cassandra. You have intelligence and ability. You have been challenged to use them."

"That isn't fair," Adam said quickly. "You make it sound as if it really is up to Cassandra to stop this killer."

The glance that Running Stream turned on Adam was calm and calculating. "You want to protect her, but you cannot. This is for her, Mr. Raleigh. You can help her, but you must not interfere."

Those words chilled Cassandra more than any others she'd heard. The full burden of her responsibility settled on her shoulders.

Adam saw the way she slumped. It had been a bad idea to go to Sheriff Beaker. Coming to visit Running Stream had been an even worse idea.

"I have only my dreams," Cassandra said softly.

"And the earring Bounder told me about," Running Stream said. "You must not give up. This killer has to be stopped."

"And I must do it?"

"Listen to the dream. Yield to it. Remember all of it," Running Stream said. She grasped Cassandra's hand. "Allow Mr. Raleigh to offer you comfort and support. Call on me and Bounder to help you." She smiled. "You aren't alone. And how is that fine black cat?"

"Controlling the household," Adam answered. He was rewarded by a slight smile from Cassandra.

"He and Adam are the nice things that have happened to me. I somehow feel that Familiar was sent to help me, too."

Running Stream laughed. "Talk like that will get you burned at the stake, Cassandra."

"Another visit to Sheriff Beaker with a dream, and he'll probably be glad to oblige with the stakes and firewood."

"Tell him. You must tell him everything. Then ignore the way he reacts to you." Running Stream shrugged. "Your responsibility is to tell. You cannot make him listen."

"That's some comfort," Cassandra said, finishing her tea. "We'd better go. It's getting dark and one of the things I don't want to do is go up that mountain when I can't see."

"Bounder will be watching, in the woods," Running Stream said.

"No!" Cassandra's refusal was sharp. "If someone is out there, lurking about, Bounder could get hurt."

"He can see in the dark," Running Stream said with a smile.

"Promise me he won't try to protect me." Cassandra could already see tragedy building. "It's too dangerous to have him out there. Promise me."

"I will tell him not to," Running Stream said reluctantly.

"Cassandra's right," Adam agreed. "If we see someone around the cabin, we're going to assume it isn't a friend. We'll be safer with that attitude."

"Perhaps," Running Stream said carefully. "The best thing you can do, Cassandra, is to fight to remember the dreams. Each detail. If you are seeing the future, then you can prevent it."

"I'll try. If only I could see the killer instead of the young women. That would be a lot more helpful."

Running Stream touched her heart. "No, Cassandra, do not wish for that."

"Why not?" Adam asked. "It would make things a lot easier to look for the killer."

"Simpler, perhaps. But if Cassandra sees the killer in her dream, then she will be the next victim. She will be dreaming her own future death."

ADAM HELD OUT HIS HAND to stop Cassandra on the porch. "The television's on," he said softly. "We didn't leave it on."

"This way." Cassandra signaled him around to the side of the house. Hugging the log exterior, they moved silently, looking in each window as they passed. When they were finally at the den window, they saw the bluish blur of the television screen. The room appeared to be undisturbed. Familiar sat on the back of the sofa staring at the screen.

"He can turn it on," Adam reminded her.

"We did leave him alone. Maybe he got lonely."

"There's something very weird about that cat, Cassandra."

Her soft chuckle was delighted. "You step into the life of a woman who has prophetic dreams, is involved in serial killings, and you find it strange that a cat can turn on a television?"

"It's a matter of degree," Adam said. In the dusk, crouched at the window of her home, Cassandra had never looked more appealing. Before he had time to reconsider, Adam grasped her shoulders and kissed her. She responded with a tentative warmth that made him draw her closer.

The kiss wasn't unexpected. She'd thought about it for several days, since she'd first felt that curl of feeling for Adam. She'd wondered how his lips would feel on hers. Wondered and wanted. The sensation was more than she'd expected. She found herself opening her mouth, inviting him to kiss deeper. His hands moved along her arms, down her back, pulling her against him. She yielded. The feel of his body was pleasurable, exciting. She was alive with sensation.

WELL, WELL. *Miss Locks and Lancelot must be pretending they're at the drive-in movies. They're standing at the window staring in at the television. Uh-oh, they're not staring at the TV anymore. They're smooching! I knew it would come to this. I have to admit, too, that I'm glad. Goldilocks ain't the type of dame to stay up here on a mountain all alone. What a waste of nature's bounty, if you'll pardon the pun! Now Lancelot can help look out for her. He's going to stay for the duration, I do believe. That's good, cause I don't like what's been happening up here on this mountain.*

Our uninvited visitor has got my hackles standing. Everyone thinks he dropped that earring accidentally. I think it was deliberate. I saw him standing there, his hands hanging at his side. The fingers on his right hand went slack. Mixed in with the rain, the earring hit the ground. Very subtle. Very deliberate. He was leaving a mark, a sign that he'd be back.

And he will.

And we'll be waiting, Lancelot and me.

I don't know for certain who that guy was. Too bad we couldn't get a better look at him. Maybe I couldn't see who he was, but I know what he was. A killer. He's different from my old enemy Cal Vrenner. It's a difference of degree. This guy's worse. Cal kills for profit, to benefit himself. This guy, he kills for the pleasure of the kill. It's enough to tingle a cat's tail just thinking about it.

I don't know what he was doing up here on the mountain, but I know it doesn't bode well for Cassandra. Looking and watching. Dropping little clues. Why? That's the sixty-four-million-dollar question that everyone is asking. Why?

I'm just glad that Lancelot has been smitten and is hanging around. Now that Miss Locks has some help, I could use a little myself. There hasn't been a word on the news about Eleanor. My leg is getting stronger and stronger. It's almost time for me to leave, but I don't know where to go.

I'm afraid to leave here. Once I'm on the road, there's no guarantee that I can get any news. It's a quandary. I've thought of calling Eleanor's friends. It's not a simple matter—getting Ma Bell to make the connection. Reach out and meow at someone just isn't effective. I hardly think even the most talented information assistant would be able to give me Magdalena's number.

While Lancelot and Goldilocks were gone, I did call Dr. Doolittle's office. Drat! Lucille answered. I did my best to talk to her—what a waste. After twenty years of working for a vet, you'd think she'd pick up the rudiments of a few feline vocabulary words. Nope! No capacity whatsoever for languages. She squawked and snorted and then hung up.

*I'll try again at another time. Eventually Dr. D. will have
to answer. Until then, I've got the television remote in one
paw and one ear cocked for trouble on this front.*

*Now that the two adult delinquents have stopped making
out, they'll be heading inside. Good. I'm ready for a little
evening snack before dinner. I hope Cassandra stopped by
the store and got a supply of sardines. This country life has
reawakened some odd hankerings.*

THE KISS left Cassandra breathless, her mind fogged by the
surge of sensations. Only her tight grip on Adam's shoulders kept her standing as he gradually lessened his hold on
her.

There was a look of wonder in his eyes as he stared down
at her. "Running Stream implied you were a witch. I believe it." He smiled. "You just put a mojo on me, I think."

The lighthearted remark gave Cassandra the time she
needed to compose her own emotions. Her blood coursed,
and she heard her own pulse. Slowly, it subsided.

There were things she wanted to tell Adam. She wanted
him to know that she was afraid of her dreams, of what she
saw. But that when he was with her, she was less afraid. He
was a visitor, though, and to burden him with such a con-
fession would be unfair. He had his own business, his own
concerns. And he would have to leave soon, especially when
she could not do the one thing he requested of her.

She dropped her gaze from his and turned away. "Let's
go see what that crazy cat is up to," she said carefully.

Adam had watched the play of emotions in her eyes. He'd
seen the tenderness, the yielding, and then the closing, all in
the span of a few seconds. For an instant she'd been his
completely. For whatever reasons, she'd shut off those feelings. He didn't know why, but he intended to find out.

He followed her into the house, half intending to ask her
then. But her nervous behavior made him desist. Cassandra McBeth was a very complex woman. It would be better
to let her come forth with what was troubling her.

Not to anyone's surprise, the television was silent when they entered the den. Familiar had given up his perch on the arm of the sofa and had curled up on a cushion for a nap.

"It's almost as if he were watching for something specific," Cassandra said.

"Is it time for that talk show guy?" Adam picked up the controls.

"Adam!" Cassandra was appalled. "Surely you aren't going to watch Martin West. He's a waste of time."

"Only because he's having some FDA experts talk about false advertising. This is one of the issues I've been fighting with the FDA about. Some of those packagers put anything on their labels. They make all sorts of claims that aren't true. If they would force the companies to be accountable, then consumers would be able to know when they're buying healthy products and when they aren't."

Cassandra picked up the remote control and flipped it through the air to Adam. "Enjoy. I'm going up to my study to work on my book for a while. I can't take Martin West."

Adam grinned as he punched the on button. He turned the volume down and stretched out on the sofa beside Familiar. It had been a long, long day with a lot of emotions.

The show made several points which impressed Adam. One federal food inspector infuriated Adam. The man, Harry Robbins, claimed that all "health food companies" were public rip-offs.

Before Adam knew what he was doing, he had the telephone in hand and the number of the show dialed.

"Go ahead, caller," Martin West's practiced voice said.

"As owner of a natural food company, I'd like to say that some companies take it very seriously when we advertise our products as healthy. In contrast to what Mr. Robbins implied, my company is accurate in labeling and conscientious in production of our natural cereal products."

"Whoa, if it isn't Yul Gibbons with a bite!" Martin West said with a laugh. "What is your product?"

"Good Stuff Cereal." Adam felt slightly foolish.

"You're one of the good guys, right?"

"Right," Adam said, feeling even dumber. What was he doing calling in to a television show?

"Well, there must be some companies who take their products seriously. It's good to know that you're one of them."

Adam heard the disconnect, and he watched on the television screen as Martin West went back to his panel of experts. Harry Robbins was commenting in a nasty tone how companies were more concerned with the bottom line than with what sediments and preservatives gathered in the bottom of a cereal box. Adam put the receiver back in the cradle. How had he ever gotten caught up in such a ridiculous confrontation?

He clicked off the set. On his way to the kitchen he paused by the stairs to the loft. He could hear Cassandra's fingers pounding furiously on her computer keyboard. She was working on her tenth Nature's Bounty book. A smile touched his features as he decided to surprise her with a light dinner.

In the kitchen he made tuna salad and brewed a pitcher of fresh raspberry tea. He was cracking the ice trays open when the telephone rang. A moment later, he heard Cassandra coming down the steps. She was in a hurry.

"That was Martin West," she said evenly, but the corners of her mouth were tight. "He wanted to know if you'd be a guest on his show Friday. Something about how natural products are grown and refined for wholesale purposes. He said you'd called in to his show today." The look she threw him was an accusation.

"I did, but I didn't leave this phone number," Adam said.

"Then how did he happen to call here?" Cassandra asked.

"Good question, but I don't have an answer. Would they record the number automatically?"

"He knew who I was when I answered," Cassandra said. "In fact, he asked if I would appear with you, along with a nutritionist and a representative from a holistic clinic. He said the show this afternoon was 'very, very hot.' He said the networks had called again and he wants to do a follow-up show."

"Good for Martin West," Adam said.

"Well, he can count me out. I don't do that sort of public thing, and I don't like people like West calling my home."

"I'm sorry, Cassandra. I had no idea. I felt that I needed to comment on a remark one of his expert guests made, so I called in. I didn't mean to start something that dragged you into it."

Cassandra pulled out a chair at the big kitchen table. "It's just that my privacy is so important to me, and I can't think of anything worse than spending time doing one of those horrible shows with Martin West." She took the glass of iced tea Adam offered.

"It does sound pretty dismal, but from my point of view, it could be worthwhile."

"You have a product to market. I don't," Cassandra reminded him.

"In a way you do. Your books. And you have a duty to educate the public. The things you know could make a difference in someone's life. Don't you think you should teach them better?"

Cassandra put the glass down on the table in a very gentle way, but the gaze she turned on Adam was blazing with anger. "No, I don't. I don't owe people anything except that I live my life in a way that does as little harm as possible."

"I didn't mean duty like—"

"Yes, you did," Cassandra interrupted. "It's just like this dream business. I have to stop the killer. The responsibility is mine, whether I like it or not. I should go on television and try to convince people how to eat and live a healthy life. That's what you're saying, that I ought to do it."

Adam rubbed his hand over his chin. "I guess that was what I was saying, and I owe you an apology."

"I write books about natural foods," Cassandra said, her voice calmer. "I put the information out there for the public to read and learn about. That's enough."

"It is," Adam agreed. "But sometimes the public needs a little jolt to make them interested. You're a beautiful woman. You have presence. I think you could shake up a few people via television. That's all I meant to say, even though I worded it poorly."

Cassandra sighed. "I'm sorry, too. I flew off the handle. It's just that I'm feeling a lot of pressure with this killer, and the idea that Martin West had my telephone number is unnerving."

"I'll call back and tell him no."

"Wait a minute." Cassandra stood up. "By all means, you go ahead and do the show. Tell people about your cereal. Just keep me out of it, okay?"

Adam shook his head. "I'm not interested in a television appearance." He took the two steps that closed the gap between them. "And I agree with you, at this particular time I think it might be best if you avoided all publicity."

"Because of my dreams?" Cassandra didn't follow this abrupt change.

"Mostly because Sheriff Beaker already views you with some lack of credibility. If he sees you on West's television show, he might think you're a publicity hound."

"True," Cassandra said, unable to stop the smile that changed her face from angry to amused. "I'm such a publicity seeker!"

"He doesn't know you," Adam reminded her. "Now that we've settled this, I'm going to call West and find out how he got this telephone number."

"Forget it, Adam. It doesn't really matter."

"I want to know for certain how he found out I was here."

Cassandra shrugged. "Ask him."

"I intend to."

"The salad looks great. I'll slice some tomatoes and how about some corn?"

"Great. I'll be back in a minute."

Adam was prepared for the high voltage of Martin West's determined personality. The guy's show was popular because he got the guests he wanted, and for some reason he wanted Adam.

"Since you're here in town, it would give the show some broader-based interest," West said. "Your company will get exposure in this part of the country you couldn't buy with advertising dollars."

"I realize all of that," Adam said, "but the answer is still no. My visit to Gatlinburg is personal, not business."

"You and Ms. McBeth going to collaborate on some product?" Martin had a nose for news.

"I wouldn't attempt to speak for Ms. McBeth," Adam said carefully, "and she doesn't care to speak at all right now."

"How'd you two meet?" Martin pushed.

Adam hesitated. The questions were harmless, but he didn't want to say anything that might jeopardize Cassandra. "I've admired her work for years," he said. "We're both sorry to decline, but we must. First, though, I'd like to ask you a question."

"Let's meet for a drink," Martin suggested. "I'm sure we can iron out this issue. If you don't come on the show Friday, I'm going to have a hard time filling that hole."

"Sorry, Mr. West," Adam said carefully. "I can't do it."

"Not even a drink?"

"My question was, how did you happen to call me at Cassandra's number?"

"Sheriff Beaker told me where to find you," Martin said quickly. "It's no secret that you're staying with the mountain witch." He laughed. "And it's no secret that several guys are envious of you."

Adam was astounded. He'd never lived in a small town where gossip was battered back and forth like a shuttlecock.

"Beaker told you this?"

"Sure, when he was on the show the other day. He said Ms. McBeth had been in his office to tell him about her dreams." West laughed. "It did make her seem a little . . . eccentric."

"Cassandra may be a lot of things, such as bright, intelligent, and sensitive, but she isn't eccentric." Adam clenched the telephone cord.

"No offense, I was quoting the sheriff. So, if you'll come on the food show, maybe we could get Cassandra, uh, Ms. McBeth, to do a show on her dreams. Now that would provoke some interest!"

"No." Adam's refusal was adamant and cold.

"Beaker said she thinks she witnesses the murders before they happen."

"Beaker has an extraordinarily big mouth."

"He's a lawman, and he's pushed to the brink right now. Two young women dead and the summer season hasn't really started yet. He's desperate."

"Desperate and not very discreet," Adam said. "I can tell you without consulting Ms. McBeth that there is absolutely no way she'd consent to that television show. Forget it."

"She might be able to save the lives of several young women—"

Adam cut him off abruptly. "It isn't Ms. McBeth's responsibility. She told Sheriff Beaker everything she knows. He chose to ignore it, and even worse, repeat it. That's as far as her responsibility goes, Mr. West."

"I didn't mean to imply that she should do anything else." Martin backpedaled. "You're sure you won't reconsider the food products show? It would make my Friday."

"Thanks, but no thanks," Adam said firmly. "Maybe another time."

He hung up the phone to find Cassandra standing in the doorway. Although she was leaning against the door frame, her posture was tense. "Beaker told him about the dreams, didn't he?"

"Yes," Adam said. "He wanted you for a show on that subject. I took the liberty of telling him no."

"Thanks." She focused her attention on a pattern in the rug.

"Are you okay?"

"Sure." She looked at him, her eyes clouded. "I'm like some freak in a carnival."

"That isn't true. West was genuinely interested."

"I've seen how interested the people around here are. Three years ago, when two little girls disappeared in the woods near here on a picnic, the locals came out and threw bricks through my windows. They found the children three hours later playing near a stream five miles from here. But the first assumption was that the mountain witch had taken them."

She took a deep breath and continued before Adam could say anything. "The year before that, someone chopped trees across my driveway, all the way down. The year before that, someone painted a hex sign on my front porch."

Adam was still. He'd never realized to what lengths the local people had gone to isolate and punish Cassandra. Her trip to the sheriff had taken tremendous courage. He pulled her into his arms and held her tight.

"The only thing that matters is that you know you're a good person," he whispered into her silky hair. "You and me. We both know it."

"I don't want to be blamed for the deaths of these women," Cassandra said. Her body grew still in his arms. "I'm afraid I'm going to."

"Beaker wouldn't be that irresponsible. He wouldn't let the things you've told him get out to the general public."

"He already has," Cassandra pointed out in that same dull voice. "The consequences are going to be even worse, this time."

Chapter Seven

"I shouldn't be doing this." Delight in her own mischief rippled through the young woman's voice.

From beneath the murky depths of the heavy water, Cassandra tried to reach out to the young woman. She had to get her attention, to warn her.

"It's only for an hour or so. You'll be back before anyone notices."

Cassandra strained to catch the inflection in the man's voice. He was smooth, practiced in his lines as his hands gripped the steering wheel of the car. She could feel the strength in his fingers. His nails were immaculate.

"They'll notice. But I did Sarah a favor the other night. She'll cover for me as long as she can."

"Sarah's the blonde, isn't she?"

"Right."

"She's older?"

"That's her. She's a great person. Really a good friend."

"Did you tell Sarah where you were going?" His voice teased.

"I said I was meeting a handsome prince," the girl answered.

Cassandra screamed in her mind. *No! No! No! Tell him you told someone. Tell him everyone knows.*

"How flattering. Do you really think I'm handsome?"

The girl laughed softly. "That's really fishing, mister. You know women find you attractive."

"It's always nice to hear, though. Just like I'll bet all the men tell you you're beautiful. What hair! I love hair."

Cassandra could feel the silky strands as he ran his hand through the chestnut lengths. She knew the hair. She'd seen it before. Shoulder-length, straight and heavy. *Oh, please let me wake up! Please!*

"Better keep both hands on the wheel," the girl said. She was handling the situation with ease. "Where are we going?"

"Eagle's Roost. It's the best view in the entire area. You'll love it."

"I have to be back at nine."

"Oh, you don't have to worry about your job."

Cassandra heard the sinister tones, the threat in his voice. The water held her prisoner, frozen in the thick depths. She could see the car, feel the evening wind against her face. She turned to look at the girl, and for the first time she saw her clearly. Nice profile, smooth skin. Her brown hair tangled behind her head as the wind blew. She wore a blue cotton blouse with a pointed collar and short sleeves. The glimmer of a necklace could be seen against the collar, and in her ears were small pearl studs. Very conservative attire.

"Where do you come from, Ellen?"

"Georgia. My folks have a small farm down below Atlanta. I got a scholarship to the University of Georgia for my senior year, but I have to earn some money this summer for rent and food."

"Here we go." He turned the car to the right down a tree-covered path.

Cassandra could see it, but it was like looking through an ancient telescope. There was the center of vision, which was fairly clear, but the edges were blurred and foggy.

"This is pretty isolated."

For the first time Cassandra could hear unease in the girl's voice.

"That's why it's such a special place. You wouldn't want me to take you somewhere that everyone went."

"I don't know."

The man knew she was getting nervous. His grip on the steering wheel tightened and he pressed the gas a fraction harder. The car moved under the canopy of trees, headlights cutting through the darkness to reveal a jungle of trunks and heavy foliage on either side.

Cassandra knew the car had taken one of the thousands of isolated paths that cut along the mountains. It was one of the most beautiful things about where she lived, the ability to find solitude. Now, though, her heart was pounding with fear for the girl.

The man was watching. No, not exactly watching. He was coveting her fair skin, her luxurious hair. His fingers reached out to touch the silken lengths again. "So soft," he whispered.

The girl knew then that he had lost sight of her as a person. Her fingers clutched on the door of the car, as if she wanted to open it and jump into the forest that grew so close to the road.

Jump! Cassandra commanded, but the girl did nothing except tighten her grip on the door. *Jump! The farther into the woods you go, the less your chances.*

But the girl was too afraid to try.

The car jounced and bumped. Suddenly it cut to the left, crashing through small shrubs and underbrush. Headlights illuminated a heavily overgrown clearing as the car blazed though the night and the high grass.

"Take me back," the girl said softly, pleading. "I'm afraid."

"You haven't seen the sights, yet," the man said. His foot pressed a little heavier; the car lurched forward. He turned to her and gave a smile. "Fear gives an experience a little edge, doesn't it?"

"For the person who's in control." There was more strength in the girl's voice. She was thinking now.

The man's hand snaked across the seat and stroked her hair. "I know this is unsettling, but I want to show you something. You aren't really afraid, are you?"

"No, I suppose not." The girl shifted in the seat.

His fingers looped through her hair and continued to stroke it. "Your hair is so beautiful."

"Yours isn't bad, either. Is it natural or dyed?" She chuckled. "It's okay these days for men to change their hair color, you know. Hey, this place we're going is really in the boonies. Maybe we should head back. I do have to check in. Sarah's a good friend, but even friends don't like you to take advantage of them."

The car stopped. "She's waiting for you? Really?"

"If I don't show up, she's going to have to call the manager. It's a rule. Sarah isn't a very good liar. She'd have to tell him I was meeting someone."

The man leaned back in the seat. The leather headrest supported him. Cassandra could feel the anger building in him. His hands tightened on the steering wheel, knuckles whitening.

"NO!" CASSANDRA'S scream echoed off the pine ceiling of her bedroom. "Run! Run!" She screamed as she struggled against the sheet and quilt. "Run!" she finally sobbed as she clutched the tangle of bedclothes and forced herself awake.

She heard the pounding of Adam's feet as he burst into her room with a power that sent the solid pine door flying against the wall.

"Cassandra!" He had her in his arms and held her tight. "Wake up. It's only a dream."

"No," she said, her voice almost composed. "It isn't only a dream. It's the future. I saw the girl clearly. I saw her. This time I have to do something." She struggled against Adam's grip as once again the sensation of the young woman came back to her. "Let me go!" she demanded.

"Hey, easy now." Adam increased his grip and held her until he could see that the panic had passed. "You're awake, Cassandra," he said calmly. "You're safe. You're safe." He eased her back against her pillow and leaned down to kiss her forehead. It was cool against his lips. All of his concerns for her came back in a tidal wave of anxiety. What was happening to this bright and sensitive woman?

"I'm okay." Cassandra drew in several deep breaths. She was in her own room. She was safe, with Adam—and the concerned cat that had hopped up on her bed to inspect her.

"Tell me the dream," Adam said. The past evening there had been nothing to upset Cassandra. They'd played some of her favorite classical tapes and had a lighthearted conversation.

Cassandra grew suddenly still. "That's it," she said. A calmness stole over her expression. "I have to remember, just like Running Stream told me. This dream was long, intense. It was as if I were there. Right there behind the wheel of the car."

Adam stared at her.

"As if I were the killer," she said, remembering the way his hands had gripped the steering wheel, touched the young woman's hair. She looked down at her own hand, expecting to find a few brunette hairs there. "I was with the killer, very clearly this time. I woke up just before he murdered the girl."

"Do you know who she was?"

"Ellen." She thought hard, pulling her memory of the dream together. She described the young woman, and as she spoke, Adam went to the bedside table and took the notepad and pen she kept there. He began jotting notes.

"She was from Georgia. A farm south of Atlanta," Cassandra finished triumphantly.

Adam put the pen aside for a moment as he picked up Cassandra's hand. "I hate to ask this, but if this dream is real, has it happened yet?"

"I don't know." Cassandra swung her legs off the bed and sat up. "With the other girls, I dreamed the murder before it happened, if we can believe the information Sheriff Beaker gave us."

"Then she might be alive." Adam felt a surge of hope.

"Maybe. And she had to be at work in the evening, so she's working the night shift." She glanced at her watch. It was midnight. "Maybe a bar or lounge."

"Her clothes?" Adam asked.

While Cassandra described the rather severe outfit, she mentally flipped through places that might hire a waitress with conservative dress.

"Wait a minute." Adam hurried out of the bedroom and returned a moment later with a telephone book. In the Yellow Pages he turned to restaurants.

"It wouldn't be a family place, not if she were going to work at nine," Cassandra said. "Most of those close at eleven, so she wouldn't be working a two-hour shift."

"It has to be a . . . what about her skirt?"

"I don't know." Cassandra focused on the dream. She saw the blouse, the necklace, the stud earrings. But her gaze didn't go below the waist. "He didn't notice what she wore, and neither did I."

The thought was a revelation to both of them. It told them something about the killer that was chilling. Once his victim was selected, he failed to actually see her as a total person.

"It was her hair he noticed. Her hair and skin and neck," Cassandra said slowly. She felt as if some tremendous sickness had brushed against her. "I want to take a shower."

"I'll start making some calls," Adam volunteered. "When you're dressed, maybe we should take a ride into town."

Cassandra nodded. She wanted to feel the spray of hot water against her skin. Shampoo. She wanted to scrub and scrub and scrub until she couldn't remember the feel of Ellen's hair ever again.

"I CALLED TWELVE PLACES, but there wasn't an Ellen working there," Adam said as he put the phone down. Cassandra was dressed and ready to go.

"Try Crockett's," she said. "It's a strange place. Lots of locals, real down-home, but supposedly the best food in town."

"Let's go there," Adam suggested. "Neither of us can sleep, and maybe we'll poke around and find something."

Cassandra wanted to run, to fight, to scream. The horrors of the dream had given her tremendous energy. Driving down the mountain to Crockett's was the best substitute she could find. It was probably a wild-goose chase, but it was better than doing nothing.

In a small town where the population grew by thousands on a daily basis during the summer, it was going to be hard to find a young woman named Ellen. Hell, it was next to impossible. But once they were down in the town, Cassandra had plans to go on over to Sheriff Beaker's. He might laugh at her and ridicule her, but she was going to tell him about this latest dream. She was also going to warn him not to talk about her or her dreams to anyone, especially not pushy television talk show hosts.

"Have you thought of something else?" Adam asked as he held the door for her.

"No." She stopped. Familiar was standing at the door as if he couldn't decide whether to go in or stay out. "Your choice, fella," she said. The cat walked past her onto the porch. "Just remember to stay close to the house. There are owls and panthers and bears out in those woods."

SO NICKNAME ME Toto and let's get on the road to Oz. It isn't the wildlife I'm concerned about. I thought I heard someone in the woods earlier. Hard to tell, since whoever it was was walking very carefully. I just thought I'd check out the territory while the humans gallivant around town.

I'm getting antsy hanging out here in the wilderness. Goldilocks has her own set of nightmares, but I had a dream about Eleanor. She was all in white. There were white bandages wrapped around her head, and her beautiful hair was gone. But she was smiling, and she had new glasses. Battered but undefeated. I just wish I knew where she was.

I've racked my brain to think where she might be. Nothing. The answering machine was on at Dr. Doolittle's office, so I left a vocal imprint. If Dr. D. gets there in the morning, he'll know it's me. I know he will. How can I be certain Lucille won't erase the tape?

I've made a firm decision to drive her to a nervous breakdown when I get back to Washington. Just punishment for hanging up on me. I've never liked her since the day I met her. She probably teaches her dog to chase cats.

Well, the big folks are gone and there's no time like the present to scout the perimeter. If it weren't so vulgar I'd get one of those coonskin caps—fake coonskin of course. Since I'm a creature with what is commonly known as a luxurious pelt, it makes me sick to think that humans actually derive pleasure from skinning small animals and wearing their furs. My, my, there's such a lot of room for civilization in this savage race of bipeds.

There's that slight movement in the woods again. I'm going to stroll that way. Few people realize that the cat and the owl have the best night vision of any creatures. We are nocturnal hunters.

Yes, I see that slight movement behind that clump of underbrush. About a hundred yards from the house, I'd say. Very discreet. Whoever it is is watching the house. They're relaxed, probably waiting for Adam and Cassandra to return. I wonder if I should frighten them away or merely observe. Best to check it out before I render a decision.

Well, well, it's that Indian. He's tucked up in the brush as if he intended to spend the night. He sees me. No point in slithering along in the dark anymore.

Strange, the way he's assessing me. It's almost as if he were aware of my thoughts, my intelligence. A perceptive young man with a troubled spirit. He's angry. I could sense it the other day when he was visiting. Angry and afraid.

Oops. He dropped something in the dark. What? Let me give him the old friendly cat trick and see what it is. A little brush across the shins with my body, and I'm in close enough for a look. Yep, there it is.

The earring! The one he and Lancelot found. I thought they took that to the sheriff's department. There, he's got it again, and he's putting it in his pocket. Patting his shirt to make sure it's at the bottom. And now he's settling back to give me a few pets. Nice touch, very strong fingers, but gentle hands. He likes the feel of my fur. It's a pleasure to meet a man who can appreciate the finer things in life. But what's he doing lurking out behind Cassandra's house? This bears closer scrutiny.

"I DON'T KNOW," Cassandra came back to her table and sat down. "There must be a hundred people in here. The waitresses move back and forth like flies."

"Not a very appetizing comparison," Adam commented dryly, "but the dress is casual, jeans and all."

"That's true." Cassandra was scanning the crowd. She knew she'd recognize the brunette named Ellen if she ever saw her. If she was there.

"Hi, my name's Sarah, and I'll be your waitress tonight," a good-looking blond woman said as she put two napkins on the table. "Can I get you a drink?"

"Two white wines," Adam said as Cassandra nodded.

"Is Ellen here tonight?" Cassandra asked casually.

"There's no one here by that name." Sarah's face grew a fraction less friendly. "I'll get that wine." She turned abruptly away.

Cassandra started to rise, but Adam grabbed her arm. "Hold on, there, Cassandra."

"She knows her!" Cassandra could feel the blood surging through her heart. "She knows her! I remember more of the dream. Ellen was talking about her friend Sarah who was going to cover for her."

All of the color had drained from Cassandra's face, and Adam could see the tension spark in her crystal eyes. He also knew that such behavior would scare Sarah away from telling them anything they wanted to know.

"Calm down," he ordered, tightening his hold on her hand for emphasis. Sarah was coming back through the crowd with their drinks. "Don't blow it," he whispered.

"Here you are, and would you like a menu?" Sarah asked. There was a practiced smile on her face, but she didn't look directly at either of them.

"Not tonight," Adam said easily. He put the money on the tray, and an extra twenty on top. "We're looking for a young woman with shoulder-length hair, a brunette. The name she gave was Ellen, but it may not be her real name. It's very important."

Sarah glanced around the room. "I don't know any Ellen." She picked up the twenty and put it back on the table.

Adam touched her wrist beneath her tray. "We're trying to help her. We think she might be in danger."

Sarah's face betrayed no expression. "I swear. No one named Ellen works here."

"She's seeing a man," Cassandra broke in. "He might try and hurt her."

Sarah looked from Cassandra to Adam. Her eyes were shuttered. "I don't know what game you two are playing. Angry ex-wife, angry ex-lover, I don't know. If there was an Ellen here, I'd send her over and let her settle this with you herself. Since she doesn't exist, I can't help you." She tapped the twenty on the table and turned away.

Cassandra watched her leave with an expression of frustration. "She knows something."

"Maybe, maybe not," Adam said. He watched Sarah's retreating back. "She seemed afraid, at first, but there was something about her... I believed her."

"She spoke with conviction," Cassandra agreed. "But why was she so edgy, then?"

Adam sipped his wine. "We could follow her."

"That's a great idea!"

"What if we're wasting the night? What if this is a dead end?"

"If she knows Ellen, we've given her enough information to warn her friend." Cassandra tried to think it through. They could follow Sarah, a potential lead, or they could continue to look for Ellen. Neither option seemed very promising.

"Ladies' room," Cassandra said as she stood. "I'll be back."

When she was around the corner that led to the rest rooms, she paused. Adam was scanning the crowd, and there was no sign of Sarah. The door to the kitchen was just beyond, and she went quickly toward it and pushed through. In the bustle of chefs and waitresses moving back and forth, no one took notice of her as she walked to the back of the room.

The noise was overwhelming and the heat intense. Rich smells assaulted her senses. There was too much confusion. Hugging a wall, she made her way around the room, searching for Ellen's face. Sarah's familiar voice, strained in worry, caught her ear.

"They were asking for Ellen."

Cassandra paused. In a corner, tucked out of sight, were two pay phones for the employees. Pans clattered and dishwashers roared so that Sarah, who held the receiver to her ear, was almost shouting.

"No, I've never seen either of them. Look, they upset me. They said you were in danger. I'm not going to be part of this anymore. You'd better get in here to work, 'cause I'm not going to cover for you." There was a pause. "Well, break the date. Tell Romeo to get up a little earlier and meet you for lunch instead."

The receiver was slammed back on the silver prong, and before Cassandra could make an escape, Sarah stepped away from the phone and rammed into her.

"What are you doing in the kitchen?" Sarah asked. She glared at Cassandra. "Guests aren't allowed in the kitchen."

"I don't care who your friend is. I don't care what she does, except that if she sees the man she's been dating again, he is going to kill her."

Cassandra knew her words sounded like the ravings of a crazy woman.

"Listen, lady, I've had enough of you." Sarah waved her hand. "Hey, Freddie! Come here!"

A burly cook with arms the size of small hams hurried to her side. "What's the problem, Sarah?" He gave Cassandra a belligerent look that meant trouble.

"This woman and her friend have been bothering me. She followed me back here and eavesdropped on my phone conversation."

"There's only one way to fix this," the big man said. He wiped his hands on his apron. "I'm calling the sheriff."

"Wait," Cassandra said quickly. "I'm only trying to help. I promise."

"You're trying to intimidate me and my friend," Sarah said. "I don't play these kinds of games." She looked at the cook. "Call the sheriff."

Chapter Eight

"Harassment is a serious charge." Sheriff Beaker rubbed the bridge of his nose as he pushed up his glasses. "Ms. McBeth, I don't know why you've decided to make a public nuisance of yourself, but this is the worst time you could have chosen. My men are worn out from working two murders. I'm up all night, and when I do get a few minutes to sleep, the telephone rings off the hook with mothers who're worried about their daughters. We've been getting calls from all over the United States."

"I explained the dream to you. If Ellen isn't dead now, she will be soon." Cassandra clasped her hands in her lap.

"There is no Ellen," Beaker said impatiently. "Ms. Welford—Sarah—insists that she doesn't know anyone by that name. She gave a sworn statement."

"She was talking to her on the telephone," Cassandra insisted. She leaned forward in her chair. "I'm not crazy, and I'm trying to stop a murder, not make trouble for you."

"The manager and the other waitresses all said there was no Ellen working there." Beaker's patience was growing thin.

"Maybe the woman's using a fake name." Cassandra stood up. "I can describe her perfectly, if you and your men would help me hunt for her."

"Stay out of this." Beaker stood up, too. "Now I'm going to let you go home, but I want your promise that you'll stay out of Gatlinburg for a few days."

"I can't promise," Cassandra said stubbornly. "I . . ."

"Ms. McBeth will remain at her home," Adam said. He stood and went to Cassandra's side. "Whatever you need in town, I'll take care of for you."

"I didn't hire you to baby-sit me," she snapped.

"Well, you might be thankful that someone is willing to assume responsibility for you," Beaker said. "I've had about all of this witchy stuff I can stand." He turned to Adam as if Cassandra had suddenly vanished from the room. "I try to be a tolerant man. As long as I've known Ms. McBeth she's been a local oddity, but never any serious trouble. There's been talk about her—" he looked at her slowly "—instability, but she's always minded her own business and let the town mind its own. That's the way it has to stay. For her own safety."

Adam didn't like the implied threat in the sheriff's tone, but he knew that argument was futile. Cassandra had put her whole heart into trying to explain her dreams to Beaker. He didn't buy into it at all. There was really nothing else to be said.

"Cassandra?" Adam held out his hand to her. "It's time to go home."

She put her hand in his and allowed him to help her up. Without another word she followed him from the sheriff's office, almost like a child.

When they were clear of the courthouse and on the sidewalk, she snatched her hand free. "Don't you ever speak to me in that condescending tone again," she whispered hoarsely. "I've never been so humiliated in all my life."

"You would have been more humiliated if he'd put you in a cell in that courthouse."

"He wouldn't have done that. He couldn't have. I haven't done anything wrong."

"Except harassment."

"Oh, please!" she said, totally exasperated. "I did not harass that woman, and you know it."

"But he could have charged you, just to teach you a lesson." Adam put his arm around her shoulders and directed her toward his car. "Let's forget this whole incident and think of a new plan. We missed following Sarah since we had to come to the courthouse. Maybe someone else at Crockett's will know where she lives."

"I can't go back in there," Cassandra said bleakly. "They won't let me back in." The tiniest glint of humor touched her unhappy eyes. "I shouldn't have swung that frying pan at that big oaf, but *he* shouldn't have put his hands on me."

"I'm glad I didn't see it," Adam said with sincere relief. "Very glad. But the fact remains that *I* can go back in the restaurant."

"And I can wait in the car?" It was torture, pure and simple, to be forced to sit and do nothing.

Adam eased the car back into Crockett's parking lot. With a sympathetic smile, he left the motor running and the radio playing softly. Before Cassandra could object, he leaned over and kissed her pouting lips. "Keep a sharp eye on the parking lot while you're sitting around. You might see something worth knowing."

He walked across the asphalt and disappeared inside the restaurant.

Dutifully, Cassandra began an exploration of the cars in the lot. She remained in Adam's car, but she scouted the area. She was about to say her task was futile when she noticed a small convertible in a far corner. The dark car was parked under a tree, almost obscured by the dense shadows. Something about the car triggered Cassandra's memory.

When Ellen and the man had been driving up the mountain, the wind had blown her hair back, revealing her neck and ears. It had been a ragtop, Cassandra was certain of that! Surely there were thousands of convertibles in the state of Tennessee, but this one was parked here. She slipped from the car and began a slow weave among the parked vehicles, making sure she crouched low.

She had to get a look at the car. Maybe there was a clue she'd remember, some portion of the interior. The least she could do would be to get the license plate number.

Gravel scuffled beneath her feet, and she stopped to listen for the sounds of anyone about. Her actions were impetuous, she knew, but they were also necessary. Besides, what harm was there in looking at a car, even if she were caught? There wasn't a law against admiring a vehicle.

As she drew closer, she could see that the car was dark blue, a midnight color that reflected the stars. Expensive paint job, expensive car. She was three cars away when she heard the voices.

"I'm afraid, Ray."

Cassandra immediately recognized the waitress Sarah's voice.

"Come on, baby, you're not the type to get so shook up over nothing." The man's voice was soft, persuasive.

"You don't understand. They followed me. She did, anyway, back into the kitchen. She looked wild. She was talking like a crazy woman about someone getting hurt and those awful murders."

"So, you said she was a local with an odd reputation. I've worked with some of those fortune-tellers, and they are weird." He laughed softly. "I never could tell if they acted that way deliberately, you know, for effect, or if they couldn't help it."

"She scared me."

He chuckled. "So you called the sheriff."

"Yeah." She laughed, too. "I never thought I'd see the day when I called a lawman. Especially not since I met you."

They laughed together, a warm, intimate sound.

"See there, you're feeling better already."

"Because you came," Sarah said. "You always make me feel better, Ray. How long do you think you'll be in town?" A note of sadness entered her voice.

"Another three weeks at least. The take has been good. I'm trying to talk the boss into staying longer. Gatlinburg is a great place for us. Tourists flooding in left and right. New folks every day." He grinned. "New suckers. By the way, thanks for loaning me that cash. The information I got in that note is worth a fortune. You'll get your money before we pull out."

"I know, I'm not worried about it. When you leave here, where will you go?" Sarah's voice sounded already as if she missed him.

"The plan is to head up the East Coast and across the northern states. It's easier up there in the summer. We swing south for fall and into Florida for the winter."

"I've never been out of this state," Sarah said softly. "One day I'm going to travel."

"Come with me and I'll show you the world," Ray said, his voice taking on the tones of a performer.

"Right now, that sounds like a tempting offer. Do you mean it?"

"I don't think the road is the life for you, Sarah."

There was the briefest pause. When Sarah spoke again, her voice was brisk. "Yeah, you're right. I've got my own life here, and it isn't so bad. Now I'd better get back inside or I won't have a job. Thanks for coming to talk with me."

"Don't let that woman bother you. It really isn't any of your business what your friends do."

"You're probably right." Doubt had returned to Sarah's voice. "It's just that if something bad happened to her, I'd feel it was my fault."

"She's a big girl. Let her handle her own affairs."

"I did warn her never to bring anyone home. I just wish she wouldn't go riding around with that guy. She doesn't know him. He's strange, too. He always makes some excuse for not meeting at the restaurant, like he don't want to be seen. Like maybe I'd know him."

"That's really jumping to a conclusion." Ray's voice was tense. "Women come up with the damnedest ways of thinking about things. Maybe he's just busy, you know."

"I don't think so. Maybe he's married."

"Quit looking for trouble." There was a warning in Ray's voice. "You might find it."

"I've learned to take care of myself." Resentment was evident in Sarah's voice. "I've gotta get back inside."

Ray laughed. "Don't stay mad, Sarah. I'll be here when you get off work. You promised me some fun tonight. I'm taking you to the fair. Maybe you can forget your troubles on one of the rides." His laugh was confident.

Cassandra crouched almost to the pavement. Looking around the bumper of a little compact, she saw Sarah walk out from under the big tree and head for the restaurant. Her back was erect, angry as she walked away. Cassandra held her breath. All she needed was to get caught spying on the waitress again. Sheriff Beaker would follow through on his threat and put her in jail.

The man Sarah had been talking with remained in the shadows. Rocks and grit digging into her palms, Cassandra waited. She had to get a look at him. There had been something in his behavior, something sinister. Did he care for Sarah? Cassandra got the impression that he did not. Just why, she couldn't say.

Footsteps scruffed closer to her and she pressed against the body of the car.

"Well, well," the man called Ray said softly. He whistled in the night, and even though Cassandra couldn't see him, she thought he was admiring the convertible.

A car door opened and slammed. Cassandra dared a look and saw Ray sitting behind the driver's wheel of the car. In a quick glance, she saw that his hair was overly long and straight. Thick, heavy hair. His shoulders were broad, very muscular. Ray was a man who built his body, structured it as an architect would design a building. She could see the bulge of his biceps as he threw a long arm over the back of the passenger seat, enjoying the feel of the car.

In a fluid movement, he sprang out from behind the wheel and landed beside the car. She could not clearly see his face, but she couldn't ignore the perfection of his body. Narrow waist and hips tapered down to strong legs. Whatever Ray did, he had plenty of time for himself, she thought, and plenty of that special discipline necessary to work on his appearance.

Narcissism? Taken to the extreme, it could be a sign of unbalance.

The kind of unbalance that led a man to kill women for pleasure?

She backed slowly around the car, her hands and feet inching in increments that made her leg muscles scream. Ray frightened her. He was so sure of his own physicality, his own prowess. Inch by painful inch, she made her way back to Adam's car. She eased in the door, closed it softly and then locked both doors and threw herself across the seat.

Her heart pounded as she waited for Adam's return.

It seemed like an eternity before she heard a fumbling at the locked door. She chanced a look, relieved to see Adam peering in the car window.

She sprang the lock and sat up.

"Napping?" he asked because he couldn't see the fright on her face.

"Sarah was out here with some man. Adam, I got some bad feelings from him."

"I checked the entire restaurant and didn't see her. Or anyone who looked like the Ellen you described. None of the waitresses would even talk with me. They served me coffee and avoided me like the plague."

"There's a car, a convertible, parked under the tree at the west end of the parking lot. I wanted to get the license number, but I got frightened and left."

"I can get it," Adam said quickly. "If you really think it's important."

"Watch out for the bodybuilder who was hanging around it. His name is Ray, and he gives me some bad feelings."

"I'll be back in a minute." He gave her a stern look. "You stay put."

Cassandra counted to three hundred, slowly, before Adam returned.

"The car is gone."

"What?" Cassandra peered through the windshield. "It was there just a few minutes ago. I was hiding, but I should have heard a car driving by."

"Are you certain it was there?" Adam felt strange. What seemed to be reality wasn't. Dreams foretold the future. Women were dying and cars disappeared. "Maybe it went by and you didn't hear it."

"No." Cassandra got out of the car and walked straight across the parking lot to where the convertible had been parked. Adam was right. The space beneath the tree was empty. A little-used trail led away from restaurant.

"I see where he went," Adam said, only a few steps behind Cassandra.

"At least I'm not completely losing my mind."

"Your dreams are the only clues we have." Adam reached out to her and stroked her hair. "Sheriff Beaker doesn't believe in them, but with each passing hour, I believe more and more. And I also know that this isn't something you volunteered for. You're as caught up in it as the young women who have died."

"You're a special guy." Cassandra took the half step across the darkness and into his arms. "A very special man. Let's go home."

They returned to the car and took the highway. "Tomorrow, I need to check on your car. I don't mind leaving you while I run errands, but I don't like the idea that you don't have transportation if you need to come to town. The shop said it should be ready by tomorrow, and we can pick it up."

"Good idea. Now that the phone is fixed and my car repaired, I'm back in business." The startling thought that Adam might leave crossed her mind. He'd stayed because a series of incidents had put him in a position to protect her. Would he continue to stay? He did have a business to run. He had a life that had nothing to do with her. When would he leave? It wasn't a question she was going to ask.

As they pulled into her yard, Cassandra caught sight of Familiar on the front porch. He was sitting on the railing as if he'd lived there his entire life.

"I think I should place an ad about the cat," she said slowly. "I've gotten very attached to him, but what if he's someone else's pet and they're worried about him?"

"My opinion is that Familiar could never belong to anyone. He might live with them, but he belongs only to himself."

Cassandra laughed softly. "He does give that impression, but there's something else there. He's looking for someone. I know you're going to think I'm crazy for sure, but have you noticed that he watches the news? Not local, but national news."

Adam started to laugh, but he checked the impulse. He'd been startled when he found the cat could operate the television. And it was true, Familiar turned it on and off. In fact, the times he'd seen the set on and the cat watching it, a news program had been on.

"You're right," Adam said. "That's damn amazing."

"With everything else going on, I haven't devoted enough time to Familiar, but I'm going to tomorrow. That cat and I are going to have a little chat."

"Find anything interesting out in the dark?" Adam asked the cat as he stroked his back and chin.

With lightning quick speed, Familiar snagged his hand in a gentle grip.

"Is that a yes?" Adam asked, laughing as Cassandra unlocked the door. "I think your other guest has sleuthed up some evidence."

Once the door was open, Cassandra walked to the rail and picked Familiar up in her arms. "I bet he probably has," she said, walking in the front door with him. "If only we could get this guy to talk."

"If only," Adam agreed.

Cassandra opened a can of salmon for Familiar and put fresh water down before she was ready to call it quits for the night. Adam was watching her.

"Would you like for me to stay in your room tonight?" he asked. "I know you're worried about the dreams."

"I was thinking. Maybe if I didn't dream, then it couldn't happen," Cassandra said carefully. "Do you think?"

Adam went to her and put his arms around her, holding her close. "I don't think that for a minute. You have nothing to do with the events, Cassandra. You simply reflect them in your dreams.''

"Ellen is alive. Even though I witnessed her abduction in my dream, she's still alive.''

"Possibly. It could be that the sheriff simply hasn't found another body yet.''

That thought hadn't occurred to Cassandra. "If that's true, then Sarah is a waste of time.''

"I've considered that. The important thing for you to understand now is that you are a spectator, not a participant. You have nothing to do with events.''

"Except that I might be able to stop them.''

"Maybe, maybe not. I'm not certain of that either way.''

"I don't want to dream tonight.''

"I'll stay with you.'' Adam pressed her closer. He wanted to touch her, to comfort her. And he wanted to arouse her and make her want him.

Cassandra reacted to the change in the way he held her. His hands shifted only a fraction, an awakening of touch. He had moved from comfort to desire, and her skin tingled with her own barely contained emotions.

Adam affected her in ways she'd never thought possible. He behaved as the perfect gentleman, the undaunted protector, and she knew instinctively that if she gave the slightest indication that that was the only role she wanted him to play, then he would step back into it. But it wasn't the only role he wanted to play in her life.

He wanted her. She saw it in his eyes in tiny moments when he wasn't aware that she was watching him. He guarded that desire in order to protect her. It was a humbling thought, that he would put her needs before his. As she'd come to know him, she also realized that she'd grown to appreciate so many things about him.

His hands slid down her back and she sighed softly, momentarily disrupting her thoughts and replacing them with a delicious sensation. That was what she wanted, not to think and weigh and worry. All of her life she'd lived with a need for rational thought. Tonight she wanted to yield to her emotions, her needs. She wanted him. She wanted to feel his chest pressed against hers, skin to skin. She wanted to twine her legs with his against the crisp, cool sheets of her bed.

His lips caught her neck and a sensation that made her gasp surged through her. Her own hands explored his back, the contours of his muscles and the lean planes of his hips.

She felt his fingers lace into her hair and gently drew back her head until their gazes met. Fire danced in his eyes. She opened her lips slightly for his kiss, inviting him to explore with abandon. She gave herself to the kiss, to the sensations that Adam evoked.

She felt his fingers on her blouse, working the small buttons. Her own hands were busily at work with his shirt. She had to know the feel of him, skin to skin.

He pushed her shirt down her arms, freeing it quickly, then removed her bra. In a moment she had his shirt untucked and free of his body. At the first brush of his chest against hers, Cassandra reached high to put her arms around his neck. She was stretched against him, reveling in the feel of him.

"We could finish this in the bedroom," she whispered against his collarbone.

"We could," he agreed, his hands sliding up her ribs to feel the weight of her breasts. "Maybe we should."

"That's the first indecisiveness I've ever seen you display," she said as she trailed kisses along the well-developed muscles of his chest. She slipped her fingers around his hand and drew him after her, one slow step at a time. With each step, she kissed a fraction of an inch lower.

At the door of her bedroom, she stopped. "Made up your mind yet?" Her eyes were dancing with mischief and desire.

"I think so." Adam smiled. "A few more kisses and I should be positive."

Cassandra laughed as they stepped into the bedroom.

THE HUCKLEBERRIES were firm as she poured them into the colander to clean. She'd picked them herself. She was humming when she dumped them into the muffin batter. She was still humming when the muffins came out of the oven, hot and delicious.

The tray was prepared, and she took it to the bedroom.

"Morning," she said as she placed it on the chest of drawers while she bent over Adam for a kiss.

"Morning?" He lifted his eyebrows. "It was midnight only a few minutes ago."

"How quickly we forget," Cassandra said. "And just last night you promised me you'd remember every second."

Adam pulled her down onto the bed with him. "I remember. I was hoping you'd show me again, though. There's this one part that I forget. It comes after we kiss for a long, long time."

"Breakfast first." Cassandra kissed his forehead, his nose, his chin and finally his lips. "You need to keep up your strength."

"I don't feel weak," Adam said. He wound his fingers in her hair. "I feel caught in your golden web."

"Yes, you're such a helpless victim." She laughed and rolled away from him. "I've put some special potions in this breakfast and I can't let it go to waste. You know, a little mandrake root, a few gnat's wings and chicken feathers." She picked up the tray and put it across his lap. When it was comfortably settled, she took a seat on the bed and picked up her own cup of tea.

"This is wonderful." Adam took a bite of a muffin and licked his lips. "Wonderful."

"An old family recipe," Cassandra said with a sinister tone in her voice. "A charm from a fortune-teller."

She was about to embellish more when the telephone rang. "Now who could be calling so early," she said as she got up. "That's the trouble with getting the phone repaired. People can call us." She went to the den where the only telephone was located.

Adam put his cup down. The first thing that crossed his mind was that Sheriff Beaker was calling because he'd found another body—one with shoulder-length chestnut hair. He didn't give voice to his thoughts. Cassandra was so beautiful, so delightfully carefree this morning. If it were bad news, it would come from someone other than him.

He heard her say hello, and then there was a pause. A second later she was standing in the bedroom door.

"It's for you."

"Me?" Adam was as puzzled as she was. He put the tray aside and went to the phone.

"Adam, Martin West here. Just thought maybe you'd changed your mind about appearing on my show."

"Mr. West, my decision stands. Please don't call here again." He was about to hang up when he heard Martin's voice.

"Has Ms. McBeth had any more of her dreams?"

He returned the receiver to his ear. "Those details were told to Sheriff Beaker in confidence. He violated a trust when he repeated them to you. If you continue to bother Ms. McBeth, I'm afraid I'm going to have to speak with the sheriff about the violation of his duties."

"Hey, it was just a simple question. You know it's hard to drum up business for one of these shows."

"Please, Mr. West, have some consideration for Ms. McBeth's desire for privacy." He replaced the receiver. Adam watched Cassandra's reaction. Though she tried to hide it, he could see her distaste. "Sorry about that. He's a determined man."

"Forget it," Cassandra said reasonably. She motioned Adam into the bedroom. "Let's finish."

"Let's finish breakfast and start something else," Adam said. He took her shoulders in his hands and kissed her cheek.

"Adam, I—"

The shrill ring of the telephone came again.

"I'm going to disconnect that thing," she said irritably. "Now what."

Adam held up his finger to her lips. "I'll take this one." In two strides he was across the room and at the phone.

"McBeth residence."

He looked at Cassandra. "Yes, Sheriff. She's right here."
He handed her the receiver.

Chapter Nine

Cassandra took the telephone in nerveless fingers. She could tell by the expression in Adam's eyes that Beaker was upset.

"Hello, Sheriff."

"Ms. McBeth, where were you early this morning, about three or four a.m.?"

Cassandra's heart skipped as she heard his question. Something terrible had happened. The young woman named Ellen, they must have discovered her body.

"I was with Mr. Raleigh, here at my home." There was a pause. "Why?"

"Are there any witnesses who can verify your whereabouts?" Beaker asked. He sounded tired and angry.

"No, we were alone. Once again, I'm asking why?" She felt Adam's hand on her shoulder and she gave him a wan smile.

"Sarah Welford was killed in the early morning hours," Beaker said. "We're talking with everyone who might have a reason to want to see her dead."

"Sarah?" Cassandra stumbled backward from the shock. "Why Sarah? I didn't see anything in my dream involving her." She was rocked by confusion. Nowhere in any of her dreams had there been any indication that Sarah Welford would die. "Was she strangled?"

"No, ma'am, she was not," Beaker said. "She was run down by a motorist. I was thinking you might be able to tell me something about that."

"Me? I've never hurt anyone." Cassandra stumbled slightly as if her knees were buckling.

Adam took the receiver from Cassandra's hand. Her fingers could barely hold it.

"Why are you calling Cassandra? What's happened?" Adam couldn't keep the anger from his voice.

"There's a possibility Ms. McBeth is involved in Sarah Welford's death," Beaker said coldly. "The coroner has set the time of death at four a.m. this morning. I find it strange that Ms. McBeth and Ms. Welford had a run-in, and now Ms. Welford is dead. Don't you find that odd?"

"Don't be ridiculous," Adam snapped back. "Cassandra wouldn't harm a fly and you know it. She's trying to help you, she isn't a murderer."

"Evidence points otherwise," Beaker said. "Would you bring Ms. McBeth into town for questioning?"

Adam was tempted to say no. He wanted to tell the sheriff what he could do with his questions, but he knew he had no choice. If he didn't take Cassandra to Sevierville, the sheriff would merely come and get her.

"We'll be there in an hour."

"Don't try anything stupid, Raleigh." The sheriff's voice was hard.

"Yeah," Adam answered as he put the phone down.

Still stunned, Cassandra took a seat on the arm of the sofa. Familiar went to her and rubbed against her hip. Her fingers absently stroked his back. "Is he charging me?"

"He didn't say."

"Why didn't I dream it?" Cassandra asked. "That poor woman. Maybe it was her all along and I got confused in the dream." She twisted her hands. "It doesn't make any sense."

"We don't know all the facts," Adam pointed out. "Sarah Welford's death might not be related at all."

"I don't believe that," Cassandra said. "You don't, either."

"Beaker didn't say the word murder, you know," Adam insisted. "He might be making this more dramatic than it should be. Maybe he's trying to upset you."

Cassandra went to Adam and gently kissed his chin. She stood on tiptoe to do so. His arms circled her and held her to his chest. "Thank you," she whispered. "Thanks." Adam was the mooring that kept her safe. He was so steadfast, and she was so battered by the shifting winds of her life.

He kissed the top of her head, letting one hand stroke her hair. "We'll get this figured out, Cassandra. We will."

"One way or the other." A terrible darkness settled on her mind. It had been bad enough when she felt she could foresee the murders. Now, though, she wasn't even much use. Sarah Welford's death indicated that her "talent" was partial, at best, and perhaps not reliable at all.

"Could you identify that Ray character if you saw him again?"

Adam's question halted her bleak thoughts. Ray. She'd forgotten about him. He was such a sinister figure. Maybe she did have some way to help solve Sarah's death.

"I didn't see his face," she said. "His body, yes. Very distinctive."

"I'm not sure that's enough," Adam said carefully. He could tell by the way Cassandra latched onto the idea that it had reawakened her hope. But for criminal purposes, he didn't know if such an identification was good enough.

"We might as well face Sheriff Beaker," Cassandra said, shifting back from the haven of Adam's chest. "I'll get dressed."

"I wish we could lock the door and stay here until all of this was resolved," Adam said. He held her close, unwilling to let her go. The feel of her in his arms was something he didn't want to lose.

"I've spent most of my life doing just that," Cassandra said. There was no bitterness in her voice, only mild amazement. "I thought I had developed a perfectly reasonable life. I gardened, I walked, I wrote, I studied. Now it seems so…incomplete. I think I was hiding, safe in my own little world with no room for anyone who might hurt me again."

Adam couldn't resist. He stepped closer and brought her back against his chest. His life, too, had been "perfect." Goal after goal had fallen before his assault. He had his own company, structured and operated the way he felt was best. He had respect, prestige to a certain extent, satisfaction in his work, always invitations to dinners and parties. And a very empty life other than that. Until now.

"This craziness won't last forever," he promised her. "Then, we're going to talk about the future. Things that we both have been too busy to realize we need."

Cassandra lifted her face to his. She stood on tiptoe to offer her kiss. "That's a promise," she said when they drew apart. "We'd better go to town."

They were both silent on the long, winding trip into Sevierville. Adam didn't say anything as they walked to the sheriff's office, but he held her arm in a tight grip of support. When Beaker motioned her into his inner office, Adam followed with no intention of being left behind.

As Beaker took a seat behind his desk, Adam watched the man's face. Something in the way Beaker's mouth tightened when he looked at Cassandra stopped Adam in his tracks. He gripped Cassandra's arm and drew her back out the door. Leaning in toward Sheriff Beaker, he said, "We need a moment." Then he quickly closed the door.

Casting a look over his shoulder, Adam made sure the dispatcher couldn't listen in.

"What is it?" Cassandra's brows were drawn together.

"It's Beaker. I just had a terrible thought. You told him about Sarah. Now she's dead."

Cassandra's frown deepened. "That's true."

"Don't you see? It's a real coincidence that you mention her name and bring her into this, and now she's dead. There have been several little things that have troubled me."

Cassandra's body tightened as the possibility of Adam's words struck home. If Beaker were involved in the murders, she'd given Sarah Welford a death sentence by naming her. "My God," she whispered. She looked at Adam. "What should I do? Surely Beaker's not involved in this mess?"

"Be careful of everything you say. I know we thought it was a good idea to tell Beaker everything about your dreams. Now, maybe we shouldn't tell him anything."

Cassandra put her hand on the knob. "We have to be wrong about Beaker. He's the sheriff, Adam." She didn't want to believe that Beaker might be involved in Sarah's death. If the law enforcement system was tangled up in murders ... The idea was too frightening to pursue.

"We probably are wrong, but it doesn't hurt to use a little caution," Adam insisted. "Maybe we could think up a test."

"What kind of test?"

"False information. See how he uses it."

Cassandra knew it was a good idea, but she had no idea how to implement it. And if they were wrong about Beaker, if she sent him on a wild-goose chase with false leads, another innocent woman could die. It was an impossible decision.

Cassandra opened the door. When Adam started to enter, Beaker stood up. "I'll speak with Ms. McBeth first, and then you," the sheriff said easily but with firm authority.

"It's okay," Cassandra said as she started to close the door on Adam.

"I'll be right here, waiting," he promised.

Cassandra took the chair Beaker indicated and sat down on the edge of it.

"Any dreams?" Beaker asked. There was no inflection in his voice. He watched her with sharp, alert eyes.

"Not this time."

"Is your subconscious, or wherever your visions come from, failing you?"

"I don't know," Cassandra answered. "I had no idea that Sarah Welford was in any trouble. You said she was struck by a car. Did she die instantly?"

Beaker ignored her question. "When was the last time you saw Ms. Welford?"

Cassandra hesitated. She shrugged. "Late last night. The early morning hours, I guess you'd say. Adam went back to the restaurant, and I waited in the car. I saw her in the parking lot with a man. Ray Somebody."

"Ray Somebody?" Beaker's eyes narrowed. "I'm surprised Ms. Welford let you get close enough to hear the name of her friend."

"She didn't exactly let me," Cassandra answered. She met Beaker's gaze and didn't waver. "I was looking at a car in the parking lot and she and her friend were in the shadows. They didn't see me and I left before I got into trouble."

"I told you to go straight home." Beaker shifted in his chair. "You don't listen very well, Ms. McBeth."

"No, but I hear awfully well," she said. "That man with Ms. Welford threatened her in an indirect way. He was a bodybuilder. Very powerful."

"Oh?" Beaker was interested.

Cassandra repeated the conversation she'd overheard. "That's it."

Beaker had made a few notes. He put his pen down. "I'll see if my men can't locate this guy. No last name. No mention of job."

"None. But Sarah's roommate, Ellen, might know who he is." She lifted her eyebrows as she said it, knowing it would aggravate the sheriff.

"If Ms. Welford has a roommate, she might know who Sarah was dating, that's true." Beaker refused to get rattled.

"How did Ms. Welford die?" Cassandra asked. "The truth. Did the car kill her, or did someone help?"

Before the sheriff could answer, a deputy knocked on the door. At Beaker's signal, he stepped into the room. "The car is clean, sir. No damage at all. I checked it thoroughly. In fact, the road dirt for several weeks hasn't been disturbed at all. It needs to be washed."

"And Ms. McBeth's car?"

"It's still over at Benny's Garage," Cassandra interjected. "He said he's had the front wheel off since it was brought in. It hasn't been driven anywhere."

"Thank you, Jim. That'll be all."

"Uh, sir." The deputy fidgeted. "Mayor Simpson has called four times. The dispatcher has him on hold now."

"Tell her to tell him I'll call as soon as I know something." Beaker's voice was harsh. "That's all."

The deputy left, closing the door smartly behind him.

"So, you wanted us in here so you could inspect Adam's vehicle."

Beaker didn't bother to deny it.

"We could have rented another," she said, anger making her reckless. "We could have ten cars hidden on the side of that mountain, just waiting for the chance to run down waitresses who won't answer a few of our questions."

"We have a warrant and my men are searching your home and the area around it now," Beaker said. His own smile was self-satisfied. "If there's anything to hide, we'll know it in the next hour or so. If you'll take a seat outside and send Mr. Raleigh in, I'd like to speak with him."

The idea that someone was in her house, disturbing her personal possessions, made Cassandra so angry she couldn't answer. She rose, turned stiffly away, and left. When she reached the hall, Adam could see the anger pulsing in her.

"They're searching my house," she said, her voice murderous. "Right now, they're in my personal belongings, going through my things." Her voice cracked dangerously and she knew the tears weren't far behind. "Beaker wants to talk with you now."

Adam kissed her cheek gently. "Just relax. There's nothing we can do. I'll be finished in a minute."

When Adam was seated in the same chair Cassandra had vacated, Beaker asked him the same questions. Adam's answers were identical to hers.

"That will be all," Beaker said, dismissing Adam. "Keep Ms. McBeth out of town, as I requested."

"Sheriff, there's something else I'd like to speak with you about."

"I don't have time for any foolishness," Beaker warned. Something in Adam's expression stopped him. "Okay, what is it?"

"Someone has been talking with Martin West. Some of the things they've told West have been very indiscreet."

"Such as?"

"Such as Cassandra's dreams."

"And how is that indiscreet?" Beaker asked.

"West has been calling Ms. McBeth's home, asking her to appear on his show."

"Maybe she should," Beaker said. "She'd make a helluva lot more money on television than her mother ever did in that shack on the side of the highway."

Adam's temper, normally so cool, flashed through him. He wanted to feel his fist crashing into Beaker's thin face. He wanted to feel Beaker's nose give beneath his hand.

"Calm down," Beaker said. He stood up and leaned on the desk with both hands. "Martin West has often helped me in my work," Beaker said. "Sometimes he stages shows that aid an investigation but I have never given him information that would hamper a case."

"You suggested that he ask Cassandra to come on his show?" Adam was incredulous. It was the most insane thing he'd ever heard. "You'd put Cassandra's life at risk."

"Listen to me," Beaker said. "I'd do whatever necessary to solve this case. If the maniac out there who's killing women heard the show and believed some psychic had tuned in to his killing spree, he might find it a challenge. He might leave clues for her to find, or send her messages in some way."

Adam clenched his fists. He wanted to pulp the sheriff. "Have you thought this thing through enough to realize you could be putting Cassandra's life at risk?"

"A very small risk," Beaker said. "Personally, I don't believe anyone would be foolish enough to fall for such a cockamamy thing. This killer is smart. Very smart. Some crazy recluse who claims to dream the murders wouldn't scare him."

"Then why tell West?"

"Mr. Raleigh, you don't realize what's going on in this town. We have three women murdered. Panic is just below the surface. Ken Simpson is riding me hard. If I don't get a lid on this, Gatlinburg is going to suffer one of the worst tourist seasons in history. The town's economy could be ruined. My career would be destroyed."

"That comes with your job, Sheriff," Adam said. He had no sympathy for him. Beaker was a calculating man who watched his own backside. His assumption a few moments before that Beaker might actually be involved in the murders gained new weight. If not Beaker, was the sheriff protecting someone?

"If Ms. McBeth will do the show, we'll give her complete protection." Beaker didn't smile. "It will also give us an opportunity to watch the two of you. I'm still not certain you aren't involved."

"The feeling's mutual," Adam retorted. He watched with satisfaction as the impact of his statement struck Beaker.

"If Ms. McBeth truly wants to help, she should consider going on television. If she knows anything, maybe she can flush out the killer."

"I won't have Cassandra dangled like a piece of bait." Adam was immovable.

"I didn't realize you were making Ms. McBeth's decisions for her," Beaker said. "She didn't strike me as that type of woman."

Adam knew Beaker had instinctively gone for his weak point. Cassandra wasn't the type to let anyone else make her decisions. "Ask her yourself," he said. "I'm not speaking for her, I'm merely reflecting what she's already told me."

"Martin West can do his own asking," Beaker said. "In fact, that's probably what he's doing now."

Adam jerked open the door. Cassandra was sitting on the bench in the sheriff's main office, talking with Martin West. Adam recognized the television personality immediately. Even so early in the morning, West was perfectly dressed, every hair in place.

"If anything happens to Cassandra..." Adam didn't finish the sentence. He closed the door behind him as he left Beaker reaching for the telephone.

He waited at the door, taking the measure of the room. Cassandra seemed calm enough. West was leaning forward, pressing a point, but Cassandra wasn't distressed. At least he didn't think so. Adam slowly started to her side. He didn't want to interfere.

"Adam," Cassandra said. There was the tiniest hint of relief in her face. "Mr. West was asking me to do a show."

"Yes, Sheriff Beaker said he'd given Mr. West some details."

"It's the perfect opportunity for Ms. McBeth to reveal her talents and to shed some light on the murders of those poor, unfortunate women."

"I told Mr. West that there's really nothing I can tell the public that I haven't already told the sheriff." She shrugged. "I have nothing interesting to tell, so there's no point in doing such a show."

"But you actually witnessed the murders of those women, didn't you?" West pressed.

"That isn't an accurate way to put it," Cassandra said. "According to Beaker, I had a nightmare."

"But Beaker said you claimed to see the murder happen in a dream." West pulled a sheet of paper from his pocket where he'd obviously made notes from his talk with Beaker. "You feel you're a part of the murder, as if you were with the killer and victim, right?"

"That's correct," Cassandra answered with some reluctance.

"Then you could identify the killer." Martin's voice grew sharper. "Can you?"

"Not exactly." Cassandra shifted away from the man. He seemed to be leaning closer and closer to her. "I really don't want to talk about this anymore."

"Well, you can or you can't. Which is it?"

"Ease back," Adam suggested as he stepped to Cassandra's side. His voice was pleasant, but the tension in his body let Martin know he was prepared to make his request an order.

"Hey, sorry. It's just exciting."

"Not for me," Cassandra said softly.

"Some people have no appreciation for a rare gift." Martin West put his hand on Cassandra's knee. "But I do, Cassandra. I've always believed in special talents. I mean, since I was old enough to remember, I've wanted to be in television. I think I made it happen for me, and I think that's a gift."

"Clear and focused ambition can be a gift," Cassandra agreed. "Not many people know what they want. Those who do are way ahead of the game."

"That's right." Martin West sat back, finally turning his attention to Adam. "Forgive me, I've forgotten my manners. And here is the cereal magnate, Adam Raleigh, isn't it?" He held out his hand.

Adam shook it slightly. For a big man with a large hand, Martin West's grip was annoyingly soft.

"We can leave now, Cassandra," Adam said clearly. "It's been a hard morning. We were both sorry to hear about Ms. Welford." As he spoke, Adam assisted Cassandra to her feet.

"Tell me one more thing," Martin said as he rose, also. "If you see the murders happening, and you can't identify the murderer, then he must be wearing a mask, right?"

Cassandra stared at the television host. "No. He doesn't wear a mask."

"How can you be so certain?" Martin followed through, walking with Cassandra and Adam toward the door.

"He's a vain man," Cassandra said slowly. "He worries about his looks. He wants to be told he's handsome. That's how he attracts the women, with his looks and his—" She broke off. Her voice had taken on a dreamlike quality.

"His what?" Martin pressed. He pulled his pen from his pocket.

"I'm not certain," Cassandra looked at Adam for reassurance.

Adam felt an urge to stop her, to get her away from West, but he knew he could do nothing. Cassandra was a grown woman. If she wanted to feed the frenzy of the TV host, she had every right. It was just that he didn't understand her motivation.

"His what?" Martin asked again. "His clothes, his car, what?"

"His personality," Cassandra finished. "He's good at that. He meets the public well, and he gives an aura of confidence. Like an official personage of some kind."

Martin stopped writing. "This is heavy stuff. We should get this on tape. How about we put you behind a screen, no actual photos. We could protect your identity and yet let the public know that you're solving the murder case."

It was more than Adam could take. "Cassandra isn't solving anything," he said sharply. "She's tried to help, but so far the authorities have been more interested in persecuting her than taking her help."

"Remember what I told you." Martin gave his attention to Cassandra. "You might be able to draw the murderer out."

"Enough!" Adam knew how seriously Cassandra took her responsibilities. He should have known Martin had dangled that particular ploy at her, making her feel guilty in order to get an interview. He took Cassandra's arm. "West, stay away from Ms. McBeth and her property. Don't call or we'll press harassment charges, is that clear?"

"It's clear enough you don't want to let the lady decide for herself." West grinned. "Afraid of what she'll do?"

"I make my own decisions," Cassandra said clearly. "Right now, I want to leave. I'll consider what you had to say, Mr. West. I'll give it serious thought, and I'll get back to you."

"Not many people get a chance to stop a murderer," Martin said loudly as Adam and Cassandra walked away. "Think about it, Ms. McBeth. Think long and hard about the women who might die before this thing is stopped."

Chapter Ten

"It is not a good thing." Running Stream paced Cassandra's kitchen. Her dark eyes were angry. "You could be in terrible danger, Cassandra. You must not do this."

"Innocent women are in danger," Cassandra replied. She didn't sound too forceful because her heart was troubled by the idea of appearing on Martin West's show. But her conscience demanded that she do everything in her power to stop the killer. If, via television, she could convince the killer that she was getting closer and closer to finding out his identity, then maybe he would come after her. "I have to try to stop him. Even if it means going on television."

"Even if it means putting your own life at risk?" The unexpected question came from Running Stream. "I know how much you hate the idea of going on television, but that isn't the biggest problem. Cassandra, if that killer thinks you know him, he'll have to come after you."

"It's a calculated risk," Cassandra admitted. Running Stream was bringing up the exact same points Adam had used to argue against the idea of her television appearance. She'd sent Adam into town on an errand so that she could have this discussion with her friend. Even though his absence was at her request, she still missed him.

"Adam doesn't want you to do this, either, does he?"

Looking up at the tall, statuesque Indian woman, Cassandra noticed for the first time that her friend's skin was sallow. Dark circles, like smudges, were beneath the un-blinking brown eyes.

"Where's Bounder?" Cassandra asked. She knew in-stinctively that the young man would be the source of Run-ning Stream's moments of extreme joy and pain.

"He didn't come home last night," Running Stream an-swered. "I had hoped he might be here, watching you."

"I haven't seen him." Cassandra felt a swift flurry of concern. Bounder had lately taken up with some rough companions. She censored that disturbing thought and found one more acceptable. "Maybe he's camping. Spring is coming and he loves the woods."

Running Stream shook her head. "He wouldn't take the clothes that are missing on a camping trip. Dress clothes."

"A date?" Cassandra wanted to think of all the best possibilities.

"Probably not. He would have left a note, even if he thought I would disapprove." Running Stream's smile held a sad twist. "He's a man, and I've accepted that fact. His ways are different from the way I was raised. Staying out all night with young women, traveling together for week-ends—these are things we don't agree on, but we talk about them. If it was a woman, he would've told me."

Cassandra went to her friend. Together they stood by the kitchen window, looking out at the greening meadow and trees. They were both worried, both thinking the same thing.

"Are Billy and Stalker at the reservation?" It was the one question she didn't want to ask, but it was the most impor-tant. The two young Indian men had become Bounder's constant companions. They were slightly older and a lot more unsettled. In fact, they burned with a dangerous an-ger and frustration.

"I can't find them." Running Stream took a deep breath. "I'm worried that they'll do something ill-considered. They talk so foolishly."

Cassandra knew what black thoughts Running Stream spoke about. She'd heard some of the talk Bounder's new friends had been spouting—talk of running the white people from the mountains, of frightening the tourists so that the resort town of Gatlinburg would dry up and blow away. They wanted to reclaim the old hunting grounds of the Cherokee. It was the desperate talk of young men tired of a system that offered them no opportunities. Cassandra sympathized with their emotions, but she'd never encouraged their wild talk of destruction. Now she was frightened for the young man she'd grown to love like a brother.

Bounder was not a violent man. Not in the least. But he was under the influence of Billy Buckeye Tanner and Stalker McKinney, two hotheaded men who were determined to change their world, even to the extent of destroying it.

"Where would they go?" Cassandra asked, careful to keep the worry from her voice.

"I've checked all the places I know," Running Stream said. She turned to Cassandra. Her eyes were hard and bright, a mark of her strength. "There's something I must show you."

"What?" By the tone of her friend's voice, Cassandra knew Running Stream was deeply troubled. She watched as the Indian woman drew an object from the pocket of her skirt.

Metal shimmered as dangling crystals caught the light.

"Carla's earring," Cassandra said with an intake of breath.

"I suspected as much," Running Stream said. Her eyes brightened with tears as she continued. "I found it in Bounder's pocket."

Cassandra grasped the top of a cane-bottomed chair for support. "You couldn't have. I gave the earring we found to Sheriff Beaker. Bounder and Adam found one earring in the yard and I gave it to Beaker." She repeated herself, denying what the appearance of the earring might mean.

"Then this is the second earring," Running Stream said. She was never one to walk away from the truth, even when it meant grave danger for herself or those she loved. "We need an explanation."

"My God," Cassandra whispered. "Do you think Bounder found out something about the murderer?"

Running Stream had composed herself. "I have thought that, yes."

"Then he could be in grave danger."

"One way or the other," Running Stream said. "If his companions have broken the law, then he is an accomplice. If he has discovered their actions, illegal actions, then he might be in danger of harm from them."

"Billy and Stalker..." Cassandra left the thought unfinished. The two were angry enough to do almost anything. Almost. But surely not to come up with a plan that involved killing innocent young women.

Surely not that.

Cassandra thought back to the most recent conversation she'd had with the three young men. Bounder had remained quiet, watching Billy and Stalker argue with her. An attempt to get support for research into the history of the Cherokee people had gained only a small following outside the younger members of the tribe.

Billy and Stalker were resentful, and angrier than usual, and they blamed the local merchants and tourists. She could clearly hear Billy's words. "They like the reservation nearby. Indians with their feathers and dances are colorful, great tourist attractions. But no one wants to know the truth, to learn about what the Cherokee nation once was. We should scalp a few of the tourists. Give them a real lesson in history," he'd said.

"Yeah," Stalker had agreed. "The only way for an Indian to earn any respect around here is to make people afraid."

Cassandra understood the deep source of their anger and had done what she could to try to ease some of the bitter pain. The economic and social problems facing the young Indian men were tough, and she didn't have any panacea. Not even a comforting answer. She and Running Stream had encouraged Bounder to leave Cherokee, North Carolina, and go to college—a solution he'd steadfastly refused. He wasn't leaving his heritage. He wasn't leaving his friends. Not even if Cassandra helped him. Not even if his mother begged him.

Cassandra sighed. The day-to-day reality of Bounder's future was hard enough, now it was doubly complicated by the beautiful earring she held in her hand. What had the young man gotten himself into?

"What do you think we should do?" she asked Running Stream.

"I don't know." She stared out the window. "I'm afraid whatever I do will be wrong."

"And if we do nothing, more young women will die."

"In your dreams, this man that you hear, how does he talk?"

"He's charming. Very quick. I think he's very good-looking. The women all look at him as if he were. You know, they're attracted to him."

Billy was a handsome man. Almost as handsome as Bounder. Cassandra felt herself begin to tremble.

"Could he be Indian?" Running Stream asked.

Cassandra swallowed, but her throat was dry. She'd never given it a thought, actually. She'd assumed... like everyone else. She'd never considered that an Indian man might be involved. She thought back over the sequences of her dreams.

"I don't know," she finally answered. "The killer has strong hands. They're tan. I remember them on the steering wheel, but it was more the feel of them than the look."

"Billy is a very handsome man. He's well educated, very successful with the ladies, so I've been told. And his father was a white man. Like Bounder's."

"Yes. Billy is a very handsome man." Cassandra nodded. She'd never discussed Bounder's father with Running Stream. She knew only that he was the reason Running Stream moved off the reservation and closer to Gatlinburg. Recently Bounder had defiantly returned to the reservation. Bounder's white heritage could be found in his face, even though he, like Billy, hated his father's culture. In her heart, Cassandra had suspected it was a large contributing factor to the discontent she saw in the young men. It only added to their feelings of being cast away and cheated.

"My son is very handsome, too." Running Stream spoke slowly. "Women find him irresistible."

"Bounder wouldn't hurt anything." Cassandra didn't raise her voice. She knew she could have more impact on her friend by remaining completely calm. "We both know that." The look on Running Stream's face tore at her heart. She saw a mother's love warring with a need for truth. Running Stream had more courage than anyone she'd ever known.

"I can't believe that he would," Running Stream answered. "But—" she held out the earring "—this tells me otherwise. I believe your dream, Cassandra. I believe this is the earring of a dead woman. And I want to know what my son was doing with it in his possession."

"That's something we both need to find out," Cassandra agreed.

ADAM LEANED AGAINST the white oak tree. To a casual observer, he looked as if he were taking a break on a beautiful early spring afternoon. The beauty of the small town shimmered in the afternoon light. Only a careful observer would have seen the surreptitious glances he threw at the back door of city hall.

Sheriff Beaker, Police Chief Charles Haggin and another man Adam didn't know had all disappeared into the office. Adam wanted a word alone with Beaker. He was ready to punch out the lawman's lights for the harebrained scheme of putting Cassandra on television. If he couldn't stop Cassandra from doing it, then he wanted to make sure that Beaker was good for his promise of protection.

His wait was rewarded when Beaker and the unknown man came out of the door. As soon as they crossed the street, Adam followed. He couldn't help but notice that the second man was well built. He was in his mid to late thirties, Adam guessed, but he could easily be taken for ten years younger at first glance.

He walked with a spring in his step that embodied fitness. Beaker was fit, also, but he lacked the buoyancy of his companion.

Adam had hoped for a private moment with the sheriff, but as he followed, he could see the two men were headed for a local coffee shop. He closed the distance between them, intending to stop Beaker. It might work to his advantage to have a witness to what he intended to say.

"What about that muscle man the mountain witch mentioned?" the stranger asked.

Adam instinctively dropped back, waiting to hear more. The mention of Cassandra's name, especially in such a derogatory reference, made him want to hear as much as possible.

"No leads, yet. We don't even have enough information to make a case for deliberate homicide. My personal belief is that some drunk hit her on the side of the road. Anyway, we're going to stake out Ms. Welford's funeral this afternoon." Beaker checked his watch. "In an hour or two."

"The boyfriend didn't even come by to ask if you'd found any leads?" The other man shook his head. "Some boyfriend."

"No, Ken, he didn't. If he was her boyfriend, he wasn't the kind who stays around in times of trouble."

Beaker's humor produced a short laugh from his companion. "That's too bad. I liked Sarah. I'd known her for a couple of years from Crockett's. Her family was from north of here, pretty far out in the woods. Getting to Gatlinburg was an accomplishment for her, and she had plans to go farther. Did her family show?"

"Yeah. They're torn up, as you might imagine. They're also riding me pretty hard to find the driver who killed her. Since it was probably an accident, it could take a while. Crimes without a motive are always the hardest to solve." Beaker rubbed his chin with the back of his hand. "Like this maniac killer we have."

"You've got plenty on your plate. At least it's been quiet for a few days. Tell me the truth, has Cassandra McBeth been able to spook up any idea who the killer might be? Any good dreams or visions?" he laughed.

"Don't even say it," Beaker said. "You'll bring the creep out of the woodwork again, and I'm hoping he's moved on. Cassandra's dreams are interesting, especially in their accuracy, but she hasn't named any names. Do me a favor and don't go around spouting off about Ms. McBeth. Her male friend chewed on me about unprofessionalism."

Adam sauntered behind the men, his ears straining. Beaker was terribly free with details about his investigation. It seemed a bad habit with the man.

"Haggin says the crimes are out of his jurisdiction, but if you need help, don't hesitate to ask. I'm sure that with my influence, the city could declare some type of emergency and loan you some policemen and cars."

"Thanks." Beaker rubbed his chin again. "We're exploring every lead we find. My men and I believe the crimes are committed somewhere else, then the bodies are brought to different ravines and dumped. Hell, it's over now. I'm hoping the guy's moved on and we're left with two unsolved murders."

"That's not the best solution," the other man agreed, "but I like that better than a continuation of the murders. You aren't holding out on some evidence, are you?"

Beaker slowed his pace. "Not at all, Mayor. We're considering the possibility of putting Ms. McBeth on Martin West's show. There's a chance, if the murderer's still around, we can draw him out."

"Using Cassandra McBeth as bait?" The mayor considered the possibility as he spoke. "This could end up looking bad for the city. I mean murderers and psychics. We don't want to look ridiculous."

"But we do want to catch the killer."

"Just don't go overboard. You know West likes to exaggerate everything. He could make us all look like a bunch of hillbillies."

"Ken, if we don't catch this guy, then the next murder will bring the national media in here. Serial killers are big television."

"How much does Ms. McBeth actually know?" The mayor stopped and shifted his weight from foot to foot. A sheen of perspiration touched his upper lip.

Beaker shrugged. "Who knows for sure?"

"Do you really believe she knows anything?" The mayor wiped his forehead with the palm of his hand. The afternoon was not hot, but he was uncomfortable.

"I don't buy into this mumbo jumbo crap. She's an eccentric. But she doesn't have to convince me, only the killer."

"Well, let me know if the city can be of any assistance." The mayor looked up and down the street with some anxiety. "I'd better be getting back to the office."

Adam ducked behind a trash can. So that was Mayor Ken Simpson. Adam didn't particularly care for the way Simpson had referred to Cassandra as the mountain witch. Neither man had much concern for her welfare, either. They were both too caught up in protecting their own little niches.

The mayor and sheriff parted ways. Beaker headed for the small café where coffee and fresh hot doughnuts were a specialty. Adam followed close behind. He waited for the exact moment to speak.

"Sheriff, if Cassandra does this Martin West show, how many deputies will you put on her for protection?"

Adam's question stopped the lawman in the door of the café. Beaker turned, one hand still on the doorknob. "Enough to take care of the job. We have no intention of setting Ms. McBeth up as a sitting duck."

"No? How about a cooked goose?" Adam felt his temper begin a slow burn. Beaker was so damned superior. "I think this is a serious mistake. If anything happens—"

"Can the melodrama," Beaker interrupted. "Ms. McBeth knows the dangers. She agreed to do this because she wants to help. My suggestion to you is that you either stay out of the way or, in general, make yourself scarce."

"I'm not some local you can intimidate," Adam said. Beaker's attitude was infuriating. It was almost as if the man wanted to put Cassandra in the worst position possible.

"That's right, Mr. Raleigh. You aren't a local. As far as I'm concerned, you're becoming a troublemaker. If it becomes necessary, I can have you locked up tight." He took a step closer. "I want this case solved. It isn't my intention to endanger anyone, especially not Cassandra McBeth. But you forget, she came to me and volunteered information. Now I'm just going to use it in the way I deem most beneficial to my investigation."

Adam held his ground. "You'd better make certain the protection you give her is adequate."

"I don't take too kindly to threats."

"I don't give them lightly. And while you're at it, it might be nice if you asked the mayor not to refer to Cassandra as the mountain witch."

Beaker smiled. "Ken Simpson and Cassandra went to school together. He knows her family history as well as I do. We both remember when her father fell in the apple orchard. Some folks said it wasn't an accident." Beaker let the implication hang.

"I guess the law enforcement was about as good then as it is now." Adam smiled as he saw Beaker's face grow red. "If foul play was suspected, someone should have done something then. Besides, Cassandra isn't responsible for the past."

"You'd better stay clear of me and my work," Beaker said carefully. He opened the door of the café and stepped inside, slamming it behind him.

Adam checked his watch. He had one last idea. Sarah Welford's funeral. He would have liked to go back for Cassandra, but there wasn't time. Besides, she was too well-known. He hurried to a drugstore where he could find a telephone directory and a list of funeral homes. He had only half an hour to find what he needed before the funeral was set to begin.

SITTING ON THE BACK PEW, Adam scanned the crowd. He saw no one who even remotely came up to the physical description of the man called Ray. There were weeping relatives, and some of the waitresses from Crockett's that he remembered. No bodybuilders, though. He was about to give up the hunt when a slender woman entered. She wore a black veil and took a seat on the pew opposite him. Adam could hear her sniffling as she sat down.

His heart rate increased as he scrutinized the woman. He'd come looking for Ray, but he might have found the mysterious Ellen. He couldn't be certain about her hair. It was done up in a bun and covered with the hat and veil. It was dark, though. And there was something about her, a sadness that went beyond loss of a casual friendship.

Throughout the service, Adam kept his attention on the young woman. As soon as it was over, she stood up and stepped toward the door. He made it a point to be right behind her.

"Excuse me," he said.

She turned, her eyes hidden by the veil. She couldn't disguise the intake of breath.

"Leave me alone," she whispered.

"Ellen?" he asked.

"My name is JoAnn Reed," she said, her voice shaky but clear. "I was Sarah's roommate. Whatever you want, please leave me alone."

Adam felt a moment of confusion. "Could we talk for a moment. This is terribly important," he said, taking her elbow and guiding her away from the front of the chapel. Sheriff Beaker, Chief Haggin and several other law enforcement officials had been at the memorial service. He wanted a chance to talk with this young woman without interruption.

He felt her tense, as if she intended to pull away. Suddenly she started to cry. Adam put his arm around her in a gesture of comfort and drew her to the side of the chapel where a hedge allowed her some privacy. For a few moments, he held her while she cried.

When at last her sobs began to diminish, he shifted her toward a wrought-iron bench that had been placed in a small secluded garden beside the chapel.

"What do you want?" she finally asked. "Why are you hounding me?"

Adam searched her face behind the veil. It was swollen and splotchy. Was she the woman Cassandra called Ellen? Did that woman exist? He realized for the first time that he was on the verge of accepting everything about Cassandra. He'd never really believed in special talents. Now, though...

"I have a friend who's been worried about you, I think," he said. "It's a long, rather strange story, but I have no intention of harming you in any way."

"Sarah told me about you. You and that woman." She touched beneath the veil with a crumpled tissue. "She said you bothered her. The night she died . . ."

"Ms. McBeth and I were looking for a young woman we thought was named Ellen." He saw the girl flinch slightly at the name. His hopes rose. "We wanted to warn her about something Ms. McBeth dreamed." He put his hand on the girl's forearm. "I know this sounds bizarre, but at least listen to me."

"I don't know." She started to rise, but Adam's hand gently restrained her. She resumed her seat, her head bowed.

"Cassandra saw a girl like you in a dream. She was riding with a man in a car. The man intended to kill her." He waited for a reaction, but JoAnn Reed didn't move. "We only wanted to warn the young woman to be careful. That's all."

"Sarah thought you were from my parents." She looked up at last. A tear dropped from her chin beneath the veil and landed in her lap. "She thought you were someone my folks had hired to make me come home."

"No." Adam shook his head.

"She was only trying to help me." JoAnn's voice cracked. "I feel like it's my fault that she's dead." Her voice rose and then she started to cry again.

Adam put his arm around her, giving her his shoulder to cry on. "The sheriff said it was an accident. A hit-and-run driver."

The young woman struggled away from him. "Hit and run? Yeah, it was a hit and run. But it wasn't an accident. What was Sarah doing on the highway alone? That wasn't the way home and she would never have gone that way. What happened to her car that it broke down? Sheriff Beaker doesn't want it to be a murder, so he's acting like it isn't. But I know Sarah. Somebody killed her!" JoAnn's voice rose to a high note of hysteria. She backed away from Adam. "She was afraid of you. Maybe it was you!"

"Raleigh!" Beaker's voice cut through JoAnn's hysteria. "I warned you about causing trouble."

The sheriff stepped through the small black iron gate and stood at the bench. "Harassing young women in town is not something I'm going to put up with."

Beaker motioned JoAnn to his side. She rose, turning from one man to the other. Before Beaker could stop her, she ran through the gate and disappeared.

"You need to talk with that woman," Adam said.

"You need to mind your own business. I warned you about making trouble."

Adam stood up and faced the sheriff. He was desperate to track JoAnn Reed, but he couldn't afford to let Beaker see his intentions. "Are there any charges?"

Beaker waited, watching Adam closely. "What were you doing with that young woman back here all tucked away?"

"Talking. As you clearly saw and heard."

"Sounded to me like she was crying."

"Her friend was murdered." Adam hit the last word hard.

Beaker rubbed his chin with two fingers. "Take a word of warning, Raleigh. Don't nose into business that isn't yours."

Chapter Eleven

It's time someone took things in hand around here and found some answers. Lancelot is down the mountain, and Miss Locks has gone off the deep end with this television idea. Geez! Humans are such creatures of emotion. If I understood the conversation I just heard, Running Stream and Cassandra both think Bounder is involved in the murders—by choice or happenstance. Now, let me put my thinking cap on and assume the pose of E. A. Poe's inspector in my favorite, "Murders in the Rue Morgue." Excellent title. Macabre twist. Those French have such wonderful street names.

I must have been an expatriate writer in a past life. Paris promises so many exciting things. Clotilde, the little calico feline who holds my heart, had a bit of Parisian blood. No, she wasn't long-haired and prissy. Not Persian, Parisian. Her great-great-great-great-great-grandmother was an immigrant. Clotilde had that bit of French...chic. It was in the way she held her tail when she walked. Elegant, yet a tease. Ah, Clotilde.

Anyway, back to Poe. Inspector Dupin knew the difference between inductive and deductive reasoning. Now think back with me. The earring is, of course, the crux. Both earrings. Why would Bounder find an earring with Adam if he intended to keep his involvement secret? This is the part that doesn't fit. I mean, Bounder didn't have to find that ear-

ring in the mud. He could have ignored it. Why find something that would be better to be lost?

How did Bounder get the second earring? My conclusion, or I should say that I deduce that if Bounder's friends are up to criminal behavior, he didn't know in the beginning.

Before you clap me on the back in congratulations, consider the implications. If Bounder is missing now, then he might be in danger. That is, if he found the earring in the possession of his two Indian friends, he might have found more than he should have. Another possibility is that he found the earring somewhere else. So where?

He had it the night he was watching this house—another example of behavior that could be interpreted a number of ways. Was he protecting or plotting? If he is a psychotic killer, my normal feline instincts might not detect it. I can sniff out bad guys sometimes, but the psychotics are impossible. They don't reek of guilt. It's a frightening thought. I remember how gentle Bounder's hands were when he stroked me. Once again, evidence that is either very good or very bad. Gentle. Tender. Sensitive... Abnormal. Geez! I need a bit of fresh air.

The thing to do is go back to the bushes where Bounder was hiding. Maybe I can detect something there, some lingering odor or emotion. I've got a lot on my mind, too. I was thinking—if I could get on television with Cassandra, Peter or Eleanor might see me. It's a slim chance. Martin West's show isn't nationally syndicated, but it might play on some of the cables. If Eleanor is as sick as I think she is, maybe she's watching television.

Whatever happens, I can't panic. So, I'll saunter over to the door and demand an exit. I can explore while the humans thrash around in complex emotion.

"MEOW."

Cassandra looked up from her intense conversation with Running Stream. Familiar was at the front door, asking to be let out. "Coming, boy," she said as she stepped away from her friend.

"Stay close to the house," Cassandra admonished the cat as he exited. "No telling who's out there watching us."

"Meow," Familiar agreed, walking to the edge of the porch and taking a seat. He yawned and stretched his body full-length across the wide boards. He sat up and began to clean himself.

"Stay close." Cassandra watched him a moment longer and then shut the door. She'd never seen a cat who took up with a place so readily. Familiar had never budged from his new home. He hadn't even given a thought to leaving. In fact, his only aberrant behavior was his passion for turning the television on and off.

"What is Familiar up to?" Running Stream's casual question broke the tension the two women had shared in their concern for Bounder.

"I don't know." Cassandra had returned to the kitchen, but on an impulse she went back to the front door. When she opened it, the porch was empty. "It was almost as if he knew I was watching him," she said. "Like a little boy, he pretended to settle on the porch, but the minute my back was turned, he disappeared."

Running Stream nodded. "Familiar has his own agenda. He came here unexpectedly, and his behavior is unique." She started to say something else but stopped. "I'd better go home. There's a chance Bounder has returned."

"Maybe." Cassandra didn't hold out much hope. "If he isn't home by tomorrow, we'd better notify the authorities."

"Don't dream tonight, Cass." Running Stream put a hand on her shoulder. "For both our sakes." She smiled, but it held only sadness.

"That's one request I'd gladly oblige. The trouble is, I think Sarah Welford was murdered, and I didn't dream a thing about that. So my dreams, or lack of them, don't seem to mean much."

Running Stream paused before she spoke. "I'm not certain what this means. The other girls were strangled, Cass. Sarah Welford was struck by a car. I agree, I don't think it was an accident. But why the change in the method of killing?" She shook her head. "We must try hard to think of every possibility. No closed doors."

"No closed doors." Cassandra forced a smile. "As soon as Adam gets back, I'll tell him everything. We'll come up with a plan."

Running Stream nodded as she opened the front door. Tears glimmered in her eyes and she brushed them away as she hurried down the steps without looking back.

Cassandra watched the car disappear down the lane. She took another look around for the cat, who was nowhere in sight. She'd give him an hour, then look for him in earnest while she waited for Adam to return. He was far later than she'd anticipated. Worry gnawed at her as she slowly climbed the steps to the shade of the porch. She felt as if her entire life had narrowed down to the minute passage of time, minutes ticking slowly by.

The brisk shrill of the telephone drew her back into the house. She felt a sinking sensation as she recognized Martin West's voice.

He gave her the instructions for the afternoon filming. The show was broadcast live and she had to be at the studio early. She was to bring a list of questions she wanted him to ask, and he had some tips for handling audience questions that he thought would help her. He assured her he was thrilled with her participation.

"This could be the show that sells the networks on me. Have you had any more dreams?" he asked eagerly.

"None." Cassandra couldn't keep the note of depression from her voice. As much as she hated the dreams, she'd come to feel they offered her only chance of solving the murders. Now, even they had abandoned her.

She hung up feeling more and more trapped by the circumstances of her life. How valid was it to go on television now, when Sarah Welford was dead and Cassandra hadn't even had an inkling of her murder?

For a few moments Cassandra paced the house. She straightened cushions, picked up her gardening gloves only to throw them aside, went to make tea, turned off the kettle and finally walked out the front door. If she couldn't do anything else, she could look for Familiar.

She took the path that lead to the upper orchard, moving on instinct. The cat could be anywhere, but she felt he'd taken the path she and Adam had used on their picnic. She didn't like the upper orchard. It was lovely, with one of the best views anywhere. But it was also where her father had died, and when she went there alone, it made her sad. Her life had changed so radically when Blake McBeth died. All permanence had evaporated. Sylvia, never one to love the settled life, had finally given up any attempt to make a home. Cassandra allowed a smile to play across her face as she thought of her mother. Where was she this week? Budapest? Prague? Or was it Brussels?

She received postcards on an irregular basis. They were loving and filled with Sylvia's adventures, both psychic and of the flesh. It wasn't the kind of life that Cassandra had ever wanted, but she loved her mother and wished her only happiness. After all, Cassandra had learned to take care of herself long ago, when she was just a teenager.

The past led to the present, and Cassandra gave in to her need to think about Adam. He'd begun to fill a void that she'd never even acknowledged before.

That was the thing that made him so special. Somehow he'd slipped into the tightly woven fabric of her life without disturbing a single thread. He was the element that had been missing. Someone to share with. Someone to... love. Yes, if she had to admit it, she did love him.

How was it possible that she'd fallen for a man who came from the opposite end of the world from her? Adam was business, profit, production, quotas. He lived the city life of an executive. Those things were anathema to her. She wanted solitude, isolation, the privacy of her mountain home and her garden and study. She could no more survive in a city than she could learn to fly. And Adam couldn't run his business from the top of a mountain, either.

She sighed and called Familiar. Listening for a moment, she heard nothing. She walked on, her determined strides covering the ground and moving her along the little used path. It was time she checked the apple trees anyway. She allowed the other farmers to come in and harvest the crop. She wanted only the apples she could use herself, and she had no desire to oversee the picking and selling of them. But she liked to look at the trees. Her father had taught her so much about husbandry. It was the growing that gave her pleasure, not the selling.

The sight of a sleek black tail bobbing out of some huckleberry bushes put all thoughts of the past or future from Cassandra's mind.

"Familiar, you bad cat. I told you to stay close to the house." Cassandra left the path and went after the bobbing tail. Familiar was obviously going to lead her on a merry chase through the orchard.

Well, the sky was blue and the sun warm and pleasant. Chasing the cat was the best option Cassandra had at the moment. Laughing, she darted toward the shrubs, willing to play Familiar's game of hide-and-seek.

"Come here you black devil," she called as she ducked around a tree. Familiar stayed just enough ahead of her to lead her through the orchard.

The grass had grown with the first hint of warm weather, and it brushed Cassandra's bare calves with a whispering sound. For a moment she remembered the way it felt to be a child, to run in the orchard playing without worries or concerns. It was a memory that brought sadness and delight.

"Meow!" Familiar called her back to the game. With a spurt of power from his hind legs, he bounded into a tangle of vines.

Cassandra laughed, then doubled around the vines, hoping to cut him off on the other side. He was a wily creature and one that obviously had spent plenty of time playing with humans. Where was his family? How had he come to be in her car?

It seemed that her entire world was questions without answers. She pushed that depressing thought aside and renewed her attempts to corner the cat.

"Familiar, if you don't come to me, I'm not going to give you any cream when Adam brings the groceries back," she threatened.

"Meow." Family pounced out of the vines and butted the back of her calf with his head. Then he was gone again, bouncing over the tall weeds and hiding in the grass.

"I'm not going to give you any of the fresh fish Adam's bringing." Cassandra crouched down and listened for the cat.

When he sprang out of the weeds at her, she fell over backward laughing. "I'm going to get you, Familiar," she cried as she jumped up and ran after him. She could barely see his black tail above the weeds, but this time she wasn't going to let him win.

He disappeared a moment and when she crashed through a waist-high plot of black-eyed Susans, she found him standing perfectly still in the middle of two tire prints. Two ribbons of light green grass led away in either direction. Her heart began a steady, high-paced drumming.

She stopped beside the cat. The tall grass had been pushed down by the weight of the car. A small car, judging by the width of the tires. Cassandra looked up and down the tracks. Who had been on her property? Perhaps the man who'd been watching her house had driven in and hidden his vehicle in the upper orchard. It was a thought that made the goose bumps march across her skin.

Only Familiar's total calm kept her from panicking. If there was a stranger around, Familiar would let her know. He was the best watch-cat she'd ever seen. She had to think of other alternatives. She'd promised Running Stream no closed doors.

It could have been Bounder, looking out for her. It wasn't uncommon for him to patrol her property, but she'd never been aware that he did it in his car. He loved to walk in the woods. Cassandra looked at the cat. Familiar sat in the scrunched-down grass, licking a back leg.

"Why do I get the impression that you wanted me to see this?" she asked him. "Let's take a look and see where the tracks lead. My guess is that the southern direction hooks up with my driveway. And the northerly route . . . I don't know for certain."

Before she could take a step, Familiar's claws sank into the top of her tennis shoe. He held her with both paws and an unblinking feline stare.

"Come on, Familiar, let's go." She tried to shake her foot free, but the cat held on with all his might. Her persistent jiggling of her foot only made him dig his claws in deeper.

"Wait for Adam?" she asked. She hesitated as she met his gaze. He was one determined creature. "Okay, we'll wait for Adam and show him."

Familiar released her shoe.

"Then let's get back to the house." She started down the trail with Familiar at her side. With each step, the possibilities of someone hiding out on her property increased her dread. Who had been in her private orchard?

It could have been Beaker's men, when they'd searched her house. It could have been one of the farmers, checking on the apple trees. But the farmers always stopped by her house and had a cup of tea. Beaker's men had no reason to ride around her apple orchard. The only thing she'd ever found in the orchard was the past. Besides, the path had been used more than once, the grass was crushed, not merely pressed down.

Ducking through the branches of the trees as she headed home, Cassandra knew she was escaping from her memories as much as from the idea of an intruder. She had a terrible image from the day after her father died. The dream of his fall, and the emotional turmoil that was a result of that horrible incident, had put her in bed, unable to utter a word. She'd awakened the next morning before anyone could stop her and gone running to the orchard. She'd gone looking for her father, hoping that it had all been a nightmare and that she'd hear him whistling in one of the trees.

The apple orchard had been as calm and peaceful as she'd ever seen it. Morning birds were chirping and the hint of frost had been on the ground. There had been no sign of the accident—except for the impression of the ambulance tracks in the orchard grass. She'd known then that he was really dead.

She felt a lump in her throat and broke into a jog. The past was nothing to think about now. It was over and done. Blake McBeth had been dead for nearly twenty years. It was the future that she had to worry about. The present.

As soon as she got to the house, she was going to…what? She could only pray that Adam was there waiting. The next step was to find Bounder. He could answer a lot of questions.

When she broke through the last of the trees, she was delighted to see Adam's car at her house, along with her own little convertible. Adam was standing at the fender of the Miata, examining the paint job.

"The mechanic followed me here," Adam said by way of greeting when he saw Cassandra jog into the yard. "He said it was repaired, and he put the bill on your account. It must be nice to live in a town where you can charge bills without a piece of plastic."

"Adam…" Cassandra was breathless from her run. "I found…"

"Cassandra, I found the girl I think is Ellen."

She stopped just out of his reach. "Ellen? Really?" The emotion that struck her was something akin to relief mixed with fear. "She's alive?"

"Very much so. And badly shaken."

"Did she tell you who she was seeing?" Cassandra felt as if the ground had shifted under her feet. Edges in the puzzle that didn't fit were close to dropping into place.

"I didn't have much of a chance to really talk with her. Beaker showed up and she ran away like a startled deer. I came up here to get you. I thought maybe we could look for her. If we can find her and get her to talk, maybe we can actually begin to solve some of this."

"Oh, Adam." Cassandra took a seat on the top step. "I was going to suggest we look for Bounder."

"Look for him?"

"He's missing, and Running Stream is afraid he's in danger." She told him about the second earring Running Stream had found in Bounder's room.

"That's hard to believe," Adam said. "I never suspected that he could be involved in anything illegal."

"I don't think he is. I'm more concerned that he might be in danger."

"What should we do?" Adam sat down beside her.

"We could split up. You could hunt Ellen, since you've seen her. I could begin to search for Bounder."

"No!" Adam was emphatic. "I don't like that at all. If we hunt, we hunt together. And Ellen's real name is JoAnn Reed."

"We have to split up—we don't have much time." Cassandra thought of the tire marks. Someone was watching her. It would be wiser to stay with Adam, but what if Bounder was in danger? What if he'd stumbled onto something because he was trying to protect her? Time was the enemy, and she knew she had to do everything she could to find the young man and the woman whose life she'd clearly seen in danger. She made her decisions—to keep her knowledge of the tire marks secret awhile. No point in upsetting Adam further. He was already overprotective.

"Adam, it couldn't be too dangerous if we both went around asking questions. You've got Ellen's real name. Find her, get the man's name who she's been seeing and then meet me at the trading post at the Cherokee reservation. Or leave a message there."

Adam started to protest, but he knew what she was saying made sense. He also knew by the look on her face that nothing he said would change her mind. For a woman as beautiful as an enchantress, she had the tenacity of a pit bull. "What do you think you can do there that Running Stream can't?"

"I knew some of Bounder's friends. Some his mother didn't know or didn't want to know." She smiled. "As close as those two are, there are still secrets a young man has from his mother."

Adam allowed a rueful grin. "I suppose. These friends, are they troublemakers?"

"It depends on whose perspective you see them from," Cassandra said with a sigh. "I don't think they'd bother me. After all, I may be a white woman, but I'm not accepted by the local community. I have a lot in common with them." She pushed her long hair back from her face and stood abruptly. "It isn't so different, you see. Bounder's friends understand that I'm an outcast, too."

"You wouldn't be if you moved somewhere else." Adam rose also and put his hands on her shoulders. "Anywhere else in the world, you'd be accepted for the bright, interesting, and beautiful woman you are."

"Anywhere except my hometown?" There was an edge of bitterness in her voice.

"You could make a new home. Any place can be home as long as there's someone there who loves you."

"I've never been one to run away." Cassandra held her chin up and met Adam's gaze. She knew it would come to this conversation, this hurdle. She simply hadn't expected it so soon.

"Wisdom is knowing the difference between running and starting over. There's no shame in taking a different path, Cassandra."

"No, there's not." She had to find the right words. "But I'd have to know in my heart that I wasn't running away. If I wasn't certain of that, I wouldn't have any respect for myself." She placed her hands on his chest, where she could feel the beating of his heart. "Besides, I don't know if I could live anywhere but this old mountain. It's part of me, Adam.

I'm part of it. The plants and animals and the way the seasons come here . . ."

"There are other places, other ways of living to experience." He'd reached a wall with her, one that he was going to have to be very careful in how he scaled it. She was so much a part of her surroundings; did he even have a right to suggest that she leave them?

The bigger question was whether he could leave without her, if it came to that.

She saw the struggle in his eyes. He, too, was confronting the vast differences that stood between what they felt for each other and reality. His heart beat strong beneath her palm, and she felt the longing build inside her to step into the safety of his embrace. She remembered too well the sense of security she could share in his arms. When their bodies touched, reality was pushed away.

"We both know we can't make any decisions until we find out about these young women. And Bounder." She spoke so softly that he inclined his head to her. "Let's not talk about this now, Adam. Not now. Neither of us is ready for that kind of decision."

"Come with me to hunt JoAnn. Then we'll go to the reservation." He wasn't inclined to premonitions. Maybe it was living with Cassandra that made him more attuned to his senses. For some reason, though, he didn't want to let her get away from him. Not even for an hour.

"Give me two hours. If you get tied up, call the trading post's main number and leave a message for me. I'll check there if you don't come."

"Be careful." Adam pulled her into his arms and held her. She was so delicate. How was it possible that she had so much strength?

"Hey, I'm going to be a television star tomorrow. I wouldn't risk a hair on my head." She put her arms around his neck and clung to him. It was a second of pleasure. She pushed herself away. "See you in a while."

Adam watched as she swung into her little red convertible. She waved as she pulled out of the yard.

The nagging sensation of impending doom settled on his shoulders with a vengeance. He had an irrational impulse to follow her, even if he had to do it clandestinely. But Cassandra would deeply resent such an action. And JoAnn Reed's life might rest on his taking the proper action. He got into his car and started down the long, tree-lined drive.

He'd just rounded the first curve when he saw the man dash out in front of the car. He had only a brief glimpse of the stooped old man in a hat before he put all of his attention into stopping the car. Adam hit the brakes and cut the wheel sharply.

There was a thud as he struck something and the car skidded into a tree.

The sudden impact jarred him with such force that a groan escaped his lips. His seat belt took the full force of his body flying forward, and then he was thrown back into the seat with a back-jolting whiplash. Stunned, Adam sat in the seat for several moments.

When he finally got out, he hurried to see what he'd struck. Beneath the front wheel of the car was a scarecrow. It looked as if it had been pulled from one of the tobacco fields anywhere along the road. Straw escaped from the tattered body and spilled beneath his car.

"Son of a…" Adam looked around the woods. His mind was working clearly again, aware now that danger was imminent. Someone had thrown the dummy out of the woods in an attempt to wreck him. Why?

"Cassandra!" He knew then.

The front of his car was totaled. Fluids dripped onto the leaf-filled ground. He tried the key, but the motor only sputtered. Slamming the steering wheel with his hand, he swore.

He'd fallen right into the trap. In dodging the scarecrow, he'd wrecked his car and now he was trapped on the mountain with a good two-hour walk ahead of him. Two hours when Cassandra might need his help.

He slammed out of the car and started jogging. At least it was downhill. Ducking low limbs and concentrating on establishing his breathing, Adam set his course toward the highway. With any luck, he might catch a ride. If his luck ran against him...if he had to crawl, he'd get to Cassandra.

Chapter Twelve

About ten miles from the Cherokee reservation property, Cassandra waited in the shelter of an old chestnut tree. Perched in the branches, several small finches sang, unafraid of her presence. She was so taken by the brave songsters that when she heard her name called, she jumped.

She swung around into the handsome face of Billy Buckeye Tanner. He'd stolen silently through the woods until he was only six feet from her. She'd never even heard a twig snap.

"I heard you wanted to see me," he said softly.

The tree's shade put Billy's eyes in shadow. Cassandra searched them, but she could see nothing, not a hint of anger or fear or remorse.

"Where's Bounder? When I asked around with some of your friends, they were all reluctant to say anything."

"He's a grown man. I don't keep tabs on him." A flicker of contempt touched Billy's lips. "You and his mother are so afraid he's going to grow up. You're smothering him."

"I care for Bounder, and for his mother. I don't want to see him make a mistake that could ruin the rest of his life. I don't want to see you do that, either, Billy."

"I don't need a baby-sitter!"

Anger only intensified the handsome angle of Billy's jaw. Cassandra couldn't help the ghost of a smile that touched her lips. Those were exactly the same words she'd spoken to Adam when they were with Sheriff Beaker. "Bounder could be in serious trouble. Please help me," she said. "If he isn't with you, then he's disappeared."

Billy's face gave nothing away. "What do you want to know?"

"Has Bounder been in my upper orchard?"

This time she struck pay dirt. Billy's reaction was split second, but it was there nonetheless. "Has someone been in your orchard?" He tried to act as if he wasn't surprised by her question.

"I found the car tracks. All I have to do is follow them."

"We put some things up there." He gave up the pretense. "For safekeeping. Bounder didn't think you'd mind."

"Basically, I don't mind if Bounder uses my property." Cassandra felt her pulse quicken. "I would like to know what things."

Billy shrugged. "Stuff we needed for later. Nothing important."

"I'm going straight home and find whatever you've put there." She started to move past him, back to the path that led to the highway.

Billy's hand gripped her arm. "You don't want to see that stuff."

Cassandra met his gaze in the shade of the tree. "It's illegal, isn't it? What? Guns? Money?" She couldn't believe it.

"Wire and stuff." Billy was vague. "Leave it alone and we'll get it tonight."

"Whatever it is, Sheriff Beaker and his men were all over my place," Cassandra said. "They might have already found it."

Billy shook his head. "No, they would have arrested you if they had." He smiled. "If they'd known what it was."

"Don't touch it." Cassandra felt her anger build. "Whatever it is, leave it there and I'll take care of it later. Whatever plan you had, forget it, Billy. No matter how right you think you are, violence is no solution. Now where is Bounder? Is he up there guarding that stuff?"

Billy shook his head. "We haven't seen him since yesterday. He said he had something he had to do. He wouldn't tell anyone. Not even me. What do you think he's up to?"

Cassandra hesitated. This latest development made her almost certain that Billy was not involved with the murders of the women. "He found something. An earring. I think it belonged to one of the murdered women, but I can't prove that."

"Where?"

"That's the question we all want answered."

"We're supposed to meet tonight at nine," Billy said. "If Bounder doesn't come, then you can be sure he's in trouble."

"I'll wait until tonight. I won't go to the orchard until I've heard from you. But Billy," she warned, "don't try to pull anything on me. Whatever you have up there, I'll have it removed later, when no one will be blamed."

"Tonight." He stepped back. In five strides, he'd disappeared as silently as he'd come. Cassandra was left in the woods, wondering what plot the young men were involved in. And if Bounder wasn't with his friends, where was he?

She took the long path back to the place where she'd parked her car. She'd been gone more than the two hours she'd told Adam. He'd be worried.

To her surprise, when she checked at the trading post, there was no word from Adam. As she drove back to Gatlinburg, she hit on the idea that he might be at Crockett's. She drove through the parking lot, but she didn't see his car. Knowing she'd probably end up in trouble again, she went inside. Many of the tables were empty, and a cluster of waitresses were gathered near the kitchen door talking.

"I'm looking for JoAnn Reed," she explained.

"JoAnn quit this morning." One woman stepped forward, signifying that she was the person in charge. "I'm the hostess. Is there some trouble?"

"No. I'm a friend." Cassandra took a chance. "I heard she might be looking for a roommate or a place to stay."

"Yeah, she was staying at Sarah's, but . . ." The hostess looked around. "That was such a tragedy."

Cassandra liked the woman, and she felt guilty for tricking her. But she had to find JoAnn. "I thought I might be able to help JoAnn out. Until she gets things put back together. She was very upset about her friend's death, and I've got some extra room."

"Well, if you'd been here earlier, you could have helped. As it is, I think she's leaving town. She said she had her stuff packed and she was moving on."

"Was she going home?"

"How good a friend are you?" the woman questioned suddenly. "Nobody who knew JoAnn would ask that question."

"Well, I mean, I didn't know if she had a choice. After everything that's happened, I thought maybe she'd be forced to go home. And I wanted to give her an option." Cassandra improvised as she went along.

"One thing you can be certain, she won't be going home. Not a chance."

"Do you know where she might have gone?" Cassandra felt her thin hope beginning to break. To come so close and lose the young woman would be hard to take.

"She didn't say. Check up at Sarah's. You might catch her there yet. She said she had a lot to pack."

"Could you give me directions?"

"How well did you know JoAnn, or Sarah?" the woman demanded.

Cassandra looked her in the eye. "Not very well. But I like her. I'd like to help."

"Okay," the woman relented. "She needs some help."

Cassandra wrote on a napkin as the hostess directed her to a small house that was part of a resort development. Sarah had rented the cabin for several years and had been considered a regular tenant.

Cassandra knew the area well, and she left the restaurant determined to find JoAnn Reed. What she couldn't answer was what had happened to Adam. If he'd gone to Crockett's as he'd planned, then he would have found the girl at work. Maybe he had tailed her home.

THE CHALET that Sarah Welford had rented was ideally located. The view was excellent, and the isolated cabin was perfect for two single women to share. As Cassandra took the steps, she found it hard to believe that Sarah was dead. According to the police, she'd been struck by a hit-and-run driver on the highway outside a local bar. The police report indicated she'd been drinking, and the assumption was that she stumbled onto the highway in the path of an oncoming car. Contrary to Beaker's accusations to Cassandra, no charges had been filed against anyone. Sarah's death had never been listed as a homicide.

There were other things that troubled Cassandra. Sarah hadn't struck her as the kind of woman who got drunk and stumbled along highways. It didn't make much sense. The more Cassandra thought about it, the more certain she became that either Beaker was stupid, or he was hiding something. With that thought in mind, she'd taken care to hide her bright red car in a dense copse of trees half a mile from the chalet.

Cassandra knocked at the door, not knowing who she expected to answer it. If JoAnn did, then she had to convince her that her life might truly be in danger. Minutes ticked by and she knocked again. After the fourth attempt, Cassandra edged around the porch and checked the back windows of the chalet.

White curtains still hung in the kitchen window. She could see a sofa and table in the den, but there was definitely an air of abandonment in the place. Against all of her upbringing, she pushed at the sliding-glass door. To her surprise, it opened readily. One deep breath and she was inside. The earth-tone interior gave a sense of warmth and easy living. Remorse at Sarah's death struck Cassandra hard as she looked around. It was difficult to believe that the young woman who'd lived here only a few days before was dead.

Forcing her feet forward, Cassandra moved into the kitchen. There were still dishes in the drain board, and a check of the refrigerator showed a few condiments. Someone had gone to the trouble to throw away things that would spoil.

Stairs led to the bedrooms, and Cassandra stilled her doubts about invading another's privacy and went up. As she'd begun to suspect, one bedroom still contained Sarah Welford's personal items. The other had been cleaned out. JoAnn had fled.

With great reluctance, Cassandra began to open the drawers in the empty bedroom. A thorough search of the entire chalet would take a while. As she shook off her feeling of wrongdoing, Cassandra wondered again where Adam was. She held onto the bright hope that he'd found a better lead and was pursuing it.

She searched the chest of drawers and the closets. Each bedroom had a bathroom, and the one JoAnn had used was cleaned out. When every corner had been searched, Cassandra finally went to Sarah's room.

Lingerie spilled from a drawer and the top of the dresser was covered with bottles of perfume and powder. It was as if the woman had stepped away for a date. But Cassandra knew she would never be coming back. She forced herself to search the drawers, moving aside personal items and clothes as she looked for an envelope with an address or any scrap of information that might lead to JoAnn.

She was so engrossed in her search that she didn't hear the car pull up in the drive. She was deep into the third dresser drawer when she heard the sliding-glass door open. It was a sound she recognized instantly. In that same instant, she also knew that it wasn't Adam's footsteps. Without a second thought, she rolled under the bed.

She felt as if her heart was pounding so loud the bed above her shook, but Cassandra held herself rigidly still. One by one, slow and methodical, the footsteps came up the stairs. The pace was steady, regular, without hesitation.

They went to JoAnn's room first, and then came toward the bedroom where Cassandra hid.

In the half inch between the dust ruffle and the carpeted floor, Cassandra saw two feet in black running shoes. Worn denim, ragged at the bottom as if it had been worn and washed a hundred times, touched the tops of the shoes. Some distant part of Cassandra's brain registered the fact that the jeans had a deep crease, as if they'd been pressed in a laundry. A man who took his jeans to a laundry. It was a thought that stuck with her and she concentrated on it to keep her breathing steady.

The feet moved toward the bed, then turned as if the man were surveying the room. "I guess you won't be taking any of those rides with me, Sarah, sweetheart," he said. "Now that's a real shame."

Cassandra's lungs clenched up. Breath caught in her throat, and for one horrible instant, she thought she was going to choke. Praying that he wouldn't hear, she took in short, ragged gulps of air and tried to calm herself. She knew the voice. She knew the man. It was the bodybuilder, the one from the parking lot. Ray!

Pressing her palms into the carpet, Cassandra squeezed her eyes shut and concentrated on remembering everything he'd said. What rides? She thought back to the conversation she'd overheard. He was in town for a brief spell. Then he'd be traveling on. What did he do?

The crash of a drawerful of clothes onto the floor almost made Cassandra scream. One of Sarah's slips fell partially under the bed. Inching backward, Cassandra moved as far as possible from it. Peering from the tiny crack, she could see other clothes cascading from the drawers as Ray searched through Sarah's belongings.

"Damn!" he muttered as he finished the dresser and moved on. "Now where could it be?" He turned, making a circle in the room before he ripped the sheets off the bed. The mattress whumped from the force of his jerk, and Cassandra squinched into the tightest ball she could make.

Systematically, Ray tore the room apart. When he'd emptied every drawer, thrown the mattress off the bed and torn every piece of clothing out of the closet, he kicked the wall with an oath.

"Sarah, where did you put it?" he asked angrily. "You said you'd put it someplace safe. Where? Or did you give it to someone? Like your roommate." He cursed again. "She could pay for this mistake with her life." He left the room and took the stairs two at a time. The sliding-glass door banged shut.

Terrified that he was still in the house, yet determined to see Ray's face, Cassandra hurried to the bedroom window. Instead of the blue convertible she was expecting, a brown Jeeplike vehicle roared out from behind the chalet and tore down the road.

"Damn!" Cassandra said as she pressed her forehead to the window. She'd only caught a glimpse of the man. He had dark hair and the narcissistic body she remembered. The features of his face still eluded her. "Damn!" She bumped her forehead against the glass in frustration. She might have had the killer in the same room with her, and she'd failed to get even a glimpse of his face.

She turned back to the mess around her. With a sigh of discouragement, she continued her search, but she knew it was futile. If there'd been anything that gave a clue to JoAnn's whereabouts, Ray would have taken it. Thirty minutes later, she was ready to give up. Another dead end.

As she walked down the steps, she felt an intense need to see Adam. Where was he, anyway? It wasn't like him to fail to show up. On an impulse, she picked up the kitchen phone and called the trading post. Yes, there was a message for her from an Adam Raleigh.

The clerk's voice grew concerned as she read. "Don't go home without me. Trouble. Wait at the Ruby Inn."

"It's my boyfriend. He likes to play practical jokes," she explained with a forced laugh. She wanted to avoid any further questions. She hung up and started toward her car. Concern for Adam made her run the half mile, and in less than five minutes she was tearing down the dirt road toward the small, cozy restaurant Adam had named.

Adam was on his fifth cup of coffee when Cassandra pushed through the door, sending the brass bell into a wild jingle. He noted the anxiety in her wide eyes as she searched the restaurant for him. He had a pang about the wording of the message he'd left for her, but he'd had to make it strong enough to keep her from running back up the side of that mountain.

She saw him, and the joy and relief that spread across her face made him flush with pleasure. When Cassandra cared about someone, she cared with her whole heart. Adam knew by looking at her that she cared for him. It was a feeling that was totally reciprocated. He was out of his chair and halfway across the dining room to meet her when she rushed into his arms.

"I was worried silly," she said, lifting her face for a kiss. She was oblivious to the people staring at her or the single whisper of disgust that came from one of the booths.

Adam led her to the table he'd taken in the rear of the small establishment. He'd chosen it for privacy. When he told her about the scarecrow incident, he wanted to be sure that no one else heard. Thoughts of his own news were pushed aside, though. He could tell from her face that she had exciting news, and as soon as they were seated, he asked her what she'd learned.

"I didn't know they served witches in this restaurant."

The ugly comment drifted to Adam from another booth. Still talking, Cassandra didn't hear the remark, but several other diners had heard it and conversation in the small restaurant stopped.

The Gatlinburg mayor stepped out of the booth and stared directly at Adam. He shook his head in disgust and went to the cash register.

Adam kept his face in a mask, not showing the anger he felt toward Simpson. Torn between taking the matter up with Simpson or hurting Cassandra's feelings, he focused his attention back on Cassandra's story.

"I don't know what to do now," Cassandra continued. "We have Ray, Bounder and JoAnn to try and track down. I don't know where to start." She had carefully omitted any reference to the stash that the young Indians had hidden in her orchard. If the men were involved in illegal activities, it was better not to drag Adam in, too.

"I don't know, either, but I know we shouldn't split up again. Whatever we do, we have to stick together. And I don't want you taking off hunting for Bounder by yourself, not even on your own property."

"Why?" She had a feeling that he knew about the tire tracks.

"There's someone on the place," he said, and told her about the scarecrow being thrown at his car. "I had your mechanic go up and tow it to town, and I'm making arrangements to rent another." He gave a twisted smile. "We seem to be hard on cars."

As the waitress brought more hot tea for Cassandra and a cup of coffee for Adam, he reached across the table and took her hand. His touch was light on her fingers as he turned her hand over to explore the palm.

"What are you doing?" she asked, surprised at his behavior. He'd been uncharacteristically quiet. There was something troubling him, but she couldn't be certain what.

"Look at this line right here," Adam said, pointing to her palm. The truth was, he was fighting hard to control his emotions. He cared for her so much, and she'd come very close to finding herself in a position where she might have wound up dead.

"What line?" Cassandra bent closer to her hand.

"This one here. I've been studying from a very ancient palmist, and I've learned that this is the line of destiny."

Cassandra laughed. "There's no such thing. There's a fate line, but—"

"Okay, the line of fate," Adam interrupted. "It says right here—" he used his forefinger to gently mark a spot "—that you will meet a man from Michigan, and that you will do everything he tells you from now on in order to protect your life.'' At last, Adam looked at her. "You will get on a plane and go away with him. Tonight. Without any quarreling. You will obey him."

Cassandra reached across the small table with her free hand and rested it on Adam's cheek. "I wish I could," she whispered. She could see how troubled he was. He hadn't reacted to her information because he was too upset. She could see it now.

"You can, Cassandra. Let Sheriff Beaker handle this. It's his county, and it's their town. Get out now, before you get hurt."

She shook her head. "You know I can't."

"Marry me. We'll find a place where you can be happy."

She stroked his cheek, lingering on the feel of the day's growth of beard. "I won't consider that a proposal. To marry a woman to protect her is a noble thing, but it isn't the kind of marriage I want."

"You know it's more than that!" He caught her hand and pressed it against his lips. "I love you. And I do want to keep you safe. More than anything."

"I can't." She blinked against the tears in her eyes. "Ask me again, Adam. When all of this is over. If you still want to."

"Will your answer be any different then, or will it be something else, some other reason that ties you here?" There was no bitterness in his voice, only acceptance of reality.

"I can't see beyond this mess," Cassandra said. "I honestly can't. We both know there are very real differences between us. When this is over, we can talk about them. If there's a way around them, we'll find it. Together." She captured both his hands in her small ones and pulled them across the table to her. She kissed one and then the other.

"I didn't realize the mountain witch had taken to casting spells in public places."

The voice was harsh, ugly.

Cassandra looked up into the face of the city mayor.

"Sheriff Beaker tells me you've been helping on his murder cases." Simpson smiled, but his eyes were deadly. "I never figured you for the helpful type, Cassandra."

Adam started to push back his chair, but Cassandra held tight to his hands.

"Nothing you ever thought about me was accurate," Cassandra said easily. "In fact, I'm surprised to hear that you actually think." She put Adam's hands down on the table as she straightened in her chair.

"Why you..."

Adam stood with slow deliberateness.

"Why are you afraid of me?" Cassandra asked. Her blue eyes snapped with a fiery anger and a sure intelligence. She was rewarded when his face blanched. "You're terrified of me. Why? What is it that you have to hide that I might find out about?"

"You're a menace to this town," Simpson said as he took a step backward. "Your mother was a freak, a sideshow, and you're just as bad." He stepped behind an empty table as Adam reached for him.

"Let him go," Cassandra said softly as she watched Simpson retreat. "It's taken me twenty years to realize why he hates me so. He's afraid."

The bell on the door of the Ruby Inn jangled as the mayor pulled it closed behind him. Cassandra looked at Adam. "Another question for us to answer—why is the esteemed mayor so afraid?"

Chapter Thirteen

Cassandra waited in the passenger seat of her car as Adam disappeared into the lobby of the Smoky Mountain Lodge. They had decided that tracing JoAnn Reed was the most important step at the moment. Adam had come up with a plan to talk with Sarah Welford's family. It wasn't going to be pleasant, but they were the only people who might have an inkling where JoAnn had gone.

The afternoon was winding down, and Cassandra leaned her head back and closed her eyes. It had been such a day of conflicting emotions, and tomorrow she had to do something she dreaded, appear on television. The confrontation with Ken Simpson had reawakened all of the horrors she'd suffered since childhood.

She hated the limelight. Hated the thought of being in a place where people could ridicule her and hate her because she was different. She'd suffered all of her life because of it.

A faint smile played across her lips as she thought of Sylvia, who loved being the center of attention. Her mother had warned her about hiding from life. She could still hear Sylvia's melodic voice saying that she couldn't hide from her destiny, that she shouldn't be ashamed of her talent.

It wasn't a matter of hiding or shame, it was simply that Cassandra wanted to be left alone. She needed neither praise nor condemnation. She didn't need anything...except Adam.

Behind dark sunglasses, she blinked her eyes open. Her watch indicated Adam had been gone fifteen minutes. She shut her eyes again. What had Ray been hunting in Sarah's bedroom? Maybe something that identified him as the murderer.

She sat up and pushed her glasses aside. She shuddered. She had the feeling that someone had walked on her grave. She checked her watch again. Another ten minutes had passed. Adam would be returning soon.

Almost as if by command, he walked out the double doors of the lodge. His step was long, brisk, as if he had a destination.

"She hasn't left town," he said as he got into the car. "They don't know where she is, but she told them she wasn't leaving Gatlinburg. She's going to change jobs, too."

"Won't she need a reference from Crockett's?"

"I'll check with the manager," Adam said. "It's doubtful, though, with a waitress position."

"So, another dead end." Cassandra slumped against the seat.

"Why don't we take a ride?" Adam suggested. "I've been in Gatlinburg almost a week, and I haven't seen the first sight."

"Ride..." Cassandra held onto the word. She concentrated hard. "Ride. That's what Ray said. The night when he was talking with Sarah at Crockett's, he said he was going to take her on a ride." She opened her eyes. "What a fool I've been. The fair!"

"Transient, moving north for summer and south for winter. Florida. That's it." Adam pulled her across the seat and kissed her. "He's a carnie. It's the perfect occupation for..."

"A murderer," Cassandra finished. "Tan, strong, familiar to the girls he picks up. And he would know JoAnn and Sarah. Maybe he even ran Sarah down when she tried to warn JoAnn."

Adam started the car and pulled onto the interstate with a spray of gravel. "How about an evening of fun at the fair?"

"Fun?" Cassandra couldn't help the anxiety that touched her. "What if we find him? We can't exactly call Beaker and get him to help."

Adam realized what she said was true. "We'll take care of that later. First, let's find him."

Cassandra gave directions to the fairgrounds where the traveling shows set up each spring. Music from the many different rides and booths carried on the clear mountain air and they heard the fair long before they saw it. As Adam found a parking space, Cassandra watched the lights of the Ferris wheel spin and weave through the mountain dusk.

"I've always hated the fair," she said slowly. "Always. Even as a child. My father died in a fall."

"We don't have to ride anything. If Ray is a carnie, he'll be working one of the rides or a booth. He shouldn't be too hard to find, if you can really recognize him."

"His voice and his body. His hair." She got out of the car. "Let's start with the rides."

They dodged clusters of teenagers and mothers trying to keep young children grouped together. Clouds of cotton candy added splotches of pastel color to the midway. All around them, the young and old screamed as the rides bobbed and whirled. Cassandra had an image of wide open mouths and hair blown helter-skelter. It reminded her of her nightmares and she felt a knot of sickness in her stomach.

Walking slowly, they passed the Octopus, the Orbiter and the Tilt-A-Whirl. Cassandra stopped for a moment to watch the children on a merry-go-round. For one brief instant she allowed herself the luxury of enjoying their innocent pleasure, then Adam's hand on her arm moved her along.

Night was claiming the horizon, and along the mountainsides lights had blinked into existence like tiny, distant stars. "We'd better hurry," Adam said. "I'd like to get a clear look at this guy during daylight."

"I'm not so sure I want to see him," Cassandra admitted.

Hawkers called to them as they passed booths of chance and shows of the grotesque. Cassandra increased her pace. Ray wouldn't be working that section, she knew it. He'd be on one of the wild rides.

They doubled back, checking the opposite side of the midway. In the distance Cassandra could hear the screams coming from the ride called the Spider. She slowed, then remembered that Ray had no reason to recognize her.

"Let's go," she whispered to Adam.

He felt the tension in her body and he moved closer protectively.

Cassandra saw the man's broad shoulders as he heaved back on the stick that sent the ride into motion.

The arms of the ride began moving around and around, up and down, as each individual seat spun sideways. Inside the cars, people screamed with the thrill of pleasure and fear.

"That's him," Cassandra whispered.

"Are you certain? You didn't see his face."

"It's him." She was as certain as she could be about anything in her life.

As the ride picked up momentum, the man leaned on the stick with his hip. Pulling a cigarette from the pocket of his T-shirt, he turned slightly to protect the flame of his match from the wind.

"Charm him, Cassandra." Adam squeezed her arm.

Cassandra took in a breath. He was far more handsome than she'd expected. His hair, long and shining under the lights of the ride, fell across his jaw. When he looked up, he looked directly at her. He gave a slow, lazy smile.

"Want a ride, lady?"

She didn't answer instantly. She looked to her side, but the space was empty. Adam was gone! She stepped to the wooden deck that surrounded the ride. "Yes. I'd like a ride. Where do I get my tickets?"

He leaned down to her. "Don't tell a soul, but *you* don't need a ticket to ride this machine. Step on up here and I'll give you a spin for free."

Cassandra mounted the four steps to the platform. She stood beside him, close enough to touch. Her gaze wandered to his feet. He wore the same shoes she'd seen from under the bed.

"How long is the fair in town?" she asked. She thought her voice would crack, but it didn't.

"Another two weeks. I'd sure like to spend that time getting to know you."

Cassandra lifted her eyebrows and made her eyes wide. "Oh, what makes you think you would?" She felt like a complete moron. She'd never attempted to play the coquette before, and her lack of practice was burningly apparent.

"Aren't you cute?" he chuckled. "You're one of those gals who need a lot of compliments. Well, I could make a list of reasons, all of them exciting." He let his eyes wander from her hair to her throat and down. "But I'd rather do that over a drink tonight."

"Don't you have to work?" She spoke so fast, she realized she sounded scared. "I mean, the fair stays open until so late. I'm a working girl. I have to get up early."

"Now that's just the opposite problem that my last girlfriend had." He smiled, a confident animal used to the courting routine, and used to winning.

"Last girlfriend?" The words escaped before Cassandra could help herself. "What happened to her?"

"Oh, I left her down the road. That's my business, and I won't pretend otherwise. The fair moves, and I go with it. Some girls take it better than others. Some—" he shrugged "—get real upset. But I never lie. I'm up-front from the very beginning, just like I am with you."

Cassandra recovered. Thank heavens he'd thought she was jealous. "It must be hard, leaving all those women behind." She smiled, looking up at him through her eyelashes. Where the hell was Adam? The ride was spinning wildly behind her. Ray gave her most of his attention, but he was pulling back on the stick, slowing it down. The passengers had gotten an extra long ride as it was. It was time for the next shift.

A line had formed just below the steps, and she knew her time was growing short. "If you could get off a little early, I might meet you."

"You might, huh?" He leaned down close to her. "Where?"

"Well, I'm visiting here with some friends. I don't know the area very well, but I heard this place called Crockett's, you know, after Davey," she giggled, "was a good place."

"It's a bit crowded," Ray said. He was signaling to the people to get off the ride. He shifted his weight, knowing he should make the rounds and help undo the safety bars. "How about another place?"

"I don't know..." Cassandra knew why he didn't want to go to Crockett's. Someone might be able to identify him as Sarah's beau.

"Meet me at Blue Ridge Lounge, just off the main road. At nine. I'll get someone to fill in for me here for a hour or so." He reached a hand out and touched a lock of her hair. "Be on time, okay? I hate it when women are late."

"Okay," she breathed softly, wanting nothing more than to escape. In a hard way, Ray was a handsome man. He had the jaw and the carefully developed body. Long clean hair, impeccably groomed. But his eyes—they were so cold and assessing. Everything came to him on his terms, or he didn't fool with it.

"Even Sarah," Cassandra whispered to herself as she let the eager crowd push her forward until she was standing beside one of the gondolas for the ride.

"Step up."

She felt strong hands on her waist and started to turn. She expected Adam. The touch was unfamiliar and she felt her spine tighten.

"You forgot to tell me your name," he said softly in her ear.

She shivered. "Ellen," she answered. "Ellen Mc-Knight." She watched his reaction carefully, but he gave nothing away. She climbed into the car and let Ray hook the safety bar. She put a smile on her face. "Thanks."

"See you later, Ellen," he said, stroking her hair again.

She watched him disappear around the other gondolas, buckling the safety bar in each one to make sure his passengers rode safely.

The ride started to move, and Cassandra prepared herself. She'd never liked the fast, tumultuous rides, but she had no choice but to stick this one out—and look happy about it. She'd concentrate on plotting her strategy for the upcoming meeting with Ray.

The lounge he'd selected as a meeting place was dark and isolated. More of a local hangout than a tourist bar. How had he learned of it? Sarah Welford, no doubt. She was a local girl.

The gondola started to pitch up and down. Gripping the bar, Cassandra pushed into the back of her seat, hoping for some sensation of steadiness in her revolving world. She gritted her teeth and kept her eyes open, fighting the sense of complete loss of control. She focused on her fingers gripping the bar. She felt like . . . Ellen in the convertible as it sped down the woodland trail.

She felt her control slipping. The dream crept onto the edge of her consciousness, pushing hard against her. It was like the day she'd nearly totaled her car. There was nothing she could do to hold it back. Her head fell back against the rest, and as the gondola sped and whirled, Cassandra drowned in her dream.

"I HATE this place."

She heard a woman speak, but the voice was unfamiliar. The woman was standing in shadow.

"It's beautiful here. The only real beauty is that of nature." The man spoke with deep regret. "I'm sorry."

His hand touched the woman's face. The fingers were soft and cool. She was facing the view and there was no place for her to put her feet to get away from him. The mountain dropped away. It was a sheer cliff.

Cassandra had never seen the dream so clearly before. The night was crusted with stars, and below the lip of the mountain where the woman stood, only blackness could be seen. She could sense the woman's terrible sadness, her fear and her worry.

The man stepped up behind her, closer, and she tried to turn around to face him. He grabbed her arms. "Don't turn around. I told you. Don't! You know the rules."

"Why?" she asked. "Why are you doing this? It can stop now, if you'll let me help you."

Held beneath the dream, Cassandra struggled to help the unknown woman. She was new, a different victim. She wanted to encourage her to stay calm, to think. The killer never forced the victim over the edge of the cliff, but that was how he controlled them. If they struggled too much, they might fall. So they died like cattle in a slaughterhouse line. No real struggle. *Fight!* she mentally urged the woman.

"It doesn't matter. It's my destiny. Would you like some champagne? I brought some, just for you. A toast to Eagle's Roost." The man laughed, an easy, practiced sound. "You're the kind of woman who should go out in style."

"Yes, I'd like some champagne."

That's right, Cassandra urged her. *Do the unexpected. Get him to move away from you.*

"I knew you wouldn't be a baby. Not like the others. You're a beautiful woman. Beautiful skin. Beautiful hair." He picked up a strand and let it slide through his fingers. "So beautiful. I'm surprised you haven't asked about JoAnn. She hasn't gone far, you know."

"Have you hurt her?" The woman inched away from the cliff. A rock slipped beneath her foot. It echoed in the night as it struck several outcroppings of stone before it disappeared into the black void.

"I sent her . . . to a safe place." He laughed a little at his own cleverness. "Until I could finish this with you. You've put me through a lot of trouble, you know. But it's made it all . . . interesting. A worthy adversary, and one with such beautiful hair and skin. I almost hate to kill you.''

"HEY! HEY, ELLEN! Wake up!'' Ray brushed Cassandra's hair out of her face.

Cassandra felt the hand on her shoulder. Someone was shaking her roughly. There was a din of confusing noises all around her, smells that made her reel. She tried to open her eyes but lights throbbed and pulsed at her, blending with the rhythm of the pounding of her head.

"Someone call an ambulance,'' Ray ordered.

"No,'' Cassandra forced herself to say. She struggled to sit up, but there was a wooden bar across her lap. At last, she opened her eyes. Ray stood hovering over her, his eyes squinting with concern.

"What happened?'' he asked roughly.

"I don't know,'' she said. "I started feeling funny. I must have eaten something.'' She fumbled with excuses. What had happened? She had been back in the dream, back with the killer. He'd found a new victim, a woman she hadn't seen clearly at all, except for the long hair. They'd been at the place the killer called Eagle's Roost. He was ready to kill again!

"Wait a minute,'' Ray said. He unbolted the bar that held her prisoner and easily pulled her out of the car. "Calm down a little.'' He held her tight.

"I have to go,'' she whispered. Her head was pounding and her heart felt as if it were going to burst.

"You can't even walk.'' Ray helped her over to the wooden platform where he controlled the ride. "Wait here a minute. Let me get them loaded and I'll be back.''

Unable to argue, Cassandra nodded. She was feeling desperately sick. Even the solidness of the hard platform felt good as she sat on it and leaned her head forward into her hands. Beneath her headache and nausea was the drumming fear. He wasn't gone. He was only waiting, hiding out, thinking sharper and faster than those who pursued him.

He was sick and smart, and he loathed his victims. He hated women. Hated, feared, and envied them. Cassandra started to shake, and there was nothing she could do to stop it.

Ray returned and gave the controlling stick to the ride a fearful punch. The Spider took off with an unusual burst of energy.

"Maybe you'd better let me call an ambulance," he said. He sat down beside her. "You look really sick."

"I'm better," she said. "It will pass, and there's not much a doctor can do." She forced her gaze up and looked at him. Was he planning the murder of a young woman even as he sat beside her? And, dear God, what had he done with JoAnn?

"The color is coming back," he said, nodding at her. "You really scared me. I've seen people get sick on rides, but not like you. And that scream you gave. It almost stopped the midway."

"What scream?" Cassandra felt anxiety rumble in her stomach. What had she said?

"You screamed 'no' like someone was trying to murder you."

"I, uh, didn't want to get sick. Not on the ride."

"Thanks," Ray said, and there was a glint of humor in his face. "But you are looking better. How do you feel?"

"Like I'd better get out of your hair and let you earn a living." She stood up. The jackhammer in her skull kicked in a little harder, but she could walk. She could get away from Ray before she collapsed.

"If you'd rather cancel tonight…" He gave her a grin that might have charmed some women.

"Not on your life," she said, smiling at her own pun. "Not on my life, either. I'll be there. At nine. And I'll be on time," she said.

Before he could reconsider, she walked away. She needed to lie down and rest, and she needed to do it right away. Where had they parked? The little convertible would not offer much of a bed, but she had to rest. Just for a few moments.

There was so much to do. JoAnn. Where could she be that the killer would have "sent her to a safe place?" The silly woman was putting her life in danger as each minute ticked away. And the latest victim. Cassandra had no idea who she might be.

She had to think. Clearly. With her head filled with a crescendo of pain, she had no tool to work with. And where was Adam? When she found him, she was going to pickle him.

When she was certain she was out of sight of the ride, she slipped behind one of the trailers and leaned against the wall. She felt horrible.

Nausea made her double over and she fought for control. She had to get home.

"Cassandra!"

She recognized Adam's voice and tried to straighten up. His warm hands grabbed her shoulders and supported her. "What happened? Did he hurt you?"

She shook her head. "No. It was a dream. He's after someone new. He's going to kill her."

"That's why I left," Adam said hurriedly. He put his arm around her and began a hasty retreat to the car. "I thought I saw JoAnn. She was coming down the midway with a bunch of her friends and I wanted to dodge away before she saw me. But it was too late. She saw me and they scattered. I went after her, but I lost her in the crowd."

"Do you think she was going to see Ray?" Putting her thoughts into JoAnn seemed to steady Cassandra. She took a deep breath and straightened her posture.

"She was headed straight for the ride."

"He made a date to see me tonight. This may be the only thing that saves that girl's life."

"Ray's a busy man." Adam didn't like the idea of Cassandra meeting Ray anywhere, anytime. "You're too sick to do anything, thank goodness. We'll have to watch him . . ."

"I'll meet him." Cassandra's voice brooked no nonsense.

"Cassandra..."

"It's tonight or never. Do you think he'll go out with me after the television show tomorrow?"

Chapter Fourteen

Weariness tugged at Cassandra's bones as she got out of her car at the Blue Ridge Lounge. It had taken all of her reserve to argue Adam into letting her keep her appointment with Ray. Adam had finally capitulated to her logic—if they didn't find out about Ray tonight, she'd never stand a chance once she appeared on television. Everyone would recognize her as "the local whacko psychic who had some mental link to the murderer."

As it was, Adam had parked fifty yards from the lounge. While she was making small talk with Ray, Adam would take his position near Ray's convertible. They had a plan, but it was one that depended on Cassandra's ability to lie.

Lying had never been one of her strong suits, but she was desperate enough to try anything. They had to get Ray outside, alone and in his car. Then Adam could subdue him. If Cassandra could lure him outside, and then keep his attention on her for a few moments, Adam could subdue him. Once captured, he might confess. At least he'd be immobilized until JoAnn could be found.

She checked her lipstick in the rearview mirror and got out. The fear that she'd anticipated had not materialized. She didn't particularly like Ray, but she wasn't afraid of him. It was strange. In the dreams, he terrified her. He was so cold-blooded about the murders.

She pushed open the heavy door and stepped into the dim interior. It took several seconds for her eyes to adjust as she checked out the floor plan. The bar, on her right, ran the length of the room and about half of the stools were occupied. The dance floor was at the back, and the stage was empty. To the left, she saw a scattering of tables, several with couples, but the majority empty. Ray was seated at the bar, a beer in one hand and his eyes riveted on her.

Tension tightened her shoulders, but still, she noticed her own lack of fear. Even when their eyes met, she wasn't afraid. She walked forward and took a seat on a stool beside him.

"Glad you could make it." He asked what she wanted and signaled the waitress over and gave her drink order for orange juice, on the rocks. "Still feeling under the weather?"

"Just a little." She smiled and continued. "But I really wanted to see you tonight."

He chuckled. "Not bragging, but I've heard that before."

"I'll bet you have." Cassandra hid her sarcasm behind a flirtatious smile.

The waitress set her drink down with a snort of derision. "Ready for another, Ray?"

"Sure, Rita. I don't have a lot of time."

"You must come here a lot." Cassandra found it difficult to make small talk, but she had to give Adam time to set up beside the car.

"Yeah, every season when we come through, I come by here. Rita and I have known each other for a lot of years, haven't we, Rita?"

"Too long," she said. "But you never stop amazing me. I thought I knew your taste." She looked at Cassandra knowingly.

"Folks change, Rita." He grinned at her, and she turned back to her bar.

Cassandra gave her watch another surreptitious glance. She took a sip of her orange juice and put the glass on the bar. "Ray, I don't want to stay here. It's too stuffy. Maybe we could go for a ride, look at the stars. It's a beautiful night."

He stood up immediately. "You're a real piece of work. I figured I'd be wining and dining you for the rest of my stay here. You're one classy-looking lady."

"Like your other girlfriends?" she asked, leaning toward him slightly. It was too soon. She hadn't anticipated that he'd act on her suggestion so suddenly! She had to think of something to keep him in the bar a little longer. She was making a real muck of the night. "I was talking to a friend of mine and she said she'd seen you around with someone else. Like on a regular basis."

"You're worried about that, aren't you?" He grinned with pleasure.

"I just like to know the score." Play it cool, a little flirtatious, she encouraged herself. Smile.

"I was seeing someone. It's over now." A slight frown wrinkled his brow. "Who told you . . ."

"How can I be sure it's over?" Cassandra cut in, watching every shift of his expression.

"Take my word for it, there's not a chance I'll be seeing Sarah again."

Adrenaline shot through Cassandra at the mention of Sarah's name. This was the direction she wanted to go. Ray had admitted knowing Sarah—now for some link to JoAnn. "Wasn't there someone else?" Cassandra played coy. "I think her name was Ella, or Anna, or something like that. Maybe JoAnn."

Ray gave her a puzzled look. "Nope. Her name was Sarah. She's the only girl in these parts I've seen lately." He stood up so abruptly that his stool crashed over. "I thought you wanted to get out of here. How about that ride?"

Cassandra swallowed. "Any place special?"

"I know a few good places." He checked his watch. "I have to get back to work in an hour or so, but we have a little time. Let's go."

"Sounds good." Cassandra could feel her heart beating. The rush of blood was like the wind in her ears. She'd given Adam all the time she could. Now her future was in his hands. If he failed her, she'd be all alone with the man she suspected of at least three murders.

"How come you and Sarah broke up?" she asked as she led the way to the door.

"What's with you and this fixation on my ex-girlfriends? I don't grill you about the men you've seen. This is a date, not a proposal of marriage."

His anger was very close to the surface. Cassandra wanted to recoil, but she knew she couldn't. "I'm the jealous type."

"I told you, there's nothing to be jealous of." Ray's tone was softer. "The past is over and done. Let the ghosts rest."

Cassandra barely stopped the shudder that came with his words. "My friend just said you and this Sarah were very thick. How come you stopped seeing her?"

Ray's hand gripped the doorknob and held it. Cassandra was caught between his solid body and the door. Looking around the bar, she knew no one there would come to her assistance.

"She was the jealous type, too," he said. "It annoyed me. I guess I ought to warn you that it's not a good policy to annoy me."

"I'm sorry," she whispered sincerely. At last the fear had arrived, in van loads. It tingled the skin at the small of her back. Any little thing could push him over the edge.

"Everybody's allowed one mistake." He pulled the door open and ushered her into the night. On the steps, he took a deep breath. "Hey, I didn't mean to sound so tough. It's just that Sarah is hard for me to talk about. Where's your car?"

Cassandra balked. "I'm a little low on gas."

"We'll go by a station and fill it up," he said. "My, uh, clutch is acting up. I don't want to climb around on any of these mountain roads."

"Let's take your car," Cassandra persisted.

"Hey, Ellen." He gripped her shoulder. "What's wrong with you? I'll be glad to put some gas in your car. Mine's dangerous. You wouldn't want to be rushing around these mountain curves when the clutch gave, now would you? I

hate to think what a wreck could do to that beautiful face.''
He brushed his fingers gently over her cheek. ''You have the
most beautiful skin.''

Looking into his eyes, Cassandra couldn't answer. The
words lumped together in her throat. ''I, uh, thought...''

''Just leave the thinking to me, sweetheart. That will
make your life easier and mine a whole lot more pleasant.''
His fingers tightened on her arm. ''You're a tiny thing,
aren't you? Little but fiesty. I like that. Keeps life interesting.''

''My car's right this way,'' she said. She had no choice.
Either she could blow the entire plan now, or she could take
him to her car. Adam would have to scramble to keep up
with her, but she could drive slowly.

''Nice car,'' he said approvingly. ''I love convertibles.''
He plopped into the driver's seat and held out his hand.
''Keys?''

''I'd rather drive.'' Cassandra balked. She clutched the
keys in her hand. ''I've never let anyone drive my car.''

''Just for a few curves,'' Ray said. He gripped the steering wheel with his hands. ''She's a beauty.''

''I think...''

Ray reached over the side of the car and pulled her over
the door and into his arms. The keys fell on the console and
slid down by his foot. Laughing, he held her tightly.

''I told you,'' Ray said as he maneuvered her into the
passenger seat, ''let me do the thinking tonight. Take a
breather, Ellen, baby. Ray Elsworth is in the driver's seat,
so sit down and enjoy the ride. I'm going to show you the
Smoky Mountains.'' In a spray of gravel, they tore around
the parking lot.

As the car lights swung over the parked cars, Cassandra
caught a fleeting image of Adam hunkered down by the
fender of one. His eyes were wide with alarm.

Ray was intent on getting the feel of the car and didn't
notice. As they pulled onto the asphalt, Cassandra caught
one final glimpse of Adam running toward his car. He'd
never be able to catch up. Never. She was on her own.

ADAM WATCHED Cassandra speed out of sight, and he knew he'd failed her. By the time he got back to his vehicle, they'd be long gone. He blocked out the panic and concentrated. They'd taken a right on the highway, and he'd watched their taillights disappear as they'd sped around the first curve.

Adam's long strides put him at his car, and he jumped in and roared onto the highway in hot pursuit. He took the first curve with squealing tires and not a click of hesitation. If there was any way possible, he intended to catch up with the little red convertible.

He'd known Cassandra was at risk with their plan to capture Ray and question him. The whole scheme had been dangerous. Only Cassandra's determination had convinced him to try it at all. That and the fear that if the killer weren't captured, Cassandra would forever hold herself responsible.

He came to the first intersection, and gut instinct told him to go straight through. The road led up the mountain. That was the killer's modus operandi—up to the view and then the murder.

The car slewed to the edge of the road, and Adam had a harrowing view of a cliff that seemed to fall for an eternity. A thousand feet below him three tiny lights winked through the trees. He swung the wheel hard to the left and climbed back onto the asphalt.

Though he strained to see in the darkness ahead, there was no sign of any taillights. Eagle's Roost. That was the place the dream killer always mentioned. Cassandra, who knew the mountains like the back of her hand, had never heard of such a place. Where could it be?

As he drove, he turned over every possibility in his mind. Where would Ray take her?

The road ahead of him remained a tunnel of darkness. No matter how hard he wished, he didn't see the telltale red glow of her car lights. He came to another intersection, and his instinct wavered. Where had they gone?

With a sharp movement that almost put the car into a slide, he turned right. It was pointless to drive all the way to

Sevierville to argue with Sheriff Beaker. He would go to Running Stream. If anyone knew where Eagle's Roost was, it would be her.

He drove the car with abandon as he pressed on through the night to the Indian woman's home.

When he pulled into the yard, he hit the steering wheel with frustration. The house was completely black. He got out, deciding to knock anyway. Without Running Stream, he didn't know what to do.

"Hello, Adam."

The soft, low voice startled him as he put one foot on the step. Running Stream spoke from the darkness.

"Cassandra might be in terrible trouble," he said, trying to keep from shouting. "She's with the man who may be the killer."

Running Stream creaked forward in her chair. "I was sitting here, waiting for Bounder to come home. I'm afraid for my son, and for Cassandra. I've been listening to the hoot of an owl, the harbinger of death."

Her words chilled Adam. "No word from Bounder yet?"

"None. This is going to be a long and painful night for both of us."

"Running Stream, have you ever heard of a place called Eagle's Roost?" Adam blocked out the image of Cassandra, on the side of the mountain, with Ray's strong hands around her throat. He couldn't afford to lose hope now. Hope was the only thing he had—hope and his faith in one petite little woman with an unconquerable spirit.

"It isn't in the park." Running Stream motioned Adam to an old rocker on the porch. "No, Adam, I don't know such a place. The name sounds like it belongs here in the mountains, but I haven't heard it."

"Could it be a local nickname for a place? Maybe an Indian name."

"I would know it if it was an Indian name. It isn't."

Adam rubbed his forehead with one hand. This wasn't good enough. As he sat on the porch wasting time, Cassandra could be fighting for her life. "I have to go." He stood up and went to Running Stream's side. He gave her shoulder an encouraging squeeze. "Come and help me search for Cassandra."

"No." Running Stream looked up at him. "I've sat here for the past four hours, watching the light fade from the sky. I have a bad feeling, Adam Raleigh. I'll wait here for the bad news to come."

"I never would have thought that you'd retire to your porch like an old woman." Adam knew his words were harsh, but he had to do something to shake Running Stream out of her depression. She was one of the strongest women he'd ever seen. He could not allow her to sink deeper and deeper into the pit of self-pity. "I thought Cassandra's friends were made of stouter stuff. I was mistaken, and I'm afraid she was, too."

The hint of a smile touched Running Stream's eyes. "You're a very smart man."

"I try hard," he said. It hadn't taken much to shock Running Stream. She was a strong woman, an able friend. "Want to go to the fair with me? I have to find out some information about Ray, the man who has Cassandra."

Running Stream stood. For the first time, Adam noticed she was dressed in traditional Indian attire. The dress was beautiful, with a starburst pattern of beadwork.

"I dressed to meet the moment of knowing," she explained, "and then I sat down and waited for that moment to come to me. You've reminded me that it has to be sought, and fought for." She pressed her hand to his chest. "Like friendship. Let's go."

"What about Bounder?"

"Sitting here will not make him come home. I've searched everywhere I know to look. If we find Cassandra, we may find him."

"If they're together, then whoever has them had better beware," Adam said with grim determination. "They'd better look out for us."

THE HIGHWAY SPUN under the wheels like a wide strand of licorice. They'd taken several turns off the main road and were climbing at a steady pace. To her right, Cassandra could hear the rush of one of the clear mountain streams. The water pounded over the boulders, sounding a delightful challenge to daring rafters. She'd never harbored even the slightest desire to raft one of the rough passages, but at the moment, she would have given her right arm for a rubber raft and a ten-minute head start on Ray.

"Women claim that I don't treat them good." He reached across the car seat and touched her hair. "I've never really had a woman like you, though. You're like something out of a fairy tale. So pretty and tiny. So different."

"Thank you, Ray. I enjoy your company," she said, praying that she could keep him talking. So far, he'd been content to drive along the deserted roads, recounting stories from his childhood and anecdotes about the fair.

"You know..." He cut her a long look that put them off the edge of the road. For a second he concentrated on his driving, then he turned to look at her again. "Why do I get the feeling that you're saying these things to make me talk?"

"I don't know." She shrugged and tried to look perplexed. *Dear God, don't let him think I'm playing him.* She looked down at her lap.

The car cornered a tight curve, and for a few seconds, Cassandra had a respite.

"Have you ever thought about settling down?" She had to start a normal conversation. If she'd been without fear at the lounge, she made up for it now. She felt as if her limbs had become so fragile they might snap if she moved them.

Ray laughed, and it was bitter. "I've thought about it. I used to think that the only thing I wanted was a wife and three children. The American dream. My own place and my own family."

"Why haven't you?"

"Oh, I did once. Trouble was, my wife didn't take it all that seriously. She liked being married when I brought the paycheck home, and when I was at work, she liked being single.''

Cassandra felt her fear grow. He was angry. So angry at women.

"You ever settled down?" he asked.

"No. I guess I haven't thought that much about it."

"Something wrong with you?" He gave her a long look.

"I don't think so." She forced herself to smile at him. "Maybe I haven't met the right man, yet."

"You're a little pushy, but I told you before, I like my women with spunk." He took another right turn.

Cassandra knew she wasn't far from her home, but under the present conditions, it might as well have been a million miles away. She thought of the cabin, of Adam and the strange black cat that had won her heart. Would she ever see them again?

To her surprise, Ray took the next left. They were headed down the mountain again.

"I really like this car," he said. "It handles real nice."

"Where are some of your favorite scenic overlooks?" she asked. "I mean, are there any that just give you a tingly feeling?"

He laughed. "You're asking a man who makes his living with carnival rides? Looking down the side of a mountain isn't all that thrilling."

"The view, though..." She didn't finish. Ray pulled the car over to the side of the road.

"Why are you riding around with me tonight?"

The question effectively paralyzed Cassandra's brain. She stumbled over a few words, but nothing would come out correctly.

"Because I wanted to talk with you," she said at last.

"If you've got something to ask, lady, just ask it. I get the feeling you're playing with me, and I don't like it." He put his arm across the back of her seat. "Now spit it out."

"Ray, I don't know what you mean." She pushed her back against the car door, but it wasn't far enough away. He only leaned forward.

"You're not the type to chase men, especially not men like me. You've been sitting over in your corner asking questions like some doctor for the insane. You poked around about the women I've dated, and now you're poking around all over. What do you want?" He grabbed her shoulder, and his fingers bit into her flesh.

"I'm a friend of Sarah's," she said in desperation. She was frightened, badly frightened. Not a single car had passed them in more than twenty minutes, and even if she could somehow get away from him and run, he'd be able to catch her.

Her words stopped him short. To her horror, he smiled. "Sarah never told me about you. And she told me everything."

"We weren't close friends, but I knew her. I liked her."

"If you liked her so much, what are you doing riding out in the night with me?"

"I had to find something out." Cassandra knew she was digging deeper and deeper in, but she couldn't stop herself.

"What was that?"

"You weren't at her funeral. You claimed to care for her."

He nodded, but his face never turned away from hers. "Sarah's family wouldn't have been too happy to see me, you can count on that."

"Why not? If you cared for her, and she believed you did, why would they object? What were you looking for in her house?"

"Her folks weren't the kind to take to the idea of a carnie dating their daughter. She talked a lot about her family. Sarah had made her own life, but she could never quite get away from them. She was as tied to this place and them as if they'd sewn her feet to the ground."

Cassandra almost thought she heard a note of remorse in his tone. She realized she was mistaken when he asked his next question.

"So, you know I was at Sarah's? You must know what I was looking for. Where is it?"

Cassandra's fingers inched to the door handle. "I don't know what you're talking about."

"Oh yes, you do. See, I figured out who you are." He picked up a handful of her hair. "Sarah described you pretty good. Now you weren't any friend of hers. You were looking for little JoAnn. You and your friend hiding out there in the parking lot."

He grinned, and Cassandra felt her heart catch. He'd seen Adam. He knew it was all a setup.

"I'm not stupid," he said angrily. "Now where is that note?"

Cassandra felt his hand move closer to her throat.

"Could we go home, please?"

"I don't think so. I want the rest of the story. Do you know something about my sideline business?"

"I don't know anything. I was hunting JoAnn, too. I'm a friend of hers. We lost touch and I wanted to see her."

"If you were really JoAnn's friend, I'd have known about you. See, Sarah talked about everything. Her family. JoAnn's troubles and her friends. People from grammar school. That woman talked. Now what do you really know about me?"

In the darkness, Cassandra could see the glint of his eyes and teeth. He looked mean. "Only that you were seeing Sarah."

"Then why are you snooping around? What is it you want to know?"

"How she died?" Cassandra hurled the question at him as she pushed open her car door and dove into the woods at the side of the road. She had a slim chance, but it was better than sitting in the car and waiting for him to reach across and take her throat in his hands.

"Hey!" Ray made a lunge for her and for a split second his fingers caught her hair.

Cassandra gave a cry of pain, but she scrabbled into the blackness of the trees. There were rocks and roots, but she sprang over them with the grace of someone who'd spent many hours running through such terrain.

"Get back to this car!" Ray ordered. "You little fool! Get back here now, or I'm going to leave you!"

Cassandra crashed through more foliage.

"I'm not going to chase you through the woods in the dark," he warned. "If you don't get your butt back here, I'm going to leave you. I've got fifteen minutes to get back to work, and I'm going to do it. You can rot up here on this mountain. Let the bears bring you home, bone by bone."

Cassandra ducked down behind a rock. She was surprised that he'd made no effort to chase her. Her breath came in short, harsh rasps as she struggled to be as quiet as possible. It would be like him to try to sneak up on her. She had to stay alert.

"You've got to ten to come back and get in this car. Then I'm leaving. One, two, three..."

Ray slowly counted, and Cassandra gripped the rock. She'd definitely blown the whole thing. Ray had never bought into her story. Why had she ever thought she could trick him? And why was he letting her escape without even trying to catch her?

"Ten! I'm out of here, lady. I'll leave your car at the Blue Ridge. I'll give the keys to Rita. Maybe when you ask for them, you'll tell her what kind of game you were playing. You'll have a long walk home to think about it. And just remember, I can always find you if I need to."

His laughter cut through the night, followed by the sound of the car cranking.

Cassandra stood up. She could barely see the headlights through the dense growth of trees. Ray was driving away! He really was leaving her! Or was he merely trying to trick her so that she'd leave the cover of the woods and walk right into his clutches again?

Chapter Fifteen

I feel like the only adult in a Little Rascal's feature film. What the hell is going on around here? And where is Goldilocks and her knight? I've been pacing this porch for hours.

Well, enough cogitation. It's time for action. I have a pretty good idea where those tire tracks up in the orchard lead, but I'm going to make certain. No one has any business up there. No one. But the facts tell otherwise, ma'am.

I haven't had the benefit of any of those fancy K-9 schools, but I know there has been more than one vehicle through the orchard. Different tires. It just doesn't make sense, though. Why is someone going up there? To watch Cassandra? That's a possibility, but it makes for a long walk through the woods.

To hide something? That's what I've finally hit upon. The more I think about it, the more it troubles me.

Humans! They play at destruction with such glee!

When I got Goldilocks to see the tracks, I wanted her to know someone was watching her. I thought she'd get the law, or at least Adam, to go up and check them out with her. But no-o-o-oo! She can't take a hint. Now Eleanor was attuned to me. She and Dr. Doolittle. They picked up on my not-so-subtle suggestions.

Cassandra can't be faulted too much, though. She's never had a cat until I showed up, so she isn't fully aware of my superior native feline intelligence, not to mention that I'm one savvy detective. In time, she'll learn these things, be-

cause she's perceptive, too. The trouble is, I don't have the time to waste. I've made a decision. I'm getting on that television show with Cassandra if it's the last thing I do. I'll make a public plea for Eleanor. It's a snowball's chance in hell, but it's my best shot right now.

With each passing day, my fears for Eleanor increase. I dream about her. Is she hurt so bad she won't know me? Or Peter. If anything happened to him, it would kill her. She'd need me there to comfort her. Besides, there's the revenge angle to work, too.

That's another basic human flaw. They don't think animals plot revenge. Ha! And cats are the most notorious. The master's touch, though, is that most people never perceive the true motivation for feline retribution. But I want Arnold Evans to know it when I do him. I want him to know it, and know where it's coming from. I never should have left his punishment to the legal system. He killed two guards escaping. If I have my way, he won't have a chance to escape ever again.

I've got it pieced together in my mind. That bomb was meant for Kirk Ranager, the "houseguest." Eleanor and Peter could never resist a fight for the underdog. I knew they were working with someone in the political prisoner's rights area, but I didn't pay close attention. I'm a day late and a dollar short, but lately I've been scanning the national news. There hasn't been a word on my people, but Kirk Ranager has had a lot of press. His disappearance has created quite a stir. That Ranager, he was raising some hell in Ireland. Putting together conversations I heard at the house and the news reports I've seen, I believe Ranager had the goods on the treatment of some prisoners. He was about to make a speech to the United Nations.

It would seem that a certain faction wasn't necessarily thrilled with the information he was going to deliver, and so they blew him up. Or tried to. They sent Arnold to do it, and since he could earn some money and settle a score with Peter, too, he was more than happy to oblige.

I should have listened to the conversations closer. It's hard to accept, but I fell into the "Fat Cat" mentality. I had my two people to cater to my every whim. My enemies were defeated. Life was good and I let my guard down. It's partially my fault that Eleanor is missing. I didn't protect her like I should.

And where is Cassandra? God forbid that she's gone off and jumped into a mess o' trouble. I'd better get my cute black tail up to the orchard and solve "the mystery of the twin tracks." I should have done this earlier. For a smart cat, I'm sure suffering from a lot of regrets lately.

ASTONISHMENT was the reaction that set in after the fear disappeared. Cassandra leaned against the boulder that had hidden her and stared through the trees into the blackness. It was so dark, she couldn't even see the road. Sure enough, though, Ray had driven off in her car and left her.

"And what are you going to do, Miss Genius?" she asked herself. She was so disgusted with her stupidity that for a moment she thought about lying down in the leaf-carpeted ground and waiting for dawn.

Only the thought of Adam's torment got her up on her feet and walking toward the road. Adam would be worried sick. By her calculations, she was closer to her house than she was to the lounge. She wasn't lost, she was just disgusted. Plodding forward, she mentally kicked herself each step of the way. There were a million things she could have done, except the ones she did. Why was it she'd picked all the wrong ones? Why?

Bounder was missing. Adam was worried, and rightfully so. JoAnn was in critical danger. Ray was still on the loose, and to put the cream on the pie, she was due on a television show in less than twelve hours.

She'd let everyone down, most of all Adam and Running Stream. Her shenanigans had cost her valuable time she'd promised to use looking for Bounder. Instead, she was out in the woods playing Girl Scout, hiking through the wilderness.

Even though the going was slower, she stayed in the fringe of the trees. She didn't trust Ray at all, and the idea that he was parked down the road, hiding, waiting for her to come out of the woods, made her take every precaution. She'd already been stupid; she could do without another go-round of it.

The incline increased, and so did her breathing. To save time, she cut directly through the woods. She'd grown up in these mountains. She knew the landmarks. The boulders and springs and giant hardwood trees were as familiar to her as her own skin.

She would have access to a telephone in a matter of minutes, and she could begin to hunt Adam down to tell him she was safe. Why hadn't she listened to him? They could be anywhere in the world now, safe in each other's arms. Was that so terribly much to ask? It was more than she'd ever expected, but now that she knew what it felt like to love Adam, she wanted a lifetime of it. That thought drove her forward.

Her house was uncharacteristically dark when she stepped out of the line of trees and into her yard. For a moment she paused, checking all of the windows. There was no sign that anyone was there, or had been there.

"Familiar!" She whispered the cat's name. He should be around the house. He'd never strayed before. "Kitty, kitty."

An eerie sense of foreboding crept over her. Even the woods seemed abnormally quiet. "Don't lose it now," she said out loud. "You've never been a namby-pamby. This is no time to start."

She forced her reluctant feet up the steps and across the wide boards of the porch. The knob turned readily, and she stepped into the foyer.

Something warned her not to turn on the light. It was a sixth sense that told her tragedy had struck. Her fingers found the switch, and then hesitated.

Ears straining to pick up any sound of another person in the house, she waited. She could hear the ticking of the kitchen clock. How odd that she'd never noticed it before. The pattern was peculiar. Tick, tick, tock. Tick, tick, tock.

Somehow she knew then. The scream was stifled in her throat, and she backed toward the door.

Tick, tick, tock.

The sound was coming from the kitchen. It wasn't the clock. The kitchen clock was electric. It had never made a noise, except maybe a tiny little whir every now and then.

Tick, tick, tock.

The ticking came from the kitchen. Each second her dread increased. Hand behind her, she fumbled with the doorknob. Cassandra's heart tightened painfully when she could not turn the knob.

Tick, tick, tock.

The knob was frozen in place. She gripped it with everything she had in her. Still facing the kitchen, she twisted with all of her might. The knob would not turn.

She expelled a rasp of breath. She knew what it meant. Someone had come into her home, put a bomb in her kitchen, and was now standing outside the door, holding her prisoner. She had to think. She had to be smarter than they were, or she could be dead.

Was there a trip wire in the house? Was that why they were holding the door, hoping she would panic and go rushing blindly through the house?

She was afraid to move forward, and someone was keeping her from leaving through the front.

The thought that at least Familiar was out of the house crossed her mind, and with it came a release. She wasn't going to cling to the door like some terrified rodent in a trap. She let go of the knob and ran across into the kitchen. As she felt her own footsteps on the wooden floor, she heard someone running across her porch. The door was free.

It was too late. She'd already made her decision. She flipped on the overhead light in the kitchen as she raced in.

A strange contraption with a clock attached to it was sitting on her table. It was exactly like the bombs she'd seen in the movies.

Her hesitation in grabbing it was short-lived. With one fluid movement, she swept it into her hand and dashed for the back door. She hurled it into the woods with all of her might. The bundle crashed into the trees and Cassandra dropped against the floor, covering her head with her arms.

Her body tensed, waiting for the explosion. There was only the sound of laughter, deep, crazy laughter, as she slowly lifted her head.

Silent seconds slipped away. Nothing. Cassandra's skin began to crawl.

"Witchy woman, I'm watching you." The laughter followed, and then there was the sound of feet running across the ground.

It had all been a joke. The bomb wasn't real. She'd been reduced to Jell-O in her own house by some sick cretin who thought he'd played the best trick in the world on her.

Slowly she got to her feet. Her body was trembling with suppressed terror. Shaking, teeth chattering, she went to the telephone. When she heard the dial tone, her anger kicked in. The creep had been so confident, he hadn't even bothered to cut the phone line.

Cassandra began the process of trying to track Adam down. She called Crockett's and the lodge where Sarah Welford's family had been registered. He didn't answer a page at either place. The Welford family had checked out, and no one of Adam's description had been seen.

She tried not to think about the fake bomb, but she couldn't stop herself. It was such a personal attack. Even more frightening was the aplomb with which it was carried out. The person had stood on the opposite side of her door and held her prisoner.

For some reason, she felt the voice was familiar. Too familiar. She couldn't remember exactly where, but she was certain it was a voice she'd heard recently. Mayor Simpson's? He'd accosted her in public, and he also knew that she was suffering from nightmares.

Whatever it was with Simpson, it was personal. She'd never understood it—she'd only tried to stay out of his way.

Did he despise her enough to play such a cruel and vicious joke? The answer was yes.

She walked to the decanter and poured a small shot of brandy as she went back to the telephone and tried to concentrate on places Adam might have gone. She called the Blue Ridge and to her surprise, her car had been returned to the parking lot.

It struck Cassandra like a blow to the head. When Ray had taken her car, he'd also had access to her purse. Her driver's license. Her real name and address. The bomb could have been his idea of a payback. Or a warning. And he'd had plenty of time while she was scurrying through the woods.

The sound of a crash against the front door made her slosh brandy all over her hand. It came again, a determined thumping on the wood.

"Familiar!" She rushed to open the door. The black cat, yellow eyes glaring, stood hissing toward the darkness.

"It's okay," Cassandra said as she scooped him into her arms and brought him in the house. "It's okay now." She buried her face in his warm black fur, glad to have something to hold on to. With a kick of her heel, she slammed the door and hastily threw the thumb bolt into place.

FOR A MOMENT, Adam thought his eyes were playing tricks on him. Ray was lounging nonchalantly against the control stick of the Spider ride. He was watching two teenage girls laughing as they whirled around and around. It was as if he'd never left his job at the fair.

"That's him," Adam whispered to Running Stream.

"Cassandra?" Running Stream's gaze roved over the crowd, searching for her friend.

"I don't know," Adam answered tensely. "If he brought her back here, then we may have made a mistake about Ray."

"What are you going to do?" she asked, her voice troubled.

"Ask him, point-blank."

"Be careful." She placed a hand on his arm and gave it a squeeze.

Adam nodded as he went to the platform where Ray stood. Ignoring the chain that was used to keep those waiting to ride in line, Adam vaulted over it and went directly to Ray.

"Where's Cassandra McBeth?" he asked.

Ray's lazy smile held a hint of anger. "I don't know what you're talking about. Now get away from this ride, or you're going to have more trouble than you can handle."

"The woman with the long, curly blond hair. Where is she? I know you met her at the Blue Ridge. The two of you got in her car, and you drove away with her."

The smug expression hardened on Ray's face. "Since you know so much, maybe you know why she jumped out of the car and disappeared into the woods. Maybe you can tell me why she used a fake name, too."

"There are lots of things I might tell you," Adam said through clenched teeth, "but you're going to tell me where Cassandra is."

"Or what?" Ray flexed his arms, making the muscles stand out.

"Or I'll tear it out of you." There was no mistaking the deadly intent in Adam's voice.

"Gentlemen," Running Stream's soft voice intervened. She stepped onto the platform and stood between them. She shot a warning to Adam with her eyes as she turned to Ray. "We're very worried about our friend. It's a long story, but she hasn't been well. We're worried that something might have happened to her."

"She was fine when she got out of the car."

Adam's face was white with worry. "Got out! She got out, or did you drag her?"

"Listen, buddy." Ray leaned forward, his chin thrusting out. "I don't know what you're implying, but you'd better watch it. She got out of her car of her own free will. She took off through the woods like she had a ghost on her heels. I called and called, but she wouldn't come back."

"Where's her car?" Adam challenged.

"Back at the lounge, where I told her I'd leave it. Her purse is on the seat. I looked through her things and found her name and address."

"Where did she get out?" Running Stream asked quietly.

Ray gave the location. "She wasn't hurt when I saw her," he insisted.

"You'd better pray she isn't hurt now," Adam said, vaulting to the ground.

"If she's sick, you shouldn't let her go running around by herself," Ray called after him.

"Thank you," Running Stream said as she caught up with Adam. "We should go to her home. I know Cassandra, and she would go there. It's closer."

"If he isn't lying. What if he's killed her and dragged the body off somewhere?" The worry he felt was more painful than anything he'd ever experienced.

"He didn't have the attitude of a man who'd just committed a heinous crime," Running Stream reassured him.

"Then why would Cassandra bolt and leave her own car?"

"We'll ask her that, when we find her." Running Stream hurried around the car and got into the passenger seat. When Adam had the motor going and was pulling out of the parking lot, she spoke again. "My son is missing, too. I know how you feel, Adam, but we can't allow ourselves to think the worst. Cassandra is fine. She's at home, trying to locate both of us, I'm sure."

"And Bounder? Where do you think he is?" Adam knew she was worried about her son. He felt a twinge of guilt. In his concern for Cassandra, he'd hardly given Bounder's disappearance a moment's thought.

"He's fine, too. When I do get my hands on him, he's going to be in a terrible amount of pain." A pair of oncoming headlights illuminated her smile.

Adam reached across the seat and patted her hand. She was a brave woman. A good ally. "Fasten your seat belt," he directed as he pushed the car as hard as he could on the winding mountain roads.

The trees were a dark blur against the headlights as they raced up the mountain. Adam refused to consider what he might do if Cassandra weren't at home.

He was tormented by the thought that he should have held Ray and called the sheriff. But Beaker wouldn't have done anything. Adam had seen the carnie leave with Cassandra, but there was no evidence yet that she was missing. He could only push the car as hard as possible and drive like a madman to her home.

The rough terrain of her driveway forced him to slow down. Running Stream did not comment, but she relaxed her grip on the door handle.

"Sorry about that," he said.

"No need to be sorry. I'm in as big a hurry as you are, Adam."

"It's rougher on the passenger, though."

When they passed the tree with the scarred trunk, Adam told Running Stream about the incident with the scarecrow.

"Any evidence who might have done such a thing?" she asked.

"Nothing solid. Whoever it is, he knows Cassandra's property."

"That's not a very comforting thought."

"Since I came to Tennessee, I haven't had many comforting thoughts." He patted Running Stream's hand. "Not to complain, because I've had some other very enlightening thoughts, especially about our mutual friend."

"You care for her deeply, don't you?"

"I do."

"Living with Cassandra would require great skill at compromise."

"That's an understatement." Adam chuckled. "We're two people very set in our own life-styles."

"Two strong people," Running Stream said. "There are bound to be conflicts in such a situation. But to find a mate with your strength, your drive, a partner in the truest sense of the word, that is something worth compromise.''

Adam waited.

''My husband was such a man. We came from very different worlds.'' She looked straight ahead as Adam piloted the car up the winding mountain road. ''He was the stronger. He gave up his life and adopted mine.''

''Did he make a good decision?'' Adam could tell that she wanted him to ask questions.

''For many years we were very happy. I don't think he regretted giving up his city life. For his family, it was difficult to accept, and that caused him pain. But for days and days we were happy without question. Bounder came to us, and Kevin could not have been happier. A son was the ultimate gift I could have given him.''

''What happened to your husband?''

''He was an advertising executive when we met, and then he became a ranger in the park.'' She folded her hands in her lap. ''He loved the mountains and the people. He studied the Cherokee history and made it his own, even though he was a white man. He was killed in the park one day while on patrol. The person who shot him was never found.''

''I'm sorry.''

''To this day, I grieve for him. But you asked me about his decision to give up the city life and live with me. For us, it was the best decision. I don't know if I could have overcome my fears and learned to live in the city, certainly not as the wife of an advertising executive. But the ultimate answer is Bounder. I have begun to wonder if we made the right decision for him.''

Adam understood the fears and worries that tore at Running Stream. In preserving her life, she'd made her son a partial outcast in the world she loved.

''Bounder has to learn, just as you and your husband did, to make his way. White or red, there are always problems.''

''He is neither one nor the other, though. And he wants so much to belong.'' Her voice caught and nearly broke.

"When we find him, perhaps I could talk with him. If he gave himself half a chance, he would find college a place where there are so many different types of people, he would see that he isn't the only one who feels alone."

"Cassandra says the same thing. If only Bounder would try."

"He has to find his own path, Running Stream, but we can help him look for the beginning of it. I promise you, I will."

"If we find him." Her worst fears were captured in that statement.

"We will. Don't worry about that."

"Adam!" Running Stream pointed through the woods on the left side of the road. "There are lights. See them?"

"I do." Adam swung around a curve and slowed so he could get a better look. "They're moving."

"Relatively fast," Running Stream said. "The woods are so dense. How is that possible?"

"Another path?" Adam had slowed almost to a stop. The lights had disappeared and the blackness of the woods settled around their motionless car.

"There's the track up to the apple orchard that the farmers use to harvest the apples. It's little more than...Bounder! He knew about it and there's on old cave he told me about. He might be hiding up there!" Hope and excitement made Running Stream lean forward in her seat.

"It could be Bounder," Adam said tersely, "or it could be someone who means to harm Cassandra."

Chapter Sixteen

"Familiar!" Cassandra saw the cat's black paw sweep along the shelf. She raced for the flashlight, but she wasn't fast enough. It crashed onto the floor and bounced on the rug. "If I didn't know better, I'd think you did that deliberately." She looked at the cat. When she checked it, the flashlight still worked, and she gave Familiar a warning glance. "You'd better behave."

Her nerves were jangling from the incident with the fake bomb. The meanness of the attack was clear to her, frighteningly so. Someone had entered her home—an assault in the truest sense of the word. He'd pointed out how easily she could be made a victim, and he'd forced her to cringe on the floor, expecting her own destruction. The final, infuriating blow was the taunts he'd hurled at her.

A muffled crash from the foyer again made her jump, and she almost dropped the flashlight she'd just rescued.

"Damn!" She hurried into the tiny room and found the coatrack lying on the floor. Familiar had dragged her black Windbreaker over to the door.

"Meow!" he insisted.

"Familiar, have you set out to torment me to death?" She picked up the jacket and righted the wooden stand. "What is it with you?"

"Meow!" His tone was strident.

"You can't go out now. Get a grip on yourself," she said, then sighed. It wasn't bad enough she was talking to her cat, she was ordering him around as if he'd deign to obey. She wasn't an expert on cats, but one thing she'd learned from Familiar was that he did only what he pleased.

"You must have been a king in a past life," she chided him. "At least, that's what Sylvia would say." The thought of her mother made her smile. Sylvia wouldn't cower down on the floor of her home, she'd take matters into her own hands.

Clutching the flashlight and her jacket, she went to the phone and dialed the number to the sheriff's office. When Beaker wasn't in, she hesitated.

"What is the nature of your call?" the dispatcher asked.

Cassandra was almost ready to leave Beaker a message, but something held her back. There had been too many co-incidences with information she'd given Beaker. Something wasn't right with the lawman. He was possibly covering up for someone. That thought made her decide.

"Tell the sheriff that Cassandra McBeth has new evidence in the murders."

"The sheriff won't be in until the morning." At last the dispatcher's interest was aroused. "I'll send another unit up to talk with you."

"No! Beaker is the only one I'll talk with. The implications of this are very serious. Only Beaker. Tell him, if he wants to know who the murderer is, to watch *The Martin West Show* tomorrow." She smiled to herself as she replaced the receiver. If she were going to set herself up by appearing on television as a psychic, then she might as well go whole hog and pull Beaker in, too.

The whump of the door rattling made her whirl angrily around and return to the foyer. Familiar was hurling himself against the door.

"You aren't going out," she said. "Enough!" She clapped her hands for emphasis.

Familiar walked directly to her feet and dug his claws into the tops of her shoes. She'd changed into comfortable jeans and sneakers. "Meow." He went to the door and threw himself against it.

Cassandra looked at the flashlight in her left hand and her jacket draped over her arm. The cat was at the door, demanding that she open it. Was it possible he wanted her to go outside with him?

She looked at the flashlight and the jacket again. Lassie couldn't have done it any better. And Familiar did watch a lot of television, especially since he could turn it on and off and switch the channels with a flick of his paw.

She went to the door and opened it a crack. Familiar shot outside, but when he got to the edge of the porch he stopped. ''Meow,'' he said.

Cassandra looked back and forth. There was no sign of anyone, or anything, in the darkness. She felt that the intruder was gone, but she wasn't willing to risk her life on a hunch. What if he were lurking on the fringe of the woods, waiting for her to venture out?

She started to shut the door, but Familiar let out a yowl. It sounded as if he'd been run over by an eighteen-wheel truck. She hurried to the edge of the porch to snatch him up, but he jumped to the safety of the yard and cried again.

''I'm going to get you,'' she whispered as she darted after him. She was suddenly struck by the memory of the day in the orchard when the cat had shown her the tracks in the grass.

It didn't make much sense, but he had shown her. Was there something he wanted to show her tonight? She had the flashlight in her hand. The lightweight jacket was perfect for moving unseen in the woods. Slipping it on, she started after Familiar's bobbing tail.

Without wasting another second, the cat moved along the path toward the apple orchard.

IT'S ABOUT TIME someone started listening to me. What with all the commotion going on around here, I didn't think I'd ever get Goldilocks on the move. There's something she's got to see.

It's going to be a long haul, and if she starts to question where we're headed, I'll lose her. She hates the orchard. I'm not certain why, but I know it makes her sad. Even worse, it makes me worried. I've got a really bad feeling about what's been happening up there.

I should have been checking around the premises more. I knew Bounder was out there, and I thought he was keeping an eye on things. That isn't exactly the case, though. His smell is everywhere, and after the things I've seen, that isn't a comforting fact.

That's one of the problems with humans. They aren't clear in their thoughts or emotions. Take a cat, for instance. Say I'm walking down the street and I see another tom. If I'm on his territory, he lets me know with a growl. He doesn't hide behind a fence and jump out and stab me in the back. It's straightforward. Humans are devious. They pretend one way and then—wham-o!—the next thing you know, there's a stiletto sticking out of the old back. I wonder if duplicity is part of the process of walking upright.

Now that's a theory for consideration. We superior four-legged animals may fight, and even kill, but it's a matter of survival and protection of territory. We also clearly signal our intention. Those two-leggers are another matter. They get into the darnedest struggles, and we're talking about environmental suicide here with bombs and nuclear attacks, and the crux of it is economic.

I'll tell you, it makes a cat wonder. When all of this is over and I'm home again, I'm going to spend some time thinking on this. How did humans end up in control? Cats are infinitely superior. Why aren't we running things?

This fascinating topic is going to have to wait until I resolve the more immediate problem of the item I've discovered. When I saw the hair, I didn't put two and two together. My mind is definitely slipping. Now I know what it means, though. As soon as Cassandra sees it, she'll know, too.

The strand of hair isn't very long, maybe about four inches, but it's a healthy hunk. Dark and gorgeous. I know it isn't Cassandra's. The way it's been placed on that rock, though, it had to be done deliberately. Some sort of sacrifice or ritual, I'd say. Just looking at it gave me the willies.

Now who would stand in the middle of an apple orchard, cut off a shank of hair and leave it displayed on some big rock? It doesn't make sense. It's so weird, I know it has something to do with those women who disappeared.

Hurry, Goldilocks! Time's a wastin'. I'd better gear up into a slow jog and keep her feet on the move. Hurry. We're alone out here for the moment, but there's no guarantee when the owner of that hair might return. And I ain't referring to the person who wore it last. I'm talking about the one who cut it off.

And frankly, my dear, I do give a damn if we get caught. I don't mind admitting that the thought of what this person might do to my incredibly sleek and gorgeous hide makes my whiskers pucker. I'd like to live to see my Eleanor once again, and I'd like to do it comfortably attired in my formal black hide.

Come on, Cass, shake the lead out, we're almost there.

"DAMN IT, FAMILIAR, slow down." Cassandra was panting heavily as she climbed the steepest portion of the path to the apple orchard. She was tired, exhausted and afraid. Now she was chasing through the woods following a cat that acted as if he were training for the Boston Marathon. It didn't make a bit of sense. Besides, she'd forgotten to leave a note for Adam when he came back. He would have no idea where she'd gone.

She lengthened her stride a bit and pushed harder. The sooner she checked out the orchard, the sooner she could go home to Adam.

She felt as if she'd covered several miles, but Familiar continued to lead. She was going to feel like a complete idiot unless she found something.

"Meow!" Familiar stopped abruptly in the middle of the path.

Cassandra snapped on the flashlight. She'd been traveling with only the light from the moon as her guide. If someone were around, she didn't want them to be able to follow her. She didn't want to be a perfect target, especially since she was beginning to feel like the perfect idiot.

The thin beam of light cut the darkness and revealed fresh tire tracks in the lush grass. Bounder had once told her a bit about tracking. Kneeling in the thick grass she felt one of the crushed blades. It was still wet where it had been broken. That meant the tracks were relatively fresh. How fresh? It was hard for her to know. She also couldn't tell if they were coming or going tracks. Bounder would have known the subtle differences, but she'd never learned.

An interesting possibility occurred to her and she scratched the waiting Familiar on the neck as she examined the ground. "Are you saying that the man who drove up here was the same man who put a fake bomb in my house?" Cassandra asked the cat.

"Meow."

"That's exactly what I thought you'd say." She shook her head at her own foolishness. It was possible, though. Not only possible, but probable. The man who'd broken into her home and tried to frighten her had been driving on her property, hiding out among her fruit trees.

And he might still be in the area.

She snapped off the flashlight. So, she'd tracked him to the upper reaches of her land. Now what? She should have left Adam a note. If someone were up here, waiting for a chance to hurt her, it might be days before Adam thought to look in her orchard. In days, she could easily be dead.

She trotted along behind Familiar for another five minutes before he veered off the path and cut through the trees. Without a light, the footing was rocky, but Cassandra followed. He was definitely leading her.

They were moving toward the edge of the orchard, a place Cassandra had not visited since her father's death. A haunting sensation of terrible loss touched her, and she pushed it aside. The past was dead and buried. She had her future to worry about, a future that might be determined by what she learned on this night.

"Meow!" Familiar called as he urged her on.

Cassandra firmed her resolve. It was almost as if that damn cat read her mind. He seemed to know she was faltering. But she wasn't. She wouldn't let the past prevent her from reaching for the future. Hadn't she done that all of her life—used the past to excuse herself from trying to find happiness and love?

She'd avoided caring about anyone just like she'd avoided this part of the orchard. She didn't want to explore the possibility of caring for anyone, and she didn't want to examine the place her father had died. She didn't want to risk further hurt.

"I'm tired of being a coward," she panted as she followed Familiar. "I'm not going to avoid this place, or my feelings for Adam any longer."

They were almost at the edge of the orchard, the place where the side of the mountain sheered away and fell for two thousand feet. It was the place she'd often come with Blake McBeth and watched the orchestrations of the stars.

Familiar stopped, as if he, too, saw the beauty of the night spread out across the horizon. Cassandra halted beside him. Sadness and loss surrounded her, and she knew again the pain of missing her father. The day he'd died, so had her childhood.

A sharp prick in her right leg made her jump.

"Meow!" Familiar demanded.

"Cat, you're too pushy." She turned away from the view and followed Familiar at a walk. He was threading his way past trees and rocks, moving unerringly toward a goal.

When he stopped by a large rock formation, Cassandra waited. The cat jumped on one rock, and then onto another. He turned back to see if she followed.

"I hate this," she said as she started to climb after him. The flashlight was awkward, still, she dragged it along with her. The rocks weren't high, but the climb was difficult in the dark. When she finally reached the top, she saw the cat crouching beside something.

"If this is some poor rodent you've caught and killed, I'm going to do something terrible to you," she whispered. She clicked on the light and aimed it at the cat. It took several seconds for her mind to accept what she saw. When she finally realized what Familiar had led her to, she felt the scream rising in her throat.

"THE LIGHTS ARE ON." Adam was amazed at the sweetness of the relief that flooded through him.

"Be careful," Running Stream cautioned as he threw himself out of the car.

He didn't bother to answer as he took the steps three at a time and rushed to the front door. The first indication of trouble was the fact that the door swung open at his lightest touch. Cassandra had agreed to keep the house locked tight.

He held up a warning hand to Running Stream, a sign for her to remain in the car. Cautiously, he moved into the house. He didn't call Cassandra's name.

He checked the upstairs and found it empty, also. When he was certain the house was safe, he went to the front door and motioned Running Stream inside.

Working together, it took them only a few moments to find the numbers Cassandra had written on a notepad by the phone.

"She was trying to find you," Running Stream said. "She called the lounge, my home, the sheriff's office. The places she thought you might be."

"And then she took off, on foot." Adam paced the room. "Why? And where?" He stopped. "And did she go voluntarily? Surely she would have left a note for me if she'd had time."

"Where's the cat?" Running Stream sat on the arm of the sofa. "And we need to check and see if anything else is missing. That would give us a clue where she might have gone."

Adam searched around the house for Familiar, while Running Stream looked through Cassandra's bedroom for any clues.

"The cat isn't around anywhere. Not inside or out," Adam reported when he returned.

"Cassandra changed clothes. Her favorite jeans are gone, and her sneakers. She's on foot, unless she caught a ride." Running Stream's gaze roamed over the den. She moved to the kitchen and foyer. "The flashlight and her black Windbreaker are gone, too."

"Maybe I should call the sheriff," Adam said with uncertainty.

"Before you do that, why don't we check the orchard? I remember when Cassandra's father told me about the cave. Blake didn't want her to know about it, for fear she might decide to explore. He was always afraid someone would hide there. Since his death, she hasn't been there at all. It's been years since I even thought about it, but if someone has been roaming around, they might have found the cave." She pulled her shawl more tightly around her shoulders.

"What are you thinking?" Adam asked.

"That Cassandra knew someone was on her property, and that she went to find out who it was and why they were there. She might have thought it was Bounder." Running Stream's fingers clutched the fabric of her shawl. "She never told me what Billy told her, but I'm afraid those young men are trouble. I think maybe they've been up in the cave."

"You think Cassandra might be there, too?"

Running Stream nodded.

"You'd better stay here and wait for her. Just a minute." He dashed out the front door and came back. In his hand was a small but powerful-looking gun.

"No," Running Stream said softly.

Adam checked the chamber and loaded six bullets. "Whether you want it or not, take it. If Cassandra comes back down here and anyone tries to hurt her, kill them." His gaze locked with hers. "I mean it, Running Stream. There's a maniac out there, and he might be after Cassandra. If someone has to die tonight, I don't want it to be Cassandra or you."

Running Stream reached her hand out slowly and took the gun from Adam. "I know how to use it, so don't worry."

"Will you?"

"If I have to."

Adam leaned over and kissed her cheek. "Thanks. Now I'm going up to the orchard. If Cassandra comes back, fire the gun once up into the air, okay?"

Running Stream nodded. "One shot and you'll know she's here safe."

"More than one, and I'll be down here as fast as I can." Adam checked his own weapon, a gun identical to the one he'd given Running Stream. He'd never owned a gun until the day before, when he'd stopped by a shop in Gatlinburg and made the purchase. One weapon had been intended for Cassandra, even though he knew she'd balk at the idea of touching one.

It was too late now for arguments over gun control. He only knew that if someone armed and dangerous was after Cassandra, he'd protect her with his life.

The moon gave fair illumination as he started the long trek up to the apple orchard. He knew how Cassandra avoided the place. What could have drawn her up there at night, alone?

His long legs and steady pace ate up the distance. Even though his lungs burned with the effort, he pushed on. At the same time he kept his ears alert for any unnatural sound.

As he ran, he mulled over the carnie, Ray. There was something about the man that didn't click. He'd used poor Sarah Welford, no doubt about that. But he didn't strike Adam as a killer.

He didn't deny having met Cassandra in the lounge, and he'd been straightforward about dumping her on the side of the road. He'd acted as if she'd gotten her due, but he hadn't lied. If he'd been killing women up and down the mountain, would he have been so blatant about his behavior? It simply didn't fit.

On the other hand, the mayor of Gatlinburg was a man who troubled Adam. Simpson's calculated attacks on Cassandra revealed a deep-seated personality flaw to Adam. The man was terrified of Cassandra.

He had something to hide, and he was afraid Cassandra would unearth it. Adam's suspicions pointed directly to the murder of the women.

Beaker was in it up to his neck. No lawman in his right mind would take confidential information such as the things Cassandra had told him and give them to a television talk show host. It bordered on a criminal action. When all of this was over, Beaker was going to have some serious questions to answer about his conduct.

Adam puffed on, forcing one leg in front of the other. He was at the beginning of the orchard. He passed the first several rows of trees and the land leveled out, allowing him to drag air into his burning lungs.

The gun was snug in his waistband with extra bullets in his pocket. Each time he drew a breath, he felt the hard steel. He slowed his pace, trying to remember the layout of the orchard as Cassandra had described it. He also had to listen to see if he could hear any sound of her presence.

Without knowing what kind of situation he faced, he didn't want to call out to her. He dropped back to a walk and began to move from tree to tree.

Night sounds were all around him. Insects whirred, their choruses broken by the flutters and rustlings of birds and small animals moving through the protection of darkness.

If there was a human sound, he couldn't detect it. He moved forward, listening, watching. Where would she go? The orchard was big, and she could be anywhere in it, if she was even on the mountain.

He was on the point of calling her name when the night was splintered by the anguish of a scream.

Adam froze, and then broke into a run. It was Cassandra's voice, and she sounded as if she were being torn apart.

The scream echoed in the night as he raced forward. He broke through a line of trees and what he saw stopped him completely. Cassandra and the cat were outlined on a huge rock. She was kneeling with the cat at her side, a flashlight beam pointed at the rock. Slowly she reached forward and picked something up.

Chapter Seventeen

Rocks dug into Adam's hands as he pulled himself up the mountain of stone to where Cassandra knelt. Against the backdrop of the starry night and the moon, she appeared to be captured in some ancient ritual of grief. "Cassandra," he said gently. When she didn't respond, he put his arms around her. "What's wrong?" he asked. She was rocking back and forth slowly, clutching something in her hand.

"She's dead, Adam. Somehow, he killed her."

"Who?" In the darkness he couldn't tell if she was injured, or confused, or coming out of a nightmare.

"JoAnn," she whispered. "See."

The hair she held in her hand was about four inches long and luxuriant, tied at one end with a red ribbon. It was obviously human hair and very much resembled JoAnn Reed's beautiful tresses.

"He left it here for me to find," Cassandra said. Her voice was soft, almost inflectionless. "He's taunting me. He was at the house tonight, and he left a fake bomb in the kitchen. He did it to prove to me that he could. He was outside the whole time, watching. He laughed at me."

"Let's get home," Adam said. They were very unprotected on the rock, and Running Stream was alone in the house. He'd known the man they sought was insane, but he'd never experienced the full reality of the killer's craziness until he saw the hair. The killer was obviously performing a ritual scalping of the women he victimized. The man was sick, and extremely dangerous.

Very gently, Adam took the hair from her hand and carefully put it in the pocket of his jacket. He helped Cassandra off the rocks, and Familiar followed, as lithe and agile as ever.

"Before we go home, I have to do one thing," he said as he led Cassandra toward the place where Running Stream said the cave would be. He had to check it out to see what Bounder was involved in. He owed Running Stream that much. There was no telling what she would have to face in the future.

He didn't like the idea of the hair. It was symbolic scalping. The first thing that had come to his mind was an Indian revolt. It would be the first thing most people thought about. Either Bounder and his friends had stepped too far over the line, or it was possible that someone was trying to set them up. For the moment, he didn't know what he believed.

"There's a cave here. I promised Running Stream I'd check it out," he said as he led the way.

Cassandra didn't ask a question. She followed him as he wound his way through the trees. For a short distance Familiar followed, then suddenly darted ahead, crying loudly.

"If we had any element of surprise, Familiar has blown it," Adam grumbled as they crept forward.

The face of the mountain was completely dark. There were areas so black that they appeared to be holes or mouths, but they were only indentations. Adam patiently searched for the opening. Beside him, Cassandra searched low while he felt high. They'd have to do it by touch.

Familiar's meow was a steady aggravation. The cat raced from them to a distance farther along the wall of the rock. Then he dashed back to them and yowled louder.

Exasperated, Cassandra followed the cat to the point where he stopped and disappeared into a crevice in the side of the mountain.

"I think we've got it," she said. "Flashlight?"

"No," Adam said. "Wait until we're inside. Someone might be out there trying to follow us. We don't want to make it any easier than we have to."

Adam stepped through the opening first, with Cassandra right on his heels. In the total darkness of the cave, the cat brushed past Adam's leg and gave a rumbling cry. Adam clicked on the flashlight.

The prone body of Bounder was flung against one side of the cave wall. His arm was twisted in a funny angle, and in the flashlight's gleam he was unnaturally pale.

Cassandra rushed to him while Adam steadied the light. A quick check of his carotid artery indicated he was still alive, but his pulse was weak. His right arm was broken, Cassandra knew that without touching him, and he was unconscious. She ran her hands along his legs while Adam held the light. They were clean and straight, but as she moved up his body she found numerous cuts and scrapes, nothing too serious until she saw the gaping head wound. He'd been soundly bashed on the left side of his head.

"He probably broke his arm in the fall against the cave wall," Cassandra whispered. "We need an ambulance. I can't tell about internal injuries."

"Could they find this location if they came up here?" Adam asked.

Cassandra thought a moment. "Maybe, maybe not. He's losing blood slowly but steadily from the head wound. We have to get him home, and quickly." She bent down to examine his arm.

Adam's hand closed on her shoulder and stayed her. "Before we do anything, consider that Bounder might be the killer."

Cassandra's hair arced around her head as she swung to face him. "I don't believe that."

"I know you don't want to, but it might be true."

"Then who knocked him out?"

Adam dropped the flashlight and moved his hands from her shoulders down her arms as he knelt beside her. "I don't want it to be true, but I want you prepared. Okay?"

She nodded, giving her attention once again to the injured man. "You're right. We have to consider every possibility. Running Stream warned me to keep all doors open. I wonder if she knew I'd be suspecting her son?"

"She's a smart woman. She knows Bounder might be involved in something bad."

"But not murders," Cassandra insisted.

"While you're working on his arm, I'm going to have a look around this place." The cave descended into cavernous blackness. Adam had no idea how deep the chamber was, or what might be hiding in there. He wanted to check it out before there was an unpleasant surprise.

The cave was narrow at the opening, but it widened out and the ceiling soared to a large cavern. The darkness ate the beam of light; the cave was bigger than he'd anticipated.

Footsteps echoing, Adam moved forward. The flashlight picked up whorls and scars in the earth where it appeared something heavy had been dragged away, but the cave was empty.

"Adam, he's coming around." Cassandra's voice echoed eerily in the empty cavern.

Adam ran the light over the interior as thoroughly as possible before returning to Cassandra's side. She held Bounder's head in her lap, and the young man was moaning and beginning to stir.

"The pain is going to be intense," Cassandra warned. "I don't have a thing to give him."

"If he can stand it, we'll try to get him back to your house."

"I can stand it," Bounder said softly.

"What happened?" Cassandra pressed her hand on Bounder's forehead, gently encouraging him to remain prone for a few moments longer. She knew the first effort to move would awaken the pain in his broken arm.

"I came up here to check on the materials." He closed his eyes and gritted his teeth against the pain. For a second, he almost fainted, but he ground out the next words. "There was someone hiding here. Whoever it was hit me with something and . . . I don't remember." His voice grew hazy.

"Then they threw you against the rock wall," Cassandra told him. "How long have you been here?"

"I don't know. I woke up several times, but when I tried to move, I blacked out again. I heard things. Crying and moaning. I knew I had to get away before I died."

"It's okay now," Cassandra comforted him. She cast a look at Adam.

"Bounder, we need the truth now. Who hurt you? Was it one of your friends?"

"No. The truth is, I don't know who it was. I never saw them." He stifled a cry as he forced himself into a sitting position with Cassandra's help. He swayed for a moment as if he might yield to the pain, but he didn't. "We have to get out of here. Now."

"What were you hiding here on Cassandra's property?"

"Parts for a bomb." Bounder panted from the pain.

"Explosives!" The word escaped Adam like a slap.

Bounder shook his head. "Everything but. We were going to get the dynamite later this month."

"Bounder!" Cassandra's whisper revealed her disappointment.

"I wouldn't have let them bring the dynamite to your land, Cassandra. We just had the housing for the bombs."

"Why bombs?" she asked.

"To scare the tourists. We didn't want to really hurt anyone, just frighten them away."

"The second earring? Where did you get it?" Adam interrupted. "What do you know about the murders?"

"I found it in the orchard. I knew it was a match to the one I found at your home."

"Then why didn't you tell me?" Cassandra's question was quietly put, but it carried a lot of raw emotion.

"I meant to. But I thought I'd watch the orchard and trap the killer myself. I wanted to do it because..."

"To show Billy and Stalker," Cassandra supplied. "Because if you could do something such as capture the killer, you'd get notice and attention. An Indian who did something important. It would make your friends rethink their plans." It all fell so neatly into place.

"I was stupid," Bounder said slowly. "My pride and my arrogance got in the way of my thoughts."

As he finished speaking, Familiar came out of the darkness and rubbed against his good hand. The cat purred loudly, then bit him gently and tugged on his hand.

"He's trying to get you up," Cassandra said. She bent down for the cat, but he dodged her hands. Familiar disappeared into the blackness of the cave.

"We'd better get him out of here," Adam whispered to Cassandra. He didn't like the cave, the feeling that something could come out of the dark from any direction and attack them.

Bounder sensed Adam's uneasiness. "Leave me, and take Cassandra to safety. Whoever attacked me could come back. I deserve whatever happens to me."

"You wanted to do the right thing," Cassandra consoled him. "The only one who has suffered is you. No matter what, we aren't going to leave you. I'm afraid the pain is going to be terrible when you try to stand."

"I've been stupid but I won't be weak." Bounder leaned forward, and Cassandra and Adam both helped him to his feet. His face showed the power of the pain, but he didn't stumble or falter.

"It's going to be a long walk," Adam warned. "If you need to rest, let us know."

Bounder nodded, and motioned for Cassandra to lead the way out. He fell in behind her, followed by Adam.

At the door of the cave, Familiar darted from the darkness and sank his claws into Adam's pant leg.

"Hey," Adam said, scooping the cat into his arms. "Now isn't the time for games. Let's get down the mountain." With Familiar protesting, he tucked the cat in his arms and hurried to catch up with Bounder. The young man looked as if he might fall at any moment, yet he continued to walk.

Bounder stumbled at a rough place in the path, and Adam was forced to release the cat so he could grasp the young man before he fell.

Free, Familiar scampered back up the path toward the cave. He gave one plaintive cry as he turned and looked back at Cassandra and Adam.

"Familiar," Cassandra called. She didn't like the idea of leaving him, but she had to get Bounder to a hospital, and fast. He was much weaker than he pretended.

"He'll come home," Adam reassured her as he put an arm around Bounder's waist and held him up. "Familiar knows the way home. He's plenty smart."

"Okay," Cassandra whispered. She eased up to his other side, careful of his arm, and offered as much support as she could. Adam was correct, the two of them were virtually carrying the injured man even though Bounder was trying to hold himself upright.

The trip down the mountain was marked by silence and an attempt to find the easiest footing. Cassandra put all of her thoughts into willing Bounder to make it.

When they were close to the house, Cassandra ran ahead. She fell into the house and collided with Running Stream. "It's Bounder. He's okay, but he's hurt. We need to rush him to the hospital. Get some towels and pillows. We'll take him in Adam's car."

"He will live?" Running Stream was motionless.

"Of course," Cassandra said, hugging her. "His arm is broken and he's been hit in the head, but he's coming down the mountain with Adam. He's walking and very much alive."

Running Stream blocked back the tears that threatened. "Thank goodness," she said as she smiled.

"ARE YOU SURE?" Adam asked as he pulled into the TV studio parking lot. "You didn't get an hour of sleep last night."

She was tired to the point of exhaustion. Bounder was in the hospital, sedated, and in stable condition. Running Stream was guarding him with her life. So far, they'd been able to keep the details of his injuries from the authorities. Adam didn't trust Beaker at all, and Cassandra concurred wholeheartedly.

To make matters worse, Familiar had completely disappeared. He'd never come down from the mountain, and Adam had been adamant in his refusal to let Cassandra go up and look for him.

"Cassandra, you don't have to do this," Adam repeated. She was too tired, but she was also the one who had to make her own decisions.

"It has to be done," Cassandra said. "The killer is still out there. We know one thing more about him, but that isn't enough to catch him."

"I read everything I could find on ritual scalping," Adam said. He reached across the car and took Cassandra's hand in his. "The most common form is a symbol of conquest, a notch-in-the-belt kind of thing. I don't get this from the hair you found."

Cassandra nodded. "It's something more. Either extreme hatred or almost envy. The traditional idea of scalping was to have proof that the enemy was vanquished, proof that he was dead. This business with the killer is more than that."

Cassandra leaned across the seat and kissed Adam on the cheek. They'd shared only an hour alone together in the past twenty-four, but the pleasure he'd given her was indelibly printed on her memory. She'd needed her sleep, that was true, but she needed his touch more. With each minute that she spent with Adam, she was more and more aware of the loneliness that had wrapped her life. Adam made her world complete.

"I love you," she whispered against his neck. "Come back for me in an hour. If you hang around the studio, it'll only make me nervous."

"Okay." Adam didn't want to leave her. He wanted to guard her, protect her—and love her. She'd shown him what it truly meant to share emotions. When she made love, she held nothing back. It was as if she'd waited all of her life to give him that special gift. It was such a precious thing, he couldn't endure the thought of anything happening to her.

"Talk to Bounder again if he wakes," she said. "See if you can connect the disappearance of his…that stuff in the cave with the hair and the earring. None of it makes any sense, Adam. There are a million questions.''

"I'll talk with Bounder," Adam agreed. "But I'll be back here at quarter of four. And I'll keep an eye open for that cat."

"Thanks." She gave him one last kiss on the cheek. Cassandra opened the car door and as she stepped out, a streak of black catapulted by her leg.

"Familiar!" She was startled to see the cat. He hadn't made a peep in the car. It was almost as if he'd been hiding.

"Thank goodness," Adam said. He was genuinely relieved to see the feline. "I think he wants to be a star," Adam said, his gaze trained on the cat. "Let him go with you. I'd feel a lot better knowing Familiar was there to guard you."

"Great. The witch woman and her black cat." Cassandra shrugged. "I might as well give the people a good show."

"That's my girl." Adam put the car in reverse and pulled away.

"Come on, Familiar," Cassandra said. "Just don't make any trouble. Sit right with me and behave. When we get home, we're going to have a long talk. You had me worried sick."

"Meow," Familiar agreed as he walked beside her, black tail waving in the wind.

The studio was pretty much the way Cassandra had anticipated. Although they'd discussed hiding her identity, Cassandra had finally decided to play it completely straight. She took her seat on the sofa that made up the set, and pulled Familiar into her arms.

The sound man miked her up, and the cameraman closed in for a reading. In a matter of minutes she was waiting for Martin West to come down to talk with her. The studio lights prevented any real ability to look over the audience. Was the killer there, waiting for his chance? She shuddered and felt Familiar stiffen. This was no time for cold feet or cowardly thoughts.

Martin West came from the wings and took a few moments to go over the procedure for her, the cues for commercial interruptions and the methods for handling aggressive questions from the audience.

"We shouldn't generate too much hostility," he said, "but be prepared for the one or two who've come here to belittle anyone who claims to have extraordinary abilities."

"I understand."

"The cat?" He gave Familiar a long disdainful look.

Cassandra could feel the fur begin to stand on Familiar's back. "A little unexpected bonus," Cassandra said. "He hid in the car and bolted in here. Don't worry. He's very well behaved and quiet."

"If he gets out of hand, we have a cage in the back."

"That won't be necessary," she said coldly.

"Well, see that it isn't." He stood up. "It's about ten minutes until air time. I'm going out to warm up the audience."

He disappeared, and the tension level in Familiar reduced considerably. "He is a bit of a bore," Cassandra whispered to the cat. "Just ignore him. He can't be helped."

"Meow." Familiar settled down on her lap and looked around.

"Don't ham it up too much," Cassandra warned. "I get the impression Martin likes to be the only star on his show."

"Meow," Familiar agreed.

Before Cassandra became paralyzed by nerves, Martin took his seat beside her and signaled that they were on the air.

"Cassandra McBeth is a local girl who's remained local and yet made a national name for herself. For all of her acclaim, she still hasn't overcome her past here in the Gatlinburg area. And today, Cassandra is going to tell us a little about a special gift she has—one with which she claims she has witnessed the murder of three women," Martin began. He stood up and started to pace the stage.

"Ms. McBeth has a special talent, the ability to dream the future. And what she sees is neither pretty nor pleasant to discuss. She sees young women as fingers close around their throats and the life is slowly, lovingly, squeezed out of them."

The audiences shifted slightly, all heads turning for a look at Cassandra. Mouth dry, hands clutched in her lap, she felt the first ripples of animosity. They hated her, feared her for what she could do. She had something secret that they didn't have.

"Ms. McBeth's visions have been so extraordinarily accurate that Sheriff Harvey Beaker has listed Ms. McBeth and her lover Adam Raleigh as potential suspects in the murders." He looked at Cassandra, smiling with the cunningness of his coup.

Cassandra started to interrupt, but Martin never gave her a chance to clarify his statement. Beaker had never formally said she and Adam were suspects. They'd never even been charged.

Martin continued. "Now the young woman who has authored a dozen books on healthy living, eating, gardening, and home remedies is here to tell us about a murderer on the loose. Cassandra..."

Before she could attempt to speak, the audience erupted into a series of hisses.

"I've actually witnessed two murders, not three," she said carefully, speaking loud enough to be heard over the din of the audience. "The third woman, Sarah Welford, was murdered. I'm positive of that, but I can't honestly say that she was killed by the same man who killed Janey Ables and Carla Winchester. But there is another young woman in peril." The audience had quieted a bit, and Cassandra spoke directly to the television camera. "JoAnn Reed, if you can hear me, get in touch with me as soon as possible. You have the key to solving these murders. You've seen the killer. You can identify him."

"I thought you had that power, Ms. McBeth?" Martin prodded. "Isn't that the claim you've made, that you can identify the murderer?"

Cassandra had expected Martin West's aggressive grandstanding. No matter who he lured onto the show, he turned on them and made himself look like the big man.

"Oh, I can, Martin. I know him inside out. I know his sick and twisted mind. But I'm not telling everything I know today. I don't have to worry about ratings and network offers." She smiled sweetly.

"What *can* you tell us about the killer?" Martin's smile was angry and he pushed the conversation back where he wanted it.

"He's strong and very good-looking. He's extremely vain and also insecure. He likes flattery, and he likes attractive women who like him. He also likes to hurt women. He enjoys the sensation of squeezing the life from them."

A hush had fallen over the studio. "He's a very sick man who can appear to be normal. I'd also say that he has a job where a lot of people know him."

"Like?" Martin persisted. He mugged to the camera. 'Like, say a . . . doctor?"

His response drew a laugh, and Cassandra knew she could hold the audience only so long. "Like a bartender, or a sports figure, or someone working at a carnival." She paused. "Someone who comes into contact with large numbers of people. That's how he selects his victims."

"You know this for a fact?"

"Yes." There was no room to quibble. Martin West would eat her alive.

"The killer also envies the women he kills. He covets their skin, their hair. He covets their beauty." She suddenly understood. "He wants to be like them, beautiful and admired as only women are allowed. He feels cheated of his adulation because he's a man."

"Since all of these killers have a reason for doing this, would you happen to know why?" Martin's skepticism was obvious. "I mean, was he abused, or deformed, or mutilated? Maybe he's just ugly—and really, really mad about it."

The audience erupted into laughter.

"He isn't ugly," Cassandra said quietly but with conviction. She concentrated on remembering the fleeting impressions of her dreams. She wanted to anger the killer, but she had to be close to the truth. Close but wrong enough—in public—to make him want to correct her.

"No, he isn't ugly. Quite the contrary. But he hates beautiful women. What does that say? Abandonment, rejection." She played the trump. "His mother was a lesbian. She rejected him for her female lover. Our killer has latent, suppressed homosexual tendencies."

The audience was completely quiet.

"That's a broad conclusion to jump to," Martin said.

"It's the truth." Cassandra sat back in her chair. The killer would never allow that statement to go unchallenged. It would strike at the core of his ego. He would have to retaliate.

"So, along with prophetic dreams, you have some aptitude for psychoanalysis." Martin reclaimed the audience and waited for the laughter to die down. "Care to tell us something about this guy's physical appearance? I mean, it's hard for the members of our audience to give everybody they meet a quiz regarding their feelings about women. If you know who the killer is, come on and give us a description."

"It's enough that he knows that I know him," Cassandra said quietly. "This is between us, now. Just the two of us."

The audience hushed and leaned forward in their seats.

"I offer a challenge to this man," Cassandra continued. "He thinks he's terribly bright. So far, he's picked on young, naive women. Let him take on someone who's a match for him."

"Someone like you?" West probed. There was a gleam in his eye as he signaled the camera in for a close-up of Cassandra's face. "That's quite a dare, Ms. McBeth."

"It's no dare," she answered. "We know each other," she said, allowing a smile to touch the corners of her lips. "Equals. Let's see how brave our murderer is when he's matched with someone who knows him."

"And I suppose that the creature on your lap is some mystical animal that helps you interpret the future? Or maybe a 'familiar'? I understand there are those around the area who believe you're a witch."

The audience was growing more unsettled. A few catcalls came from the back of the room, and people were standing up and waving their arms for a chance to get to a microphone. Familiar sat up, ears alert and tail twitching.

"No, the cat is a stray. I'm looking for his owner, so if anyone can identify him, please get in touch."

"Well, Ms. McBeth, I'm sure the audience has a number of questions for you. Say, do you go into a trance when you see these visions?"

"No," she answered, and girded herself for the onslaught.

CASSANDRA UNCLIPPED the microphone. It was over! Several members of the audience had come at her with fangs sharpened, but she'd effectively warded them off. She couldn't tell if anyone had believed her about the dreams. She could only hope that JoAnn had heard the show and would get in touch with her.

Before the killer did.

He was watching. She had no doubts about that. She didn't know if he were in the audience or at home, but he was too vain not to watch a show devoted to him. Martin West appeared at her elbow, and she gave him an angry look.

"Why don't you and Mr. Raleigh plan on having a drink with me later this evening? My girlfriend has been out of town, but she'll be back later today."

"Mr. West, I don't think I'd care to do that."

"Hey, you're not going to hold today against me, are you? That was part of the show. You've watched it enough to know that my job is to stir up the audience."

"I commend you on doing it well," Cassandra said. "There was one point there when I thought they were going to rise out of their chairs and burn me at the stake."

Martin laughed. "Not a chance. I haven't lost a guest yet."

"Thanks for the invitation, but I have to decline. Adam and I both are very busy."

"Trying to solve the murders?"

"Yes," Cassandra said.

"I know what you said on the show, but can you really identify the killer?"

"Mr. West, I'm exhausted and I want to go home." She brushed past him. Adam was standing at the door, and she wanted only to get to his arms before she collapsed.

"Sure about that drink?" Martin asked. "I'm certain you'd love to meet my girl."

"Another time." Cassandra was too tired to be mad at Martin for his outrageous behavior. Too tired and too worried. The expression on Adam's face boded no good. "Goodbye, Mr. West."

Adam signaled to her and she hurried in his direction. "How's Bounder?" she asked.

"Beaker took him into custody. He and Billy and Stalker have been charged with murder."

Chapter Eighteen

"What can we do?" Cassandra tried to sit up, but Adam's hand firmly pressed her back down into the soft pillows of her bed.

"Nothing for now. Bounder is fine. So are the other two. Even Running Stream is taking this better than you." Adam pulled the quilt around Cassandra's shoulders. There were dark circles under her eyes. Lack of sleep and the frantic pace she'd been keeping were about to make her sick. "If you'll sleep for three hours, I promise I'll have a lawyer flown in from Michigan. A good lawyer. A personal friend. I'll get on the phone and make the arrangements while you sleep."

She was too tired to argue, but there was so much to be done. For all of her brave words on *The Martin West Show*, she was afraid. She'd directly challenged the killer—and set herself up as bait. Even Sheriff Beaker had called her actions foolish.

She reached up to brush a curl of hair from Adam's forehead. He was tired, too, but he wasn't going to admit it. He'd been so angry at her actions on the TV show. Yet he'd sat with her discussing the most likely suspects. Adam had settled on Gatlinburg's mayor, Ken Simpson, as the chief suspect.

There was something odd between Simpson and the sheriff, and Simpson was unnaturally afraid of Cassandra. He was physically strong enough, handsome enough. Egotistical and mean enough, too. Sighing, she snuggled deeper under the covers. He was the most promising suspect. Adam had agreed that they would tail Simpson all night long—if she slept for a few hours.

It was late afternoon, and she had time for a nap. She burrowed down in the pillows as Adam lightly rubbed her forehead. The headache had set up housekeeping there two days earlier and showed no signs of leaving. After her herbal cures had failed, Adam had even prevailed on her to take two over-the-counter painkillers—he was a terribly persuasive man. A smile touched her mouth.

"Adam, can I ask you one more question?" She kept her eyes closed.

"No. Go to sleep." He kissed her eyelids softly. He wasn't surprised when Familiar jumped up on the bed and proceeded to curl up beside Cassandra. He stroked the cat's velvety fur.

"It isn't about any of this." She circled one arm around the cat and pulled him closer.

"Okay, shoot."

"Did you make some calls to Washington, D.C.?"

"What are you talking about?" He thought for a moment she was rambling in a half sleep.

"I got the phone bill. There are some strange calls to Washington, D.C. The person didn't talk but a minute at the most. I don't know." She shrugged beneath the quilt. "I didn't make them, and I wondered if you did."

"No, not me."

"I was just curious," she said. Sleep stretched out and touched her, luring her down into a cool, peaceful place. "I was just curious," she repeated as she fell asleep.

Adam kissed her cheek very softly before he got up and went to the telephone. His old college roommate, John Effinger, was one of the best criminal attorneys in the United States. And John wouldn't mind a trip to the mountains, especially not for a case involving a young man such as Bounder.

Adam picked up the phone and started his calls. It was a slow process, finding Effinger and working out the scheduling necessary to get the lawyer to the Tennessee mountains. An hour passed, and then two. Adam made the final arrangements while Cassandra slept.

"CASSANDRA!"

The man called her name, and beneath the quilt, Cassandra struggled. She knew that voice, but she couldn't see. It was so dark, and she was being held by thick water. She tried to move, but her arms and legs were too slow.

"You thought you were so smart, didn't you? Do you know where you are? Eagle's Roost. I see you know the name. Too bad you never realized what it meant. I named it myself when I was here one evening. I'd come to watch you. I've been watching you for some time, but I never thought I'd have you here. Not you. You were always so elusive, so distant and cool.

"But a strange thing happened when I brought that first woman here. She showed me that I could have any woman I wanted. Completely have her in a way that no one else could. With my bare hands, I could possess her life. I could make her go away, and believe me, a woman will do anything you want if she thinks she's going to go away."

Cassandra could see the outline of the man. He stood away from her, talking into the darkness of the night. She knew him. She knew him so well! Who? Her arms and legs were powerless, and so was her brain. She was like a fly in a web, caught and held, unable even to struggle.

On the edge of the dream, someone else stepped forward. It was a woman.

Cassandra struggled to wake up. She didn't want to watch. No more! she tried to cry, but she was paralyzed. She had to watch the woman in the dream. She had to look at her, but she was more afraid than she'd ever been in her life. She was too afraid to move.

"You know you're going to die." The man held two glasses of champagne in his hands. "There's no escaping now. No one to help you. Adam is dead. Your little Indian friend is in prison. There's no one at all.

"The others went fast, but not you. You said I was vain, egotistical, insecure. Those weren't nice things to say. If JoAnn had heard them, she might have been frightened." His laugh was perfect. "But I made sure she was safe. I always meant to kill her first, and then you. But she was so flighty, and you were so interfering. I decided today, what difference does it make which one goes first? None. Not a bit. So if you'll just hold still while I take a tiny little souvenir." He put the glasses down and withdrew a pair of scissors from his pocket. "One snip, just to remember you by."

Cassandra's hands clutched the quilt. It weighed a ton, and it was wet and cool. She knew the woman in the dream. She knew when she looked at her, she would see herself. She was going to die. She could almost feel the killer's hands around her throat. She could feel the life squeezing out of her, but she could not move.

ADAM THOUGHT he heard Cassandra murmur, but when he looked in on her, she was motionless, her eyes closed. He finished his call and had barely put the telephone down when it rang again. He picked it up and answered in a hushed voice so he wouldn't disturb Cassandra.

"Mr. Raleigh, this is JoAnn Reed. I have to talk with you right away."

Adam's fingers clenched a fraction of an inch tighter. "Can you come up to Ms. McBeth's home? We'd both like to talk with you very much. Who have you been seeing, JoAnn? We have to have a name."

"I can't talk now. Someone is following me, and I think they want to hurt me. Meet me at Clingman's Dome. You know the place?"

"It's in the national park, but I can't meet you right now, JoAnn. Ms. McBeth is not feeling well."

"This is my life!" JoAnn's voice was distraught. "Someone is trying to kill me. If you can't meet me, then forget it!"

"Wait!" Adam walked to the bathroom and checked Cassandra's figure through the open door. She was still in bed, still resting. He'd leave a note and risk it. "Okay, Clingman's Dome. Give me time to get there."

His only answer was the click of the telephone.

For several seconds Adam debated what to do. Finally he penned a quick note to Cassandra, telling her that he'd gone to Clingman's Dome to meet JoAnn. He told her to wait in the house until he returned. As a final precaution to keep her from jumping the gun without him, he took her car keys. With a last glance into the bedroom, he propped the note against the phone and hurried out. He didn't see Familiar, his back arched, standing at the foot of the bed, hissing as Cassandra's face contorted with fear.

SHE HAD TO WAKE UP. She knew she had to escape the dream before she confronted her own image. She knew the man. If she could only get away from the dream and think, she'd be able to identify him. If she could only wake up.

A fiery pain shot through her right hand. It was potent enough to jolt a reaction from her useless muscles, and her hand jerked. The pain intensified until she had to see what was hurting her. The dream faded slowly, like thick syrup trickling away. She was breaking through the surface, into the air—into a throbbing, burning inferno where her right thumb used to be.

When she finally blinked her eyes open, she focused on Familiar, his mouth around her thumb, his sharp teeth embedded. His amber gaze locked with hers and he slowly released her. Trickles of blood had spotted the quilt, and her entire hand was throbbing.

"The dream," she whispered. Her head was pounding and she felt as if she might die of thirst. It was the worst dream yet. She'd seen her own image, a shadow woman who showed her her destiny. She reached her left hand over to pat Familiar's head. "Thanks, buddy. If you hadn't woke me up, I might have died in my own dream."

Weak but determined, she got out of bed and went to the kitchen for a glass of water. She registered Adam's absence, but her head was pounding so severely, she couldn't think. Holding the water, she slipped into a kitchen chair and tried to focus.

Where was Adam? Had he gone to get his friend, the lawyer? She struggled to her feet and went to the den. She saw the square of paper by the phone and went to get it.

JoAnn was at Clingman's Dome, and she'd called Adam. Her mind was clearing, and the warning bell of danger tolled loudly. Why Adam? Why at Clingman's Dome? It didn't make any sense. And Adam, always gallant, had gone off to rescue JoAnn. Because that was what she, Cassandra would want.

There was no time on the note, but Cassandra dressed and began to hunt for her keys. She couldn't find them anywhere. Adam had retrieved her car from the Blue Ridge, but had he taken the keys with him? She dumped her purse onto the floor and began the process of going through the contents.

No keys. She was pushing the assorted junk back into the purse when the phone rang. Leaning across the floor, she pulled the receiver to her ear.

"Ms. McBeth, Martin West here. The piece we did on you was so exceptionally well received, we'd like a brief followup. Have you decided to reveal the identity of the killer?"

"No." Cassandra was ready to slam the phone down. "I don't have time for this."

"I'd be glad to come to your home and talk. I could bring a camera crew."

"On one condition." Cassandra was thinking fast. "Come and get me. I need to run an errand, and then I'll give you an interview, okay?" Martin West, that posturing star, was the last person she wanted to see, but he had a vehicle, and that's what she needed.

"I'll be there as quickly as possible. Don't go away."

Cassandra felt a twinge of guilt. Martin sounded truly excited to get another interview. Well, she'd make it up to him later. Now her concern was finding Adam. A fragment of the dream lingered, tormenting her with her inability to remember the entire thing. The killer had said that Adam was dead. She remembered that, but the headache had intensified a hundredfold, and her brain refused to function beyond the basic survival instincts. She had to think. She had to remember. And she had to do it fast because she knew that Adam was in danger.

She scribbled a note, just in case Adam should return, or Running Stream show up. Bounder was in the county jail and bond hadn't been set yet. It was ludicrous that Beaker was accusing the young Indian men of the murders, but Cassandra's hands were tied. Any attempt to reason with Beaker would only make it hard on Bounder, Stalker and Billy.

Luckily the sheriff hadn't found out about the young men's plans to terrify tourists with explosives. The materials Bounder said were in the cave had completely disappeared.

Bounder had sworn to his mother that he'd intended to thwart Billy and Stalker if they'd ever actually gotten off the ground with their idea. Bounder had realized all along the plan was long on romantic illusion and short on practicality. He was the safeguard between big talk and action.

She drummed her fingers on the phone, checking the time again. Martin should be there soon. Even though walking made her head feel as if it would burst, she paced the room. From his perch on the sofa, Familiar watched her.

There was something about the cat that brought her up short. She stopped pacing and turned her full attention to the feline when she heard the sound of a car.

"Watch the house. I'll be back as soon as I find Adam. If there was some way you could drive, Familiar, I'd put you on the trail of Ken Simpson right now."

She didn't wait for an answer, but hurried out the front door into the gathering darkness of the April night.

"Where are we going?" Martin asked. "I told the crew to meet me at your house."

"That'll have to wait. Adam may be in danger." She buckled the seat belt. "I need to get to Clingman's Dome as soon as possible."

"Sure," Martin said as he wheeled the car around in a circle in the grass. "We're off." He smiled at her. "Where's your little convertible? I love those cars. I usually drive mine, but I decided against it.'' He made light conversation as he drove.

''I thought you'd be upset.'' This certainly wasn't the hard-hitting talk show host of a few hours before. He actually seemed like a nice person.

''Not at all. It can wait.'' He glanced at her. ''I'm a very patient man. You'll see.''

''Thanks, Martin. You're being a lot more decent about this than I expected.'' She closed her eyes and leaned her head back on the headrest for just a moment. If the throbbing would only let up for five minutes, she might be able to think.

A GENTLE BREEZE ruffled the new green leaves, shimmering over the valley like a whisper. Adam was at the scenic overlook JoAnn had indicated. He paced the overlook. She was already ten minutes late.

Several cars had passed, all with families. For some reason, the sight of the parents and their smiling children made Adam feel anxious. Would he ever have a chance to vacation with Cassandra and their children? For the first time in his life, he saw something he wanted and wondered if it might be out of his reach.

The sound of a car approaching halted his pacing, and he assumed his position by the door of his car. This had to be her. She could kick or squeal or fight. He intended to get her in his car and get her back to Cassandra's house. She could sue him later. This time he was going to hem her up and keep her safe.

There was a sharp bend in the road that blocked his view of the oncoming car until it was almost on top of him.

The sound of the tires gave him his first clue of impending danger. The rubber squealed as the car attempted to hold the road on the sharp curve. It was coming at a fast pace. Instinct made him react. He had started away from the car, heading for the safety of a big boulder, when the black Towncar whished around the curve and into sight. The darkened windows completely hid the driver, but Adam didn't have time to look. The car was headed straight at him. Caught in the open, he had no place to go.

The heavy car was barreling down on him when he made the decision. Stretching as long as he could, he threw himself over the edge of the overlook. For a span of time that seemed an eternity, Adam felt as if he flew. When his body struck the first treetops, he clutched desperately in an effort to break his fall. A million thoughts whirled through his head, but the one he remembered was Cassandra's description of the day her father had fallen and died. So, this was what she felt, this total loss of control.

Adam's head struck leafy branches and then a trunk. He felt nothing else.

"WE SHOULD HAVE done this a long time ago." Ken Simpson leaned his hands on the low stone wall that had been built to keep drivers from flying off the overlook. There was no sign of Adam Raleigh's body. With any luck, he'd be halfway down the mountain where not even the buzzards would be able to find him.

Now there was only the woman left. Cassandra. Mountain witch. It was almost over.

"HEY, YOU MISSED the turn to the road," Cassandra said. She'd opened her eyes when she felt the car bump off the driveway and into the undergrowth.

When Martin didn't respond, Cassandra sat up. "Martin, you're off the road." She couldn't tell if his vision was poor or if he was deliberately maneuvering the car.

"Don't worry, Cassandra, I know a shortcut."

The taste of tart apples suddenly filled her mouth, a taste she hadn't experienced since her father's death. Her head turned slowly, slowly as she looked at Martin. For the first time, she saw his hands on the steering wheel, and she knew them from her dream.

"It's you," she said.

"Don't sound so shocked, Cassandra, I thought you knew all along. That's what you said on television." He gave a charming, practiced laugh. "You shouldn't make claims you can't fulfill. From what I hear of local gossip, that was something your mother did, too. I think it drove poor Ken Simpson to complete madness. She caught him stealing tools from your shed. Of course, your mother couldn't let it go as simply that. She had to imply that she knew he was stealing through her psychic powers. And she threatened to expose him as a common thief. Name and honor are important things to a young man, especially one with political aspirations. How unpleasant it would be for Ken if the people of Gatlinburg found out that his career as a thief began in grade school.''

Cassandra was too startled to ask the obvious questions. Sylvia had never mentioned the incident to her. Never.

"I see by your face that you don't believe me. Well, that really isn't the issue, is it? The people believe me, and Ken is very susceptible to public opinion. Poor Ken, I know all of his secrets, and those early years are only the tip of the iceberg.''

"What are you saying?" Cassandra asked.

"Ken has a talent for thievery. Contracts, bids, that kind of thing. As mayor, he has opportunity. See, when the city lets a bid, Ken makes sure his favorite contractor is low. Together, they see to it that they both make a lot of money.'' Martin chuckled. "The best part is that Ken thinks you told me about it. See, he thinks you and your mother can actually know what crimes people are committing. Haven't you ever wondered why he hates you so?''

"That's incredible.'' Cassandra couldn't believe Ken Simpson could be such a chump. "So you've blackmailed him over the years into doing your bidding.''

"At the moment he's performing a little errand for me. He believes your Mr. Raleigh knows about his illegal activities. He's taking care of Adam now.''

Cassandra felt sick. "The call from JoAnn.''

"Exactly,'' Martin agreed. "Clever, eh? Ken gets Adam out of the way for me, and I get you to myself.''

Cassandra struggled for control. Now, of all times, she had to be calm and alert. Don't show fear, and react in an unexpected manner—those were the rules she had to live by, if she wanted to live.

The car had picked up the tracks that she and Familiar had explored. Martin knew the area well. He drove steadily and without any hesitation. They were going to the rock formation, to the lookout.

"My God," Cassandra whispered. It had all become so clear to her. "You brought the women up here, to my property, to kill them. They were looking out over the view from the apple orchard, weren't they?"

"Give the woman an A. You finally put it all together."

Cassandra absorbed the information. That was why the dreams had come to her, because of the location. That had been the trigger. "And poor Sarah, you ran her down."

"That was your fault completely, Cassandra. She didn't have to die. Her hair was dry and coarse from all that bleach. I didn't want to kill her, but you had to meddle. You told her to warn JoAnn, and she was going to do it. Her death is on your shoulders."

That's why she hadn't gotten any dreams about Sarah's death. It had taken place far from the apple orchard. Her psychic link came from the location. "Poor Sarah," she whispered.

The car rocked across two deep ruts. Martin didn't have on a seat belt, and the motion threw him forward. With a cry of triumph, Cassandra slammed his head into the steering wheel and threw open the door.

He was quicker than she. His fingers caught the material of her blouse, and with a quick jerk, he pulled her back into the car. He slammed on the brakes and kept the motor running.

Instead of the anger, his voice was calm and assured. "That wasn't very smart, Cassandra. You're going to die very slowly. Think about that as we drive to Eagle's Roost."

Dying slowly was the one thing Cassandra didn't want to think about. "Why do you call it Eagle's Roost? That lookout has been in the McBeth family for generations. It's never had a name."

"The first time I came up here, I saw...a vision." He laced his fingers tighter in her hair to hold her. "Looking out over the view, I realized that I could be a national personality. The networks were considering me. The whole world was out there, below me, waiting. It was intended to be mine. LeAnne had promised that we would be stars together. She used me, though. Used my show to get her precious modeling career going." His fingers tangled in Cassandra's hair with a vicious jerk. "My mother was a fine person. She was devoted to me. She gave her life to me. She wasn't a lesbian and you'll pay for saying that on television. Mother gave me everything. She spent hours each day helping me to look my best, to talk properly, to prepare for my future as a television personality. She coached me night and day. It was LeAnne who betrayed me."

He threw Cassandra into the car door.

"I killed her first. In New York. Just after the network passed on taking my show last fall. It wasn't right that she was going to become a star just because she was pretty. I'd worked harder. All my life I'd worked to prepare. And the networks passed me by because I was upset over LeAnne leaving me. They said I was not ready. She was to blame—and she paid. Just like you're going to."

Cassandra pulled air into her lungs. Martin had knocked the breath from her when he slammed her into the car door. "What are you going to do?"

"We're going to the lookout. I want you to see something."

"Why are you doing this?" she asked him.

"You said you knew. You said I was sick, egotistical, that I envied the women I killed. You're so wrong, and you have to pay for that. You made me sound weak and despicable."

"You love their hair, their skin. You want to be loved like they are, isn't that true?"

His fingers clutched and gently released her hair, then clutched again. "You're the prettiest yet, Cassandra. I've watched you. Your hair. I wanted to touch it yesterday."

He drove the car to the edge of the apple trees, and then dragged her across the seat and out the driver's side door.

"Have you dreamed this?" he asked. He pulled her toward the edge of the mountain. "I want you to look out to the view. Count the stars, Cassandra. There's no escape. This is your destiny."

He had her shoulders in his hands and he forced her to look out toward the night. Inch by inch, he moved her toward the precipice. "Don't get in a rush to jump," he said. "I have to have my souvenir. One thick strand of golden hair. Maybe two, to replace the one you stole from the rock."

"You'll never get away with this." Don't show fear; keep control. That's what he thrives on, seeing the woman collapse and yield to the fear he creates. "Adam will find you and kill you. I've told him that I suspect you."

"Adam is dead." His hands caressed her shoulders, moving up her throat to feel the sensitive skin there. "You have such wonderful skin. All of those health-nut products, no doubt."

"Adam isn't dead. He's too smart to fall for your tricks."

Martin laughed. "You're so easy to deceive." He laughed again, almost a giggle. "I was going to kill you first, but it might be more interesting to show you something."

"What could you possibly have to show me?" She decided to challenge him. There was a slim chance she could force him into doing something stupid. He was much stronger than she was, and while he had her standing on the lip of the mountain, there was nothing she could do to agitate him. One tiny slip, and he might send her cascading to her death.

"Come with me, Cassandra. Remember the cave? Oh, I took that cache of toys and threw what I didn't want over the side of the mountain. Little boys playing at politics. They almost ruined my plans. But the bomb in your house was a masterpiece, wasn't it? You were groveling in fear."

His fingers kept a tight grip on her, and as soon as they had enough room to maneuver, Cassandra looked for a route of escape. With a little luck, she thought she could outrun him.

He pushed her into the total blackness of the cave, and for a split second, she was without the pressure of his hand on her arm. She ducked backward, striking a hard wall with a walloping impact. The jarring collision sent her headache to new heights of misery.

"Look who's come to pay you a visit." Martin snapped on a flashlight. The searching beam found the body of a young girl lying prone on the floor. She turned her head toward the beam and blinked.

JoAnn Reed was tied hand and foot, and a gag was in her mouth. She blinked rapidly a few times as if she'd been without any light for several hours.

"Lucky for that Indian man that he was gone. I was going to throw him over the cliff to make room for my new guest," Martin said. "Little JoAnn. She loves me, Cassandra. She wanted to live with me, until she found out about the others. She's a jealous woman, aren't you, JoAnn? Jealous, and a liar. That's too bad, because liars have to be punished, don't they?" He turned to Cassandra. "You lied when you said you knew who the murderer was."

He nudged JoAnn with his toe. "I put a little sleeping potion in her wine and brought her up here. She was in the cave when you found that Indian. There's another small chamber." He nudged her harder. "Such an easy mark," he whispered.

"Adam's too smart to fall for such an obvious trick." Cassandra drew Martin's attention away from JoAnn. She was afraid he was going to hurt her there, tied on the floor of the cave.

"He already did. He went to the meeting place."

"But he isn't dead, yet." Cassandra smiled a defiant smile. "I'd know it if he were dead."

"Then you better pray he dies soon, because I'm sure he's in tremendous pain. A fall from one of those overlooks can do a lot of damage. Actually, strangulation is a far quicker, kinder death. And it's time we got on with it." He grabbed Cassandra and pushed her down to the floor. "Get JoAnn up and bring her with you."

When they were standing, Martin roughly thrust them out of the cavern entrance.

"Remember, keep your eyes on the stars," Martin whispered, and his lips were only inches from Cassandra's neck.

Goose bumps fluttered across her skin as she walked slowly toward the precipice. She had to do something. Each step she took moved her that much closer to death.

Chapter Nineteen

The pungent odor was a sharp pain in Adam's head.

"Take it easy, there," a voice ordered Adam. There was another whiff of acrid pain. Adam struggled to sit up.

"There you go," the voice said again.

Adam opened his eyes to see Sheriff Harvey Beaker peering down at him, a worried expression knitting his bushy eyebrows together. He held a broken capsule of ammonia.

"Can you stand?" Beaker asked.

Adam wasn't sure. He looked behind the sheriff's shoulder and saw the rope that disappeared up the steep side of the mountain. The sheriff had obviously gone to some trouble to get to him.

"What..." Adam didn't finish.

"Ken Simpson tried to kill you. I was tailing him, have been for several days, and when I saw you jump over the cliff, I waited until he went on, then I came down here to see what was left of you. More than I pictured, I'd say."

"Thanks." Adam slid into a sitting position. He took an inventory of his body and found not too much permanent damage had been done. By all rights, he should have been dead.

"I wouldn't be shifting around too much," Beaker said casually, then pointed his flashlight a foot behind him. The ground disappeared. "This ledge caught you. You're a lucky man."

The full realization of what had almost happened made Adam's body tighten. "I am indeed."

"Let's get back up this hill," Beaker said. "Simpson left you for dead, but he might come back. We'd both be sitting ducks."

"Why?"

"Why was I following Simpson, or why did he try to kill you?"

"Both," Adam said as he tested the rope with his weight. It was going to be a long, hard climb, but if he wanted to get back to the road—and Cassandra—he had to do it. The idea that he'd left her alone, unprotected, gave him the strength. The call from "JoAnn" had obviously been a setup. Just a bit more surprising than Sheriff Beaker's sudden rescue.

"I was following Ken when I noticed he was acting funnier than usual. He had a real burn for Ms. McBeth. Hated her. Ken's always been a rational man. It made me wonder, and when I gave up on you as the chief suspect, I had to have someone. Besides, he poked around my office and found out some details. Later I heard those details on that television show."

"You didn't tell Martin West?" Adam gripped the rope and started the climb. It was only about fifty feet, but it was going to be a test of his will.

"No lawman gives out things he's heard in confidence. Betty, that's the dispatcher, finally admitted that she let Ken in my private office on several occasions. He musta read my notes."

"Great," Adam grunted as he slowly went up, hand over hand. He kept Cassandra's face in his mind as he struggled. He had to get to her. Before Ken Simpson did.

"What do you know about Ray Elsworth?"

Beaker's unexpected question made Adam's hand slip on the rope. He caught himself with a curse, his bruised body complaining angrily. "I thought he might be involved in the murders."

"And?" Beaker prompted.

"I'm not so sure, now."

"I saw you and Cassandra with him at the fair. I also saw him in Sarah Welford's house, along with Ms. McBeth. We'd had the place staked out for several days. What was Ms. McBeth looking for?"

"JoAnn Reed's whereabouts." Adam concentrated on the conversation. His ribs were screaming. He didn't believe they were broken, but they were badly bruised. The top of the cliff was only five yards away.

"I picked Ray up. He denies any connection with the murders. He did own up to some dealings with Simpson, though. It seems he left some papers in Sarah Welford's house. When he went to get them, they were gone."

"What kind of deals?" Adam could almost reach the top.

"Bids, contracts, city business. It would seem Simpson has been using his office for personal gain for quite some time. My best guess is that he's somehow been led to believe that Cassandra knows about his illegal activities. That's why he's after her."

Adam crawled over the stone wall and dropped, panting, into the dirt. In a moment he reached down to give Beaker a hand over the wall, but the lawman was managing on his own.

"Anyway, Ray's in custody." Beaker gave Adam a long, hard look. "Simpson's got to be stopped. My guess is that he's headed home to plan an attack on Ms. McBeth."

"Cassandra is all alone." Adam realized he'd even taken her car keys. "I have to get back to her."

"Go on," Beaker said. "I'll check at Simpson's house and hope to catch him there. In the meantime, I'll radio for some deputies. Unless you call the dispatcher with a change in plans, I'll meet you at Ms. McBeth's. We might have time to set a trap."

Adam didn't wait for further confirmation. Cassandra was asleep, alone. He had to get back to her.

"CHAMPAGNE?" Martin West asked. He held two glasses. "You deserve the best, Cassandra."

"Champagne would be lovely," Cassandra answered. She nudged JoAnn to take the second glass, but her hands were still tied. "JoAnn wants some, too."

"Such a pity," Martin said. He flicked a pocketknife open with a practiced gesture. Feinting and thrusting, he moved around them. "I always wanted to be tough, but I was afraid my face would get cut." In one quick flash of the blade, JoAnn's hands were free. She quickly removed the gag. At Cassandra's nudge, she took the champagne glass from Martin.

"So sorry, JoAnn. I should have disposed of you sooner and saved you all of this . . . inconvenience. You are a bit of a mess. That lovely hair is all matted."

"You bas . . ."

"You're taking a foolish risk." Cassandra put a restraining hand on JoAnn's arm as she spoke calmly to Martin. "There are two of us. We could take you on."

"Two women?" Martin laughed. "Hardly a risk, unless you have supernatural strength along with your psychic abilities." He laughed harder. "I thought you knew who the killer was," he taunted.

"I could see the victims, not the killer," Cassandra admitted. She watched his face in the moonlight as he sipped the champagne. "That was my advantage. I was in your mind. I could sense the turmoil and the insecurities. That was the reason I couldn't identify you. See, I thought you were a real man—confident and assured. You're so afraid, Martin. You're terrified of women. Why?"

"You shut up," Martin answered. He put his glass down on part of the rock formation where Cassandra had found the hair.

"You're taking the hair from women for some kind of silly power, aren't you?" Cassandra was guessing, but she had to keep him talking. Once he decided to kill them, he might get lucky and get at least one of them.

"I told you to shut up," he said.

She picked up her own hair and held a thick strand of it out to him. "Take it. Once you cut it from my head, it's

nothing more than dead hair. It won't give you any kind o
magic."

Martin took a short step toward her. "I told you to shu
up." He darted to the side and grabbed JoAnn. "Or she'
going to die."

"Please, don't let him hurt me," JoAnn said through he
tears. "He's already done enough. He told me about th
others. While I was lying on the floor of that cave, he tol
me how he did it to the others."

"I dreamed this night," Cassandra said softly. "Excep
it's different. It isn't happening the way I dreamed it at all.'
She looked at Martin. "We were alone in my dream. Ju
the two of us. We were drinking champagne, and you tol
me how you'd been watching me."

Martin's grip on JoAnn loosened, and she twisted away
He didn't bother to go after her.

"That's the way it should be," he agreed. "See, I kne
who you were long before this. I'd heard stories about yo
and your abilities. After you went to Beaker and said yo
could identify the killer, Ken Simpson told me your name
He said you lived up here alone. I was going to pay you
little visit the day I cut your phone lines, but Adam Raleig
showed up."

"It's been you, all along. The earrings dropped in th
yard, the scarecrow at Adam's car, the barricade. Why?"

"It dawned on me—I could get the networks interested i
me again with the right show. A serial killer on the loose. /
psychic who claims she can identify the killer. She appear
on television. Everyone knows she's after the killer, then sh
dies, just like the others. It's perfect."

Cassandra felt the fear rise up in a huge wave, and sh
held firm against it. Now wasn't the time to lose her grip. S
far, she'd managed to distract and confuse him. JoAnn wa
edging away. If there was a chance, she might be able t
make a break for it.

As if he read her mind, Martin lunged to the right
grabbed JoAnn and slammed her into the huge rock. Sh
went down in a heap. "She was going to escape," he said

He turned to Cassandra. "Now it's like it should be. Just me and you."

Cassandra took a step backward. She was near the edge of the cliff, the same place where her father had fallen to his death. Her left foot felt solid ground behind her as she took another tentative step away from the advancing Martin. Even in the moonlight she could see the insanity in his eyes. He was loving every minute. He drew power from her fear, and she had to stop it.

A movement on the top of the rocks caught her eye. It was a small shadow moving toward her. Black on black shadow. Familiar! She'd never been so glad to see anyone in her entire life. And the cat was hunkered down as if he were stalking Martin.

"You'd better kill me if you're going to," Cassandra dared him. "Adam will be here—"

"I told you he's dead!" Martin gritted through his teeth. He took a lunge forward and grabbed Cassandra by the shoulders. His hands slid up her throat, and with a rough strength, he pushed her around so that she faced the night sky.

"Isn't it beautiful!" he insisted.

Cassandra resisted the urge to struggle. He was six times stronger than she was. If she fought him, he'd kill her instantly. She had to bide her time. Would Familiar actually attack him? She could only pray the cat had really been watching Lassie on television.

"You're supposed to tell me how beautiful my skin and hair are," Cassandra prompted him. "And don't forget to cut a snip for a souvenir."

His hands tightened on her throat. "You're always making fun of me. But not much longer, Ms. McBeth. You are lovely. Such beautiful skin. Such gorgeous hair." He fingered a curl. "The finest of all my collection."

Cassandra felt the cold dread that she'd held at bay sink into her heart. She'd believed someone would come. Adam. Running Stream. Someone. She'd believed she would be able to outsmart Martin. But time was running out for her. His fingers tightened convulsively on her throat and she felt her own pulse beat hard and strong. An image of Adam came to her, standing bare-chested on her porch. A wave of tears threatened, and she fought them back.

"Adam..."

"He's dead!" Martin screamed, and his fingers dug into her throat.

"No, I'm not dead."

The voice came from the darkness above Martin. At the same time, a small black shape hurled itself through the air and landed on Martin West's head. Dangerous claws dug into the man face and eyes.

With a cry of anguish, West released Cassandra and tried to beat the black cat from his head. Familiar dug in with all four paws, riding Martin West like a rodeo rider on a bronc.

Out of the darkness, a larger shape rushed in. With the impact of a linebacker, Adam struck West in the midriff, pushing him back against the outcropping of rock.

Familiar flung himself clear as West's head flew back and connected with the rock. There was the sound of skull striking rock, and Martin slid bonelessly to the ground.

"Cassandra!" Adam's strong arms caught her as her legs started to give. She tottered on the edge of the mountain until he drew her back to safety.

"I was about to give up on you," she said, her heart pounding.

"You were never in any real danger, not with Familiar out here protecting you," he answered. Then he crushed her to him with enough strength to fuse them together. The emotions he felt were too intense for mere words.

"Meow," Familiar demanded.

With a cry, Cassandra gathered him in her arms as Adam held her. "Don't ever let us go," Cassandra whispered. "Promise me! You won't ever let us go."

"I promise, with all of my heart," Adam answered, kissing her forehead and her hair and her cheek. "Not in this lifetime."

Far in the distance, there was the sound of a siren. "They'll never get up here," Cassandra said. She felt as if she were floating. Adam's arms were the only thing that kept her from ascending far above the orchard and the tragedy of Martin West.

"Running Stream will show them the way," Adam reassured her. "But let's leave things nice and neat." He took the coil of rope from around his chest and began the work of tying Martin up. Cassandra knelt down beside JoAnn. The woman was unconscious, but she'd soon be waking up. There was a large goose egg on the back of her head, but she was very much alive.

"So, WHAT'S all the whispering about? Every time I come in a room, the talking stops. Even Bounder is whispering, and he knows better. Maybe I have something terminal and no one wants to tell me. That's humans for you. I save their butts and now they whisper behind my back. And lately, the food has been less than satisfactory. Ever since Martin West has been rounded up, Miss Locks and Lancelot have been so busy petting each other's wounds, I've been neglected. Except my feline instincts tell me that it's more than simple neglect.

Maybe I'm just too sensitive a guy. I mean, Adam has Cassandra. And she has him. Running Stream got Bounder. JoAnn got back with her family. Ray got a chance to turn state's evidence. Ken Simpson got a new black and white jail suit, and even Martin West got a date with a hanging judge and jury. What have I got? Only the memory of one sassy little Clotilde.

Uh-oh, they're calling my name. And there's this odd sound to Miss Lock's voice. I mean, she sounds happy, but it also sounds as if she's about to cry. Yep, she's one phenomenal creature all right. I heard Adam say just an hour ago that he could run his business from the top of this mountain. He said something about how Running Stream taught him what it meant to really be strong.

Good grief. Here comes Billy and Stalker. Those are two lucky dudes. Beaker never knew anything about the grand bomb plot, and no one around here is talking. Maybe they'll take Adam up on his offer to help them get into a good college.

*What is going on around here? There's a car in the front
yard. More company? They're giving a party, and no one
even bothered to tell me.*

"FAMILIAR? Is that you?"

The cat sauntered through the door into the kitchen and
froze. With a wild meow, he ran across the room and threw
himself into the arms of the strangely dressed woman. Her
head was wrapped in white bandages, and her arms were
also bandaged, but she managed to catch the cat to her chest
and hold him as she bent to kiss him.

"Familiar! I can't believe it." Eleanor Curry turned to the
tall man who stood beside her. "It's really him, Peter. Can
you believe it?"

"Where that cat is concerned, I can believe anything,"
Dr. Peter Curry answered. He went to his wife and kissed
her neck as she petted and stroked the purring cat. "It looks
like our search is over."

Standing in the doorway, Cassandra held Adam's hand.
It was the reunion she'd always hoped for, but it was also
tearing a hole in her heart. She'd known from the very beginning that Familiar was somebody's cat. In fact, she'd
hoped to find his real owners. Now that she had, she didn't
want to give him up.

Adam's arms went around her and pulled her back
against him. "There won't ever be another Familiar, but
we'll get a cat," he said. "I can't imagine life without one
now."

"Thank you both," Eleanor said as she brushed the tears
from her eyes. "When my friend Magdalena called and said
she'd seen Familiar on television, I didn't believe it could be
true. Not in Tennessee."

"Well, I wondered about those Washington phone numbers on my bill. When I found out from directory assistance that they were a vet's office, I suspected it was
Familiar's work." Cassandra swallowed her own tears and
forced a smile. "I'm so happy for you. He's a wonderful
cat."

"He saved my life," Eleanor said.

"He seems to make a habit out of that," Adam added. "Strange how it's only beautiful women that he rescues."

"I told Cassandra he was a very special creature," Running Stream added. She had her hand on her son's arm, and beside her stood the other Indian men.

Amid the laughter, Familiar accepted all the strokes and pets.

AIN'T LIFE GRAND? What cat could be luckier? From one beautiful dame to the next, and now home to my own little precious Clotilde. Arnold Evans is still on the loose, but not for long. The cops have a line on him, but even better than that, I'm on the alert. And Cassandra will help me. We're psychically linked now. And if that ain't enough, I have visiting rights whenever I want to come back here. Eleanor promised that I would never have to travel by moving van again, either. I'm thinking private limo, with remote-control TV. I'm afraid I've become a news junkie due to all of this. I've even developed a yen for those talk shows. Reminds me of the days . . . uh, day . . . when I was a star.

Yeah, I'm going to miss my mountain home, but the truth is, I'm an urban kind of cat. The feel of pavement beneath my paws. Lovely little kitties in the windows of their homes, preening and sassing. And best of all, my Eleanor. Dr. Doolittle says she'll get the turban off in two weeks, and when her hair grows back, she'll be the same old gorgeous dame. No permanent injuries. Not even a broken heart, now that she has me back—and that's a quote from Dr. D.!

A little sandpaper tongue treatment for Goldilocks. Now, now, no tears. My fur tends to flake when exposed to too much salt water. Even a little purr for Lancelot. I hate to leave a damsel alone, but even though the announcement hasn't been officially made, I think there's going to be a mountaintop union going on here soon.

Well, that's it. Watch out, Clotilde, get that cute little French-accented motor running—I'm headed home.